Greed and

"You don't really think there's anything to this stuff about changing history and wiping out the Commies, do you, Swede?" Simms asked him.

Hendricks shrugged. "It doesn't matter to us, Johnny," he said. "This time-travel stuff is our ticket to whatever we want! We'll have modern weapons. We'll know what's going to happen. And we can cooperate with the powers that be back there to get a slice of any pie we want. We could live like kings back there, man! *Be* kings!"

"Can we get away with it?"

"Why not? Once we go back there, we're on our own . . . except for the Rangers. And if they get in the way . . . " Hendricks smiled. "Hell, I killed Hunter once. I'll do it again if I have to . . . and his buddies with him."

FREEDOM'S RANGERS

TREASON IN TIME

KEITH WILLIAM ANDREWS

BERKLEY BOOKS, NEW YORK

FREEDOM'S RANGERS: TREASON IN TIME

A Berkley Book / published by arrangement with
the author

PRINTING HISTORY
Berkley edition / July 1990

ISBN: 0-425-12167-4

A BERKLEY BOOK ® TM 757,375
Berkley Books are published by The Berkley Publishing Group,
200 Madison Avenue, New York, New York 10016.
The name "BERKLEY" and the "B" logo
are trademarks belonging to Berkley Publishing Corporation.

PRINTED IN THE UNITED STATES OF AMERICA.

10 9 8 7 6 5 4 3 2 1

One

They were coming again, crawling up the road past the scattered wreckage left by their last attack. It wouldn't be much longer now.

Lieutenant Travis Hunter turned away from the slit in the wall of the command-post bunker. "If anybody has any ideas," he said, "now's the time to speak up."

"Becker might still come in time," Sergeant Roy Anderson said. The lanky Texan twisted a new barrel into place on his M-60 machine gun. Blood smeared the side of his face where a chunk of shrapnel had furrowed a deep, ragged groove.

Sergeant Eduardo Gomez chambered a 40mm grenade, snapping the breech home on the M-203 slung from the front of his M-16. "Christmas is coming early, huh?"

"I want to know what the bloody hell happened to the people we were supposed to meet here!" Sergeant Greg King's face was flushed and angry under the bloodstained swath of bandages wrapped around his head. "Where's Bravo Company?"

"Ease up, people," Hunter said. "Let's wait for Walker to get back. Then maybe we can sort things out."

The tension among the U.S. Rangers huddled in the CP bunker of Firebase Sierra was palpable. They were no strangers to combat—or to death—but someone, somewhere, had seriously screwed up and the Ranger team had been left squatting in the end product. As a practical application of time-travel tactics in a contemporary military operation, this mission had been a screwup from the beginning.

Time travel. Hunter shook his head. After seven months and several missions into the past, it was still hard to grasp. The Army's Chronos Project, a top-secret facility hidden beneath a mountain above Jackson Hole, Wyoming, was regarded by the handful of people who knew of its existence as the last hope for a free America.

Chronos had originally been conceived as a means to rewrite history, a way to eliminate Communism and the menace of a Soviet Russia which now, in 2007, dominated most of the world. Much of the United States was occupied by foreign armies, armies dominated by the Soviets, though they wore the blue arm bands of United Nations peacekeepers. Free America remained in the mountain fastness of the Rockies, guarded by what was left of the U.S. Army.

With time travel, all of that could be changed. NATO might be kept from breaking up in the mid-1990s, and the Soviet blitzkrieg across Europe a few years later avoided. The president's failure of nerve during the Mexican crisis could be prevented, and the subsequent U.N. occupation of American missile fields, military bases, and cities stopped before it happened. The Cold War might never even begin.

"Could we be seeing the results of some VBU operation?" Gomez asked. "Maybe they did something to take out Hendricks."

"Maybe," Hunter said. "Doesn't really seem like their style, though."

The Soviet counterpart to America's Chronos Project was the VBU—the Russian acronym stood for *Vremya Bezopasnosti Upravlenie*, or *Time Security Directorate*—a new secret agency drawn from elements of Russia's KGB and GRU intelligence services.

Changing history . . . that was what time travel was all about. So far, the VBU had concentrated on sweeping plots designed to alter history on a vast scale, hoping their meddling would wipe out the United States and lead to a World Communist state. Why should the VBU suddenly focus on revising a single battle only three months in the past—and one that was a major Soviet victory at that?

Of course, the Chronos Project had switched policy in exactly that way. But for Free America, the Battle of Denver represented the difference between survival and total defeat. No amount of Soviet intervention was likely to make the outcome any worse.

The Ranger mission to Firebase Sierra was a new twist in time-travel tactics. Unfortunately, it had gone sour from the moment Hunter and his men walked through the glowing portal of the Chronos facility's Time Square and materialized . . . here.

The sharp, flat crack of an explosion echoed from the canyon walls behind them. The freight-train rumble of another incoming round ended in a second explosion, then a third. "Uh-oh," Anderson said. "Here it comes."

"Probing fire," Hunter said. "One-twenty-five em-em stuff from their T-80s. They're in range now."

"I liked it better when the locals had muzzle-loading muskets." Gomez groaned. "There's no future in it for us if they've got *tanks!*"

"No future?" Anderson grimaced. "Another joke like that, Eddie, and you can go down and fight those tanks by yourself!"

"Why not? There's no one else around to do it!"

No one else, indeed. Hunter looked across the bunker to where Sergeant Daniel Malloy crouched next to a firing slit.

The man looked uncomfortable and out of place. He was the senior NCO of the six men the Rangers had found guarding Firebase Sierra. The problem was that Sierra was supposed to be held by a garrison of fifty-three men under Captain William Hendricks.

This mission was unusual in that this time the Rangers had not traveled years into the past . . . but only three months. In July 2007, elements of the U.S. III Army Corps under the command of Major General Richard Becker had been trapped and surrounded in the high country of central Colorado by three converging Russian armored columns. The Denver Massacre, as it was later called, had ended with the virtual annihilation of III Corps and the disintegration of Free America's central front. In October of the same year, the U.S. Joint Chiefs had decided to use the Chronos Project, not to erase Soviet Russia as originally planned but simply to eliminate that single, disastrous defeat.

The tactics of the change were straightforward enough. Intelligence reports suggested that Becker had been well on his way to smashing the first Russian thrust toward Denver when a Soviet tank column caught him by surprise from the rear, pinning him near Idaho Springs until the main Soviet force could reorganize and attack. The enemy flankers had taken a roundabout route behind the Shadow Mountains and down Highway 40, part of the column debouching through Moffat Tunnel while the main body smashed past a tiny garrison at Berthoud Pass to emerge in Becker's rear.

The garrison at Berthoud Pass was the key: fifty-three men described by G2 as leftovers from half a dozen shattered Army units and posted in what was supposed to be a secure area behind the lines. According to the reports, they had no antitank weapons at all, easy pickings for the Soviet armor when it thundered through the pass.

So the Rangers had been sent back through time with a small stockpile of antitank weapons and explosives. There was no time to prepare a larger force, but they could make all the difference. If Becker could be warned of the trap . . . if Firebase Sierra could hold out for only a few precious hours . . . at worst, III Corps would escape destruction and withdraw. Denver might be lost, but winter was coming and the mountain passes would soon be blocked with snow. Free America would win a little more time.

And at best, the Battle of Denver might be transformed into a much-needed victory.

Victory . . .

They'd arrived a few miles south of Firebase Sierra early on a morning in mid-July and buried the weapons and ammo they'd brought through where they could be picked up later and hauled north to their destination.

At Firebase Sierra, though, things had started going wrong. They'd found six men of Bravo Company at the outpost instead of fifty-three. They were able to radio the warning to General Becker, but III Corps was already engaged with Soviet forces and could not break away, even to reinforce the threatened pass.

Malloy and his men had returned to the temporal landing

zone with a jeep and hauled the antitank weaponry back to Sierra without incident. The firebase occupied the narrowest point within Berthoud Pass, but eleven men—the six at Sierra plus Hunter and his four Rangers—were simply not enough to hold off an entire Soviet armored battalion.

All the weapons and ammo in the world could not change that.

And so they improvised. Eddie Gomez, the team's demolition expert, had taken the jeep, five men, and a small mountain of plastic explosives north to Moffat Tunnel. He returned a few hours later with word that the Soviets would not be using *that* route to Denver . . . and that the Russian column was only a few miles behind him. The first attack had come during the night. Eleven men had managed to stall the Russian assault.

Now it was daylight, and the Soviets were moving again.

"Bloody hell!" King muttered. "Where could the guy be?"

"How about it, Malloy?" Gomez's voice was sharp, without the usual good-natured humor it usually carried. "Just where *are* Hendricks and his people?"

Malloy looked toward Hunter, an appeal in his eyes. "We've still got time to bug out, Lieutenant," he said, ignoring Gomez.

Hunter took another look through the slit. The lead Russian vehicles were perhaps two kilometers off now, edging their way past the charred hulks left scattered along the highway the night before. "Not just yet," he said. "We'll wait for Walker to get here. Then we'll see."

"Dammit, Lieutenant! There's not a damned thing more to be gained by staying here!" Malloy turned and started scrambling toward the bunker's entrance.

"Freeze, mister!" Hunter's command stopped Malloy where he was. "Until your Captain Hendricks decides to honor us with his presence, *I'm* in command!"

King reached out and gently patted Malloy's shoulder. "Best do as the Lieutenant tells you," he said. "We're all in this together now. There's a good lad."

Yeah, Hunter thought. *We're in it together, right up to our necks.*

There was a shout outside the CP, a challenge by one of Malloy's men. Moments later, a shadow darkened the bunker's open door. The fourth member of Hunter's team entered with the easy grace of a born scout.

"Good God, Walker!" King exclaimed. "Where have you been?"

The Amerindian corporal smiled grimly. "There was some . . . delay. A small Russian patrol. They had to be dealt with."

Hunter smiled. "I don't see any scalps on your belt."

Walker grinned, an unnerving gleam of white teeth behind the green-and-black camo-painted face. "Not this time, Lieutenant." He was the newest member of the Ranger team, a Dakota Indian from an alternate reality where the American Colonies had never freed themselves from England. In that world, Walker had been a member of the British SAS in the service of King Charles III of the Dominion of North America. When his world was transformed by the Rangers' intervention against a VBU plot, the Amerind had elected to join them instead. His one passion, it seemed, was killing Russians, whether they threatened his world or this one. Educated in Boston, he didn't *really* take scalps, although sometimes Hunter wondered.

"Anyway, I'm glad you made it through," Hunter said.

"I'm afraid there are more, though . . . many more." Walker frowned. "And no sign of Captain Hendricks or his men."

"What're the Russkies up to?" King asked.

"They are forming up for another attack," Walker said calmly. "At least a full battalion. I don't think this one is going to be quite as gentle as the last."

"Time we thought about a change in scenery, gang," Hunter said. He gestured to King, who drew a book-sized electronic device from a rucksack stashed in the corner of the bunker. Hunter placed the device on the floor and switched it on. Malloy was right. There was no reason to stay longer, not when all that could be accomplished was death for all of them. He switched it on.

Twenty minutes . . .

"We're boogyin', then?" Anderson asked. His eyes were on the beacon.

"We've warned Becker . . . and we held up the armored column this long at least."

"Yeah, but was it enough?" King asked.

"I don't know."

"The crazy thing is," Gomez said, "we may never know!"

It was one of the basic contradictions of time travel that the changes the Rangers introduced into the past eliminated the future from which they'd come. If they'd delayed the Russians at Berthoud Pass long enough to change the Battle of Denver into a victory, then their rewriting of history included a rewrite of themselves. Once before Hunter had seen men simply vanish when they returned to a future changed by their actions in the past . . . a future that already held duplicate versions of themselves.

If the delay hadn't been enough, perhaps they could still return to the October 2007 they remembered . . . and try again. And if they had changed history, well . . .

Vanishing into the unknown between times was almost certainly preferable to Soviet bayonets.

"We'll wait as long as we can," Hunter said. He glanced up at Malloy, who was watching him with a blank and uncomprehending stare. "The longer we can hold the Russians here, the more time Becker will have in Denver. We'll evac through the gate at the last minute. We'll either make it or—"

Another shout sounded from outside, followed by a burst of machine-gun fire. "Hey, Sarge!" one of Malloy's men yelled. "They're comin'! God, they're comin' fast!"

"Okay," Hunter said. "Let's get out there! Remember . . . make every shot count!"

It was time to get out of the bunker. That ramshackle structure would offer little protection against high explosives, and if the Soviets spotted fire coming from it, they would concentrate all their firepower against its frail sandbag walls. Better to abandon it, with the recall beacon safe inside. He checked his watch. Fourteen minutes to go.

Hunter grinned at the others. "Just one more dance, gentlemen. Then we'll hightail it for home."

Sergeant Daniel Malloy mopped his forehead with a sweat-stained rag, then peeked up over the earth rampart of the trench at the approaching Soviet line. *Damn it all, anyway!* Life at Firebase Sierra had been easy until Hunter and his Rangers came along. Now everything had changed. He hadn't felt this scared in all of the two months since he'd joined up with Captain Hendricks. The war had never come this close before.

And damn Hendricks too! Malloy knew perfectly well where the rest of Bravo Company was, but he sure as hell couldn't tell these damned straight-arrow Rangers or they'd all be court-martialed for sure, assuming they could survive what was moving up the hill! Court-martialed? Hell, they'd be *shot*! Bravo had been living high and easy for months by squeezing food and luxuries out of the civilians for miles around. It had been a good life, free of the Mickey Mouse chickenshit of the real Army . . . only now it looked like they were being shut down. Malloy shook his head sorrowfully. *It had to happen sometime*, he thought. *But damn Hendricks for leaving me to hold the bag!*

He glanced across the compound to where Hunter and two of his men were laying out LAW rocket launchers in an orderly line on the ground, tubes extended and ready to fire. Malloy still wasn't sure about the Ranger team. Their G2 on the Russian column had been right on, and they'd dragged one hell of a lot of A-T gear and ammo in from somewhere, but damned if he could figure how they got way out here in the mountains. Their talk about recall beacons made no sense at all, but he'd heard the big master sergeant mention an LZ once. Maybe they'd parachuted in. That would explain why they didn't have a vehicle for the antitank stuff.

Well, whoever they were, they were bad news for Bravo Company. Hendricks wouldn't be showing up now, not with the whole valley full of damned Russians. Maybe the chance would come to slip away, once the excitement started.

He thumbed off the safety of his M-16 and hunkered down lower in the trench. Yeah. He might find a way out yet. Let Hunter play hero if he wanted. . . .

Green-clad Russian troops moved up the road in open order, two platoons on foot followed by six slow-moving BMP-2 Mechanized Infantry Combat Vehicles. Watching their deliberate but confident advance, Hunter, crouched beside Gomez behind a sandbag wall, had to fight the urge to open fire. Sierra's tiny garrison couldn't afford to waste a single shot.

The MICVs would be the real threat. Each one mounted a 73mm cannon, a Sagger ATGW launcher, and a coaxial machine gun . . . heavy firepower against Hunter's outnumbered defenders.

He nodded to Gomez. The demo expert raised a LAW rocket launcher to his shoulder, sighting on the nearest BMP. All along the firebase perimeter the other Americans were getting ready as well. Anderson, like Hunter, manned an M-60 Maremont; the rest held LAW rockets of their own, lining up on the deadly APCs.

The Russians were within one hundred fifty yards now, well past the opening of Berthoud Pass. *Almost there . . .*

Hunter squeezed the trigger and the M-60 bucked and thundered, spraying death into the Soviet line. Empty casings glittered in the morning sunlight. Down the line, Anderson's machine gun joined the deadly chorus. Russians screamed, staggered, fell . . .

Gomez's LAW whooshed, the sleek twenty-inch rocket streaking toward its target. The HEAT warhead struck the BMP at the juncture of turret and hull, square under the cannon. The explosion was little more than a sharp crack, followed by a louder roar that seemed to last an eternity as 73mm ammunition inside the turret went off. Smoke and flame rose from the turret, and the MICV skewed to one side and lurched to a halt. Gomez tossed aside the empty tube and grabbed a second LAW in one smooth motion.

Swiveling the machine gun down the Russian skirmish line, Hunter saw two other BMPs with shattered turrets. Another had stopped dead with a hole through the right front of the hull, the engine compartment. Smoke billowed from the opening, but the turret was pivoting in search of targets. The other two vehicles continued to lumber forward.

One of the BMP guns barked, the 73mm shell streaking over the perimeter line to explode near the command bunker. Hunter continued to fire.

The Soviet infantrymen were hugging the ground now, shooting back in ragged bursts of full-auto AK fire or just trying to stay out of the twin streams of American machine-gun death. The immobile BMP fired once, but again the shell went overhead, harmless. A Russian soldier tried to retrieve an RPK light machine gun from a fallen comrade, only to sprawl across the weapon and the first body as Anderson swept his chattering M-60 back and forth across the battlefield. Gomez gave a wild yell in Spanish, picked up his battle rifle, and in quick succession fired two 40mm grenades into the Russian skirmish line.

Hunter's machine gun ran dry, the hundred-round belt exhausted. He pulled a fresh belt from its case while King reached for his FN-FAL battle rifle. Anderson's drumming fire died away a moment later, and for a few seconds Firebase Sierra was strangely quiet. The distant crackle of flames and the intermittent clattering of Russian autofire went almost unnoticed after the battle's previous fury. Figures moved again behind the ruined MICVs, re-forming to press home the attack once again.

A crewman from the immobile BMP was manning the 7.62mm coaxial machine gun now, trying to lay down covering fire for the retreating infantry. As Hunter and Anderson brought their M-60s back into play again, this time supported by Gomez and two of Malloy's soldiers firing M-16s, two more LAWs sought out the BMP. When the smoke cleared, the machine gunner sprawled backward behind his shattered weapon, body twisted almost out of recognition.

Hunter dropped the Maremont and checked his watch. Five minutes to go. He drew a flare gun and fired into the air, the signal for the defenders to fall back on the CP bunker. A few more minutes and they could all go home.

Gomez loosed a 40mm grenade into a knot of Russian soldiers, then another . . . and another. Hunter saw King and two of Malloy's soldiers scramble from their gun emplacements under the cover of the grenade attack. Grabbing an M-16 from the ground in front of him, Hunter squeezed off a quick burst of autofire. Screams mingled with chattering AK fire and a deeper rumble of heavy machinery.

Then, through clouds of smoke and dust, a clattering monster shape appeared. It was squat and ugly, a T-80 tank. Tracers whined overhead as the AFV's turret machine gun probed toward the Rangers' refuge.

"Go on, Chief! I'll cover you!" The words were hardly out before a line of 12.7mm machine-gun rounds slammed across his chest. Eddie Gomez lay very still, his eyes staring unseeing into the clear morning sky. Hunter crouched over him. It was impossible . . . Gomez was dead. With a curse he opened fire again into the Soviet line, hatred and shock numbing him to everything but the need to kill.

Walker burst from cover, his Galil spitting death as he raced for the shelter of Hunter's sandbag refuge. The corporal's face was set, determined. Then his head erupted in a bloody haze as a Russian bullet tore through his skull. He toppled and lay unmoving in the dust.

In a smooth motion Hunter was on his feet and running, firing bursts from his M-16 as he weaved across the compound. The CP bunker loomed ahead, the improvised outworks shielding a lone American defender, King. The master sergeant helped him over the low sandbag wall. Dimly Hunter realized that he could hear Anderson's Maremont roaring over the confused sounds of the battle. The Texan was crouched behind another barricade thirty yards away, his machine gun hammering into the ranks of the advancing Russians.

"Roy!" Hunter's shout brought Anderson's head around. "Fall back!"

The Texan grinned as he swept his machine gun back and forth, spraying autofire death into the Russian ranks. Hunter and King brought their rifles into play to cover him as Anderson rose from behind his bastion, still firing.

Across the compound a Soviet soldier kneeled, raising the slender tube of an RPG rocket launcher to his shoulder. Before Hunter could react, the Russian fired. The rocket grenade dipped and twisted, trailing smoke, to hit the sandbag barrier in front of Anderson.

The explosion tore through the improvised wall, spewing earth and debris. Anderson was flung backward by the force of the blast, the M-60 hurled from his hands. He landed in a limp, bloody sprawl, body twisted awkwardly. A moment later there were Russians swarming there, firing savagely into the unmoving body. Anderson was gone.

Dead. Like Gomez and Walker . . . dead.

Swearing, shouting incoherently, Greg King stood nearby, emptying his FN-FAL at the advancing Russians. Then King spun aside as a three-round burst of AK fire caught him in the stomach. He lurched against Hunter, blood pouring from a ragged belly wound.

King's eyes fluttered open as Hunter eased him to the ground. He wasn't dead—not yet—but he would be soon. *Soon . . .*

Hunter brought his Uzi submachine gun up and opened fire. A Soviet trooper shrieked, clawing at his bloody face. Another crumpled silently, shot through the heart.

Three American soldiers staggered past, unarmed, fleeing from the terror of the Russian assault. "You men!" Hunter bellowed. Dully Hunter recognized one as Malloy, limping, an improvised bandage on his leg. Who were the other two? Logan, he remembered. Logan and Marconi. "Over here!"

Dazed by noise and fear, the men complied. Hunter gestured at King. "Pick him up! Take him to the bunker! Move! Move! Move!"

He covered them with his Uzi, backing toward the bunker. The gunfire had died away. Hunter was reeling from shock and fatigue. Anderson, Gomez, and Walker . . . all dead! Why had they died, while cowards like Malloy, Logan, and Marconi lived? *My friends . . .*

"Jesus!" Logan froze in the doorway to the bunker. "Hey, Lieutenant! There's this goddamned blue light!"

"Don't worry," Hunter said, coming up behind him. "It won't hurt us!"

Inside the bunker, a whirlpool of cold light swirled above the recall beacon. The time portal to the Chronos base was open.

Hunter grabbed Malloy's arm. "You three help Greg. Get him through the portal. I'll keep them off us!"

"Huh?" Malloy looked at him blankly.

"Dammit, Malloy! Do as I say! Take Greg! Walk into the light!" King might still have a chance if they got him to Chronos.

The T-80 had rumbled into the center of the compound now, as Russian soldiers fanned out across the compound, looking for survivors. They would find the bunker soon. Hunter crouched in the doorway, watching as the three Bravo Company soldiers dragged King into the blue light . . . and soundlessly vanished. They were emerging, he knew, four hundred miles away and three months in the future. He wondered what they would think when they stepped out onto the Chronos Project's time-portal platform.

There was a shout from close by. A Russian soldier gaped at Hunter, then brought his AKM up.

Hunter snap-fired the M-16 and the Soviet trooper spun away. He turned, sprinting toward the safety of the future.

The grenade bounced through the doorway before Hunter was halfway to the beacon. There was a roar and a surge of darkness, plucking Hunter up and slamming him down again.

Consciousness returned . . . white agony. *My back. Broken.* He twisted his head, peering toward the recall beacon. The light was gone . . . the portal closed. The explosion had wrecked the beacon and with it Hunter's only hope of returning to Time Square. He closed his eyes, waiting for death.

An age or two later, his hearing returned. There was thunder outside, and the shriek of jet aircraft sweeping low through Berthoud Pass. He smiled through his pain. Those were F-117Es, American stealth fighters, probably out of Colorado Springs. He heard screams outside, and the rumbling concussions of cluster bombs.

Despite the pain, despite the grief, Hunter grinned up into the darkness. If those fighters were here, it was because the Battle of Denver was over . . . and the Soviets had never made it through the pass. It sounded as if the Soviet column was being cut to bits.

The mission, at terrible cost, was a success.

More ages passed, as Hunter slipped in and out of consciousness. The pain was receding now, but he could not move his legs at all, and the numbness seemed to be spreading, crawling up his back and chest.

Movement, the scrape of boots, brought his eyes open. Men stooped above him. Hunter saw one tall, powerfully built figure with blond hair and a short, heavy beard. There were captain's bars on his collar, and the name HENDRICKS was stenciled above the right breast pocket of his fatigues.

"Who is he, Swede?" a voice asked.

"Damfino," Hendricks replied. "Never seen him before."

"Hey, Swede," another voice said nervously. "If he lives . . ."

"Yeah. The damned brass'd know we weren't here. That wouldn't be so good, would it, Johnny?"

"Hendricks?" Hunter could barely manage to speak. His brain was fuzzy with pain and shock. Hendricks was back! Perhaps . . .

"Glad . . . you came . . . Captain." The words came hard. "Glad . . ." He closed his eyes, exhausted by the effort. A familiar *snick-snick* of a round being chambered made him open them again.

Hendricks was smiling as he brought the Colt automatic to Hunter's forehead. The muzzle flash blotted out the smile as the gun fired, filling Hunter's universe with thundering light.

It was the last thing Lieutenant Travis Hunter saw.

Two

It's good to be alive, Travis Hunter told himself, stretching languorously.

Rachel Stein stirred beside him in the narrow bed, her dark eyes opening to meet his. Their fierce, passionate lovemaking had given way to quiet tenderness, but their emotions were no less intense now.

"Raye," he murmured gently. "I still can't believe I found you . . ."

She was the daughter of the scientist responsible for creating the time portal, as brilliant as she was lovely, and Hunter had met her in the course of rescuing her father from the Russians. Shared danger in missions into the past had brought them closer together. Now it was hard to remember, even to imagine, a life that didn't include Rachel. He felt a pang at the thought.

If the mission succeeds, I could lose her forever.

"I wish there was some way to make sure we'd still be together . . . after . . ." he said aloud.

She sat up in bed, raven hair tumbling over bare shoulders. "I know, Travis. But it just won't work. It can't."

Hunter nodded sadly. Chronos was about to launch Operation Backlash, an offensive in time, a plan to rewrite history entirely

15

and erase world Communism from the planet in a single blow. If it worked, everything—past and present—would change. Travis Hunter would never have to rescue Rachel Stein and her father from the Russians. They might never meet, never fall in love at all.

"The hell of it is that we won't even know what happened," he said. "Or didn't happen."

"Maybe that's best," she said. Her hand stole to the old-fashioned locket on its chain around her neck. "And think of what we'll have . . . that we don't have now. Your brother . . . Ben Taylor . . ."

And your mother, Hunter added silently. Deborah Stein had died years before in a car crash in the mountains above Jackson Hole. Her death might not have occurred if her husband had not been involved with the Chronos Project. And Chronos, in turn, stemmed from the ongoing war with Communism. Rachel was determined to see Russia eliminated to create a new history in which her mother need never have died. It was a goal that overshadowed everything else in her life. Even—sometimes—her love for Hunter.

"I know, Raye," he said. "God knows I want to see the war wiped out, America whole. But it doesn't make losing you any easier."

"Who knows? We might still be together . . . then."

Hunter's smile was forced. "How do we make sure? Leave letters for ourselves telling us how much we love each other?"

"Sounds like one of Roy Anderson's ideas," she said with a laugh. "But I'm serious, Travis. Sometimes it seems like time is fluid, like things are *supposed* to happen in certain ways. It doesn't come out in the equations, but it's true. Look how quickly history got back on track after we stopped the VBU plot to take over the Nazi Party."

"Fate? A scientist who believes in fate?"

Rachel shook her head. "Not fate . . . but something we don't understand yet. Something fundamental to the way time works. It takes a big change to alter history, you know . . . or a lot of little ones. But putting it back on track seems, well, easier."

He nodded thoughtfully, remembering the VBU plot to change the American Revolution. Hunter and a handful of men had stopped them, though they had mortars, helicopters, spetsnaz commandos . . .

Maybe there was some kind of "fate" involved. Or maybe Hunter's Ranger team had just been lucky so far.

"I hope you're right," he said, fingers stroking her skin. "I don't see how I could just . . . forget you."

"It wouldn't be that, Travis." There was a far-off look in her eyes. "The transformation wave changes everything . . . makes a whole new universe, like the one where General Thompson lost an eye and walked with a cane."

"Or British North America with no George Washington," he added.

She nodded. "The 'you' in a new universe without Communism or the Chronos Project wouldn't have lived through any of the things we've seen. Whether we were together in that universe or not, we'd have a whole new set of memories . . . because we'd have gone through a whole different lifetime. A better one."

Better? he thought. *Could it really be better if you weren't in it?*

"I guess so," Hunter said with a sigh. "At least maybe this other 'me' won't have to make these kinds of choices. It's hell knowing I'm going back to remake . . . everything. You and me . . ."

"I . . . I know, Travis." Rachel turned away. "You think *I* don't feel the same way? I *hate* feeling like I'm choosing between you and . . ." She trailed off.

He put his arms around her. "We don't have much choice, Raye," he said softly. "Either of us. We'll just have to use the time we *do* have . . ." Their lips brushed together as she returned his embrace.

Then the room was filled with the wailing of an alarm. A voice blared from the base PA system: "Security Alert! Security Alert!"

Hunter scrambled out of bed, hands scrambling to find discarded clothes as the alarm continued its ululation. Wide-eyed, Rachel looked up at him. "All portal crew to Main Control," the voice continued.

"That's me!" she said, pulling aside the sheets. She hurried across the room to her closet and fumbled for her own clothing.

The alarm faded. Then the voice of General Thompson, head of the Chronos facility, boomed over the announcer. "Lieutenant Hunter, report to Main Control immediately. We have a Condition Seven alert. Lieutenant Hunter to Main Control . . .''

Hunter was already running through the crowded corridors for the central elevator shaft before Thompson's message was repeated.

A guard stood beside the double doors of the Main Control Room, M-16 rifle at port arms. His eyes flicked over Rachel and roved on, alert. The soldier's brief nod was the only acknowledgment he gave as she pushed through the doors and into the chamber that housed the Chronos facility's time-portal mechanism.

Officially it was Facility Level Nine, Main Control Center, but everyone connected with the project, from General Thompson on down, called it Time Square. The huge room was a beehive of people checking consoles and instruments. People stayed well clear of the raised platform on the far end of the room, where a gathering glow of shifting blue light was forming to the accompaniment of a deep, throbbing hum of energy coursing through massive busbars. Sergeant Major Jenkins and a squad of security men formed a loose cordon around the platform. Rachel saw Anderson and Gomez among them, their black berets and camo garb contrasting with the plainer uniforms of Jenkins's troops.

She looked up at the glassed-in, raised enclosure, high above the floor of Time Square, that housed the master controls for the portal. Hunter leaned on the catwalk railing beside General Thompson, a worried frown creasing his forehead. King stood nearby, his stance deceptively casual. Corporal Walker was there too. Like the guard outside, they were tense, alert, eyes roving constantly.

Once before the facility had been compromised—by a traitor. No one planned to let security lapse again.

Rachel's father, Dr. David Stein, was working inside the overhead booth, assisted by his young protégé, Brian Fitzpatrick. But Rachel's regular post—when she wasn't on outtime—was at the primary computer station on the main floor. She crossed to the console.

Sarah Grant pushed aside a wayward strand of auburn hair and looked up as Rachel leaned over her shoulder to examine the monitor screen. "God, am I glad you're here," she said. "Maybe you can handle this stuff. I can't!"

"What's going on?" Rachel asked, taking the other girl's place at the console. Sarah was her understudy for the computer station but lacked her experience as a programmer. The redhead specialized in the hardware side of portal technology.

"We picked up a recall signal five minutes ago," she told Rachel.

"But we don't . . ."

". . . have anyone out in the field right now." Sarah finished the sentence with a shaky smile. "Hence the security alert."

"Thompson ordered a retrieval?" Rachel asked. "Why?"

"I didn't ask. I've been too busy trying to answer all of *his* questions—"

"Miss Stein!" General Alex Thompson's voice cut through the babble of voices around them. "Do you have precise coordinate translations yet? Or some idea who that signal is coming from?"

"See what I mean?" Sarah turned and called back, "I'm just filling her in now, General. We'll have the answers soon!"

The recall device transmitted a simple pulse through time, a beacon that enabled the portal system to lock on and open a hole between the Chronos portal platform and any past time and location inside Earth's magnetic field. But translating the beacon's temporal coordinates into a precise position and a specific date took patience and skill, even with the computing power available to the Chronos Project.

Rachel's fingers danced over her keyboard as graphs and columns of numbers flashed on the monitor. Finally she nodded, satisfied. "Keep an eye on it, Sarah." She rose. "I'll placate the Army."

She walked briskly to the nearest ladder, climbed to the catwalk above. Thompson and Hunter both turned as she reached them.

"Well?" Thompson demanded, more agitated than she had ever seen him.

"I don't know *who* it is, General," she said. "But the signal's coming from three months ago . . . July twenty-fourth. Morning, I think . . . but we'll need more time to process that."

"Three months," Thompson said. "Why would we be getting recall signals from three months ago?'' He paused. ''What about the location?''

''First approximation rounds off to forty degrees north by one-oh-six west . . .''

''Central United States,'' King said softly behind her.

''North and west of Denver . . . but not by much,'' Rachel agreed.

''On July twenty-fourth . . .'' Thompson looked thoughtful. ''The Battle of Denver, by God! Becker's fight!''

Hunter was nodding. ''Sounds like it, General,'' he said. ''But why a beacon?''

''Russian interference there, maybe?'' King asked. ''Maybe we're intercepting one of their portals?''

Rachel bit her lip. ''That's never happened before. They use a whole different approach to time travel . . . we shouldn't be able to intercept one of their downlink signals at all. At least I don't think so. We won't really know until we get a better look at one.''

''Well,'' Hunter said, ''if it isn't Russian, it must be one of ours . . . maybe from one of our teams that hasn't gone back yet.''

''That hasn't happened before, either,'' Rachel said. ''It can't. Theoretically, at least . . .''

''Too many theories,'' Thompson said. He rubbed his forehead. ''It might be one of the beacons we've lost in the past, like the one you had to abandon last time out. Maybe the VBU recovered it. They could be planning to drop something unpleasant into the portal.''

''They wouldn't have to move it to Denver to do that, General,'' Hunter pointed out. ''Why move it up to an area we'll have trouble retrieving from when they could operate anywhere in history?''

Walker spoke for the first time, his words unhurried, precise. ''Perhaps we're dealing with time travelers from another reality.'' He smiled apologetically. ''It is not unknown, after all.''

This time it was Hunter who answered. ''There's only one history allowed at a time, Walker,'' he said, glancing at Rachel. ''If they're from a different reality, they must have replaced us for a while. So what put us back?''

''Set all that aside for the moment,'' Thompson said slowly. ''We don't have anyone out there, and anyway, I don't see why we'd have a team at the Battle of Denver in the first place. We couldn't have won it any bigger than we did. Two Soviet columns routed, a third stood off in Berthoud Pass. Why would we be wanting to change that? And if we didn't send out a team, then we have to assume it's hostile.''

"Full power in thirty seconds, General," David Stein said over the control-room PA system. "Do we continue the pickup?"

Uneasy, Rachel stared down at the portal platform. "Travis . . ."

Hunter was nodding. "It could be. God, it really could be . . . us."

Thompson looked at them blankly. "You're getting ahead of me again. What is it . . . quickly!"

"I think you should open the portal, General. That really could be one of our own teams out there."

"If it's any of us, they might not make it through," Rachel pointed out. They had learned early on about the Exclusion Principle. It wasn't possible to bring someone forward out of time if he already had a close analogue in a new universe. If Hunter, say, tried to visit a reality that already contained a Hunter, he would simply vanish, lost forever within the portal's blue glow.

"But it might not be," Hunter said. "At least we should find out . . ."

Thompson turned to the control booth and gave Dr. Stein a curt gesture. A moment later the PA boomed again, Fitzpatrick's voice this time. "Full power . . . now!"

Rachel focused her eyes on the swirl of blue light as seconds passed slowly. Then a uniformed figure took shape, staggering, a bloody rag swathing his arm. Two more soldiers followed the first, one with his leg bandaged. They stood at the edge of the platform, gaping into the brilliant lights. One of them dropped his M-16 with a clatter.

Anderson and Jenkins advanced side by side up the ramp to the portal platform, their weapons level. "Why don't you boys step on down here kind of slow and easy," the Texan drawled.

All three stared at him. Swaying, the one with the bandaged leg gripped the rail. "You . . . but you're dead!" There was a hysterical edge to his voice. "I saw you die!"

Just then a cloud of dust and smoke erupted through the blue glow on the platform. Jenkins flinched as something screeched past his head. The portal light wavered, faded, winked out entirely.

"What are you doing, Dr. Stein?" Thompson demanded as the booth door opened.

"The beacon's signal is no longer available for lock-on, General," Stein replied. "It will take at least twenty minutes to reset coordinates and build back to full power."

"The beacon must have been damaged," Hunter said.

"Don't reset, Doctor," Thompson ordered. He gestured at the men on the platform. "At least not until we see what we've got here."

As her father returned to the control booth, Rachel followed the others—Thompson, Hunter, King, and Walker—down one of the catwalk ladders and across Time Square.

The three new arrivals seemed shattered. One was sobbing; the other two were staring around them as if they expected it all to be some kind of dream. All of them were talking, but the disjointed, confused babble was all but incoherent. At the sight of Thompson's party, they became even more agitated.

"Shock," Rachel whispered to Hunter. "They weren't expecting . . . all this."

"Or us," Hunter added, nodding grimly. It was evident that they knew the Rangers, at least. Gradually, Rachel pieced together a few facts from their hysteria. Gomez, Anderson, and Walker all dead. Hunter left behind facing the Russians. King, badly wounded, dragged with them into the blue haze. . . .

The stocky master sergeant looked down at his spotless uniform. "Fast recovery," he muttered to no one in particular.

Thompson glared at him. "This isn't getting us very far," he said. Then he turned on the sergeant with the bandaged head. "You! What's your name and unit, soldier!" His voice was all authority.

The sergeant's eyes focused uncertainly on the general's rank badges. He stiffened. "Sir! Sergeant Daniel Malloy, Bravo Company, Third Battalion, Fourth Mechanized Infantry Division!"

Thompson exchanged a long glance with Hunter before gesturing to Jenkins. "Sergeant Major, will you please order the commander of Bravo Team to join us here?"

"Sir!" Jenkins hastened off. Minutes passed in silence.

"Bravo Team?" Rachel looked curiously at Thompson. "What—"

"Later, Miss Stein," the general said curtly.

Bravo Team was a new unit being trained for out-time operations, forty men drawn from a regular army unit, rather than elite troops like the Rangers. They were supposed to play a key role in Operation Backlash. General Becker, the hero of the Denver fighting, had selected them for the job and used his political influence with the Free American government to assign them to the project over Thompson's strenuous objections.

General Becker. Bravo Team . . . heroes of the desperate battle at Berthoud Pass.

Behind them, the doors to Main Control swung open. They turned as Bravo Team's commander strode confidently across the tile floor. His blond hair and short, heavy beard, coupled with his tall frame and broad shoulders, gave the man the look of a Viking walking the deck of a longship in some Norse saga. Cocky, almost arrogant, he had a commanding presence that dominated the whole room.

"Swede . . ." Malloy gasped behind Rachel.

"Bravo Team commander reporting as ordered, sir," the big man said. He sketched out a lazy salute to Thompson. The general returned it smartly, precisely.

"We seem to have some people of yours here," Thompson said. "Perhaps you'd care to help us talk to them, Captain Hendricks."

Three

"I wonder how many times this has happened before?" Hunter glanced around the conference-room table at the rest of his team. They were gathered—with Rachel, Thompson, and Dr. Stein—to discuss the questions raised by the arrival of the three refugees from Berthoud Pass. Malloy and his two comrades had been taken to another room, where Hendricks was debriefing them.

King frowned. "It still doesn't make sense to me. Those guys say we're dead . . . but we're not."

"You're just seeing time travel from a different perspective," Rachel told him. "Suppose there was a different universe—call it Universe A—where General Becker lost the battle at Denver. Didn't you say it was pretty close, Travis?"

"Damned close," Hunter agreed. "If Hendricks and his people had been overrun, that third Russian column would have caught him flapping in the breeze."

"Then in Universe A, that's what we'll say happened. General Becker was defeated. But we have time travel, and we could change something three months back almost as easily as we could fix the American Revolution. The coordinates would be harder to lock and maintain . . . but not much."

25

Thompson nodded. "The Joint Chiefs have been looking over a plan for that sort of thing," he said. "But it seemed better to concentrate on missions that would win the whole war, not tactical applications."

"But a defeat at Denver . . ." Hunter trailed off with a shrug.

"Might have convinced us to try," Thompson finished. "If Becker had lost, there wouldn't have been much left to stop the Russians."

"So in Universe A the team went back to change the battle," Rachel said. "Whatever they did . . . whatever *you* did, was enough to hold off that third Russian group. The defeat changed into a victory. It would take a transformation wave generated in July about . . . call it an hour to reach the present. History was rewritten. In Universe B, where we are now, the new reality has us remembering a victory at Denver."

"And there's no need to send us back to change the Battle of Denver," Hunter added. "Instead we're planning a totally different mission—Backlash."

King shook his head. "I'll take your word for it, Lieutenant. But it sounds like science fiction to me."

Gomez grinned. "All I want to know is whether I can collect hazardous-duty pay for this mission you say I went on. How about it, General?"

Thompson answered him with a smile. "Sorry, Gomez. I can't authorize pay to a dead man." Everyone laughed.

Then Anderson was frowning. "I'd sure like to know why we haven't heard about our part in all this before," he said quietly. Beside him, Walker nodded gravely.

"What do you mean, Sergeant?" Thompson asked.

"Bravo Team was at Berthoud Pass, General," Anderson said. "That's why General Becker picked 'em to beef us up on Backlash. So how come they don't recognize us? Why didn't their report mention anything about us? I don't like it, sir."

The general looked at Hunter. "Your opinion, Lieutenant?"

"Roy has a good point, sir," he said. "I think Captain Hendricks has some explaining to do."

He turned as the door swung open. Hendricks was there, big, smiling, confident. "Do I now, Lieutenant?" the captain asked. "I wasn't aware of having to answer to *you*."

"But you *do* answer to me, Captain," Thompson said, his voice rasping. "And I think Hunter and Anderson are right.

We heard a lot about Bravo Company holding Berthoud Pass, so why didn't we hear anything about the Rangers helping out?''

Hendricks sat down heavily. "Well . . . I'm sorry, General. I'll have to admit I was trying to cover up for some of my men. I didn't tell the whole truth." He shot a curious glance at Hunter. "I never recognized you, Lieutenant . . . you had camo paint on and . . . well, I didn't see you that long."

"Let's hear about this cover-up, Captain," Thompson said impatiently.

"Yeah . . . well, General, you read the reports. Moffat Tunnel had to be blown to slow down the Russkies. Malloy's people were out there on patrol when the lieutenant and his boys showed up and contacted him." Hendricks gestured at Hunter. "Danny . . . the sarge sent word that some Rangers had turned up out of nowhere to warn us about a Commie attack. But I told the lieutenant to stay with Malloy. Your demo man wired up enough explosives to stop a division."

"And?" Thompson prompted.

"Well, the Russkies tried to go through the tunnel, like the Rangers said they would. These guys held them off, with Malloy's men. Finally blew the whole thing. Helped put us on our toes when the bad guys showed. They saved our necks, I tell ya . . . but I guess there were just too damned many Commies."

"I'm still not hearing anything about false reports, Captain," Thompson said.

"Yes, sir. Well, ah . . . when everything was over, we sent some men to check things out. Your men were all dead. But Malloy, Logan, and Marconi turned up missing. It *looked* like they'd bugged out when things got rough. But I . . . couldn't write my boys up. We've been through a lot together, General. I figured it'd be . . . best if I just didn't draw too much attention to Malloy's bunch."

Thompson steepled his fingers on the conference table. "So you didn't know Lieutenant Hunter's men were from the future?"

"No way, General!" Hendricks looked at Hunter again and shivered. "And I'm getting the creeps just thinking about it now. I saw those men . . . all dead. I know just how Malloy and the others must feel, finding you alive."

There was a long silence. Hunter studied Hendricks, frowning. While the story sounded convincing enough, it bothered the Ranger. Parts of it didn't quite ring true.

"I will want to take up this matter of your false report later, Captain," Thompson said at length. The general was a stickler for military procedure, and Hendricks and his men were continually in trouble with him over their casual regard for protocol and discipline. "Meanwhile, there are other matters to attend to. I suppose you are satisfied with Malloy's bona fides, Captain?"

"Sir? It's Malloy, all right. Logan and Marconi too."

"Could you have been right about them being deserters, then? Did they use the recall beacon to leave Lieutenant Hunter and the others stranded? Or could they be traitors sent here by the Russians on some mission after betraying the lieutenant?"

Hendricks shook his head emphatically. "Absolutely not, General," he said. "Malloy says the lieutenant told him to use the recall beacon after everything had gone to pieces. They were trying to get Sergeant King back here for medical help. The lieutenant was supposed to follow, but . . . ." He shrugged.

"Either he vanished like Greg," Rachel said slowly. "Or . . ."

"Or the Russians got me," Hunter finished. He turned to Thompson. "I doubt if Malloy would have used the recall beacon on his own, General. One of us would have had to operate it. I think our . . . guests . . . are legitimate."

The general nodded. "Good. That confirms my own opinion." He paused, then looked at Rachel and her father. "Now . . . does any of this affect our plans for Backlash?"

Dr. Stein shook his head. "I see no way in which this incident could influence the operation, General. The two are quite unrelated."

"If anything," Rachel added, "we've got confirmation that we really can make time travel work to our own advantage. Here's a case when we didn't just hold the line against the VBU, we actually took action and made a better universe!" Her eyes were shining eagerly. "And yet we didn't know anything about it . . . wouldn't know, if it hadn't been for this accident. This whole thing just makes Backlash look more promising than ever!"

Thompson looked at Hunter. "What do you think, Lieutenant?"

Hunter shook his head glumly. "I agree with Dr. Stein, sir," he said carefully, avoiding Rachel's eyes. "This doesn't change anything having to do with Backlash."

"Including your reservations about it," the general said.

"Right," he said curtly, darting a glance at Hendricks. "The whole op just seems . . . wrong. So much rides on factors we can't control. And this 'need-to-know' spy stuff . . ."

For over a month they'd been training for Operation Backlash. So far only the broadest outlines of the plan had been released to the Rangers, with exact details remaining closely restricted. Presumably Hendricks knew more about his group's role in the operation than Hunter . . . unless General Becker, who had taken overall control of the Backlash project, was planning to reveal the information only as it became absolutely necessary. Hunter's team was to play an important role in neutralizing any possibility of intervention by VBU time travelers, while Hendricks and his larger team carried out the primary operation. Just what that part of the mission entailed was classified even from Hunter, and it still made him uncomfortable.

"Reservations noted, Lieutenant," Thompson said softly. "Believe me, I have my own problems with Backlash. I'll be taking these up with General Becker when he gets here tomorrow . . . but meanwhile we go on as planned."

"Yes, General." He looked at Hendricks again. The bearded man returned his gaze coldly. "We'll do our part. Whatever else happens."

Brian Fitzpatrick slipped into the vacant seat beside Rachel Stein in Time Square. She was staring intently at her computer monitor . . . so intently, in fact, that she didn't notice him. He watched her run her slim fingers smoothly over the console controls, watched her brush aside a strand of silky black hair. She was so beautiful.

He had been a technician with the Chronos Project for over a year, longer, certainly, than the small Ranger team that had first spirited Dr. Stein and Rachel out of Russian-occupied Boston and brought them to the Project HQ under Mount Bannon. He'd worked for the Steins as an assistant in Boston, and it had been he who got word of their whereabouts to Time Square so they could be rescued. Fitzpatrick was good at what he did and had contributed much to the government's time-travel project, but he had one serious problem he was unable to overcome.

He was in love with Rachel Stein.

As he viewed it, however, the problem could be stated differently: Rachel was *not* in love with him. In fact, she'd shown little interest in anybody since that Ranger lieutenant had come on the scene. And there was absolutely nothing he could do about it. Sometimes it hurt working so close beside her, knowing she hardly noticed him.

"Ah . . . your father asked me to help you out, Rachel," Fitzpatrick said at last.

"Oh, Brian!" She was startled. "I didn't see you there! Sorry."

"Don't worry about it, Rachel," he said. It was hard to keep from blurting out how he really felt, harder still to summon the courage to say anything that might make her reject him once and for all. "What are you working on?"

"Nothing very urgent," she replied. "The computer's running diagnostics on the recall beacons for Backlash. I'm just minding the store."

"Can I take over for a while?" He frequently offered to do her little favors, hoping she'd like him, hoping she'd notice how he felt. She usually turned him down.

"Hmm . . . I should stick with it." She frowned, then smiled. "But this stuff is all pretty routine. Okay, Brian, you're on. Thanks."

"Sure, Rachel." He paused. "Ah, maybe . . ."

She went on as if she didn't hear him. "This way I can catch up with Travis before he starts his next briefing session." She was gone before he could think of anything to say.

Fitzpatrick settled in behind the terminal and stared at the shifting readouts. If he could just find a way to spend some time with her . . . to *talk*. Surely Rachel had more in common with him than with some mud-footed infantryman.

Patience, he told himself. *You'll get your chance. Someday . . .*

Major General Alexander Thompson leaned forward in his chair. "The point, General, is that time travel is a delicate matter. We're still finding things out about it! It should be handled by people who know what they're doing!''

"Meaning, I take it, that I don't?'' Major General Richard Becker lit a cigarette and waved it expansively. "Look, Alex, we've known each other for years. I know how much this Chronos thing means to you, and I'm not here to steal it. But Denver's put me in the position to make things happen, and I'm going to make sure I take advantage of it. Backlash is our best bet to wipe the Russkies out, and I intend to see it work.''

Thompson relaxed. "I'm not accusing you of stealing the Project. But Operation Backlash is risky. Hell, anything to do with changing history is risky. We tried knocking off Lenin once and failed. If we screw up Backlash . . .''

"This time's different. Your man Hunter missed Lenin because the VBU got in the way. This time we're ready for them.''

"Agreed. But a lot could still go wrong. And Captain Hendricks and his men have no experience in time travel. Forty soldiers running loose in history . . . I still feel Hunter's team could handle this by themselves.''

Becker shook his head. "No way, Alex. Look, I know you believe in Hunter, but from where I'm sitting, things look different. I've read the lieutenant's reports and recommendations all the way back to the Lenin mission. He's consistently claimed that we shouldn't act. He wants to use the Project like a fire brigade, running around after the goddamned Russkies.''

"Hunter's never said we *shouldn't* act,'' Thompson replied. "Just that we should be careful when we do. Changing the past can wipe all of us out, you know. Dammit, Rich . . . I haven't seen one of these alternate realities, and neither have you. But Hunter and his people have! They know what's at stake. I think caution's a damned good trait for someone responsible for a century's worth of history!''

Becker's cigarette stabbed at Thompson. "Sure, we have to be careful. Why do you think we've been researching Russian history? Point is, we need someone who'll take the information we put together and *use* it.''

"But is Hendricks the right man for the job?'' Thompson demanded. "I have my doubts about him. So does Hunter.''

"*I* don't,'' Becker said flatly. "Hunter's just pissed off because Hendricks is being given the main mission. After what

Bravo Company did at Berthoud Pass, I *know* they can handle Backlash. He *deserved* that FreeAm Medal, for God's sake!''

''Can they? They're undisciplined. Hendricks has even admitted to covering up for some of his men when there was reason to believe they had deserted.''

''They've been together in the field under tough conditions, Alex. They're a close-knit team. I've watched Hunter's people, other visits . . . they're not exactly textbook soldiers either.''

''Maybe not,'' Thompson admitted. ''But they're competent. A known quantity.''

''Hendricks and his people are good fighters. They proved that. And that's all that matters here.''

''I don't care how good they are as soldiers, Rich. Time travel is a whole new kind of warfare. Hunter's team has special training.''

''You didn't train them in time travel,'' Becker said. ''They're Rangers . . . damned good soldiers, but don't tell me they started out knowing anything more about time travel than Bravo Team does now! And Hendricks was in Special Forces. Got by on his own after the Occupation. Put Bravo Company together, brought it out of Red territory. I'd say that's worth something too.''

''I just don't think Hunter should be sidelined, Rich.''

''He won't be. His team has an important part to play.'' Becker frowned. ''But the Joint Chiefs put me in charge of Backlash, Alex, and I have more faith in Hendricks than I have in Hunter. Come on, man, think! Where would we be if someone like Hunter had been in charge at Berthoud Pass? He's too cautious to pull off something like this. But Hendricks can do it.''

''I hope you're right.'' Thompson looked away. Becker's reputation was riding on his choice of Hendricks now, and he wouldn't change his mind now. *I can't turn down your orders, Rich . . . I just hope you're right.*

Four

Hunter was not yet convinced that the Russian Civil War was the right place for an American time intervention. But the Joint Chiefs and General Becker seemed convinced from their own research that events in western Siberia late in 1918 and early in 1919 offered the U.S. its best chance of eliminating Communism once and for all. That was what Operation Backlash was all about.

There was scant hard information on the war . . . few pitched battles, few major landmark events on which to pin a change of history. Spawned by the ongoing horror of the First World War, it had begun with the October Revolution of 1917, the *second* Russian Revolution, which seized power from Kerensky's socialist Provisional Government that had ruled since the overthrow of Czar Nicholas II in March. A motley array of factions and personalities led the fight against Russia's new Bolshevik masters, ranging from moderate, democratic Socialists to military officers who wanted a return to the autocratic government of the czars. Behind them all were the Western Allies, taking time and energy away from the last gasps of World War I to orchestrate counterrevolutionary activities designed to bring the Russians back into the conflict against Germany.

The war had raged across the length and breadth of Russia, its echoes lasting well into the 1920s. Lands, towns, and cities were devastated time after time after time, as one army after another smashed its way across the countryside, killing, burning, pillaging, and raping without mercy. The First World War had never seen such raw, vicious, and calculated cruelty, as Reds and Whites tortured and executed one another with a bloodthirsty enthusiasm unparalleled in modern warfare.

The Whites suffered badly in their lack of common purpose. After the czar and his family were murdered by their Bolshevik captors in July, 1918, the White cause was particularly vulnerable, with no leader, no single ideal save their common struggle against the Reds. The Bolsheviks' supreme advantage throughout the war was their ideological unity under Vladimir Ilych Lenin.

In November of the same year, however, the Whites had found a rallying point when the weak and ineffective anti-Bolshevik government, the Directory, was replaced in a bloodless coup by Admiral Aleksandr V. Kolchak. For a short time Kolchak, self-styled Supreme Ruler of All the Russias, had carried on against the Reds who, by now, were everywhere victorious. But Kolchak proved to be too little, too late. . . . and his regime had been as bloody and as vicious as that of the Reds. He was captured and shot in 1920, and his death marked the beginning of the end for the White cause.

"There was a time, though, when Kolchak might have defeated the Soviets." The speaker was a tiny blond woman, Lynn Colby, a Professor of Russian Studies at the University of Denver before the war and now the chief historian of Operation Backlash. "He gave them a central government . . . and he had the backing of most of the Western Allies. In fact, at one point, there were something like one hundred thousand Allied troops in Russia supporting the Whites. British, Japanese, Italians, French . . . even a few thousand Americans."

Hunter stirred uncomfortably in his chair. Briefings for Backlash were held almost every day, but as always, this one dealt mostly in generalities. He looked around the room. His whole Ranger team was there, along with Hendricks and his two senior NCOs, Master Sergeant Simms and Sergeant Malloy. The latter, his leg still heavily bandaged, had returned to duty with Bravo Team soon after his unexpected appearance in Time Square. Hunter's men were paying close attention to everything the professor said, but the others seemed bored, unconcerned.

"Then we're goin' in to help this Kolchak fellow, ma'am? Is that the idea, or am I missin' something?" Anderson pushed back the cowboy hat he generally wore around the base and grinned. Like Hunter and the other Rangers, the Texan was unhappy at the "security measures" that left so many details of the mission vague and ill-defined.

"I thought Kolchak turned out to be a monster," Hunter said. From the little he knew of the man, Kolchak had been as bloody-handed as the Reds.

"That point has always been debatable," Lynn Colby told him. "Actually, many historians believe the admiral to have been an honest, honorable man. The reputation he earned later was the result of corruption at lower levels of the White government . . . and the propaganda efforts of the Communists, of course."

"History gets written by the winners, eh, Lynn?" Hendricks smiled broadly.

She grinned back. "Something like that, Swede." Base gossip suggested that Hendricks and Colby were an item, though to Hunter it seemed an unlikely pairing. The petite, rather plain young historian just didn't seem the type someone like Hendricks would fall for. But it was clear that she was strongly attracted to the captain, with his rugged good looks, his record as a war hero, his dominating physical presence.

I guess Rachel and I are about as unlikely as those two, Hunter decided. He was thinking of her subordination of everything, even their love, to the chance of changing history. *In some ways, at least.*

"Point is," Hendricks said expansively, "Kolchak gives us something to rally Russia around. If his government was as corrupt as Lynn says it was, then it must mean the admiral was easily controlled. We'll do the controlling this time around."

"And if he really was a monster?" Dark Walker sounded skeptical.

"Once we're in place, we can always replace him," Hendricks said.

"What Swede means is that there were other White leaders

who could take over the government. Generals we know were good men. Deniken, Wrangel . . . lots of possibilities." Lynn smiled. "If Kolchak becomes a problem, we could persuade him to step aside."

"Ain't always that easy to persuade a ruler to step down," King commented gruffly.

"What not back one of the others from the start?" Hunter demanded.

"No one else was in the right place at the right time," the historian replied. "We need Kolchak to set up the apparatus of a central government. Then we see if we can work with him or not. If need be, we put someone else in power."

"It still sounds like we're shooting from the hip," Hunter said. "I wish we had a better picture of the overall plan."

"It was a confused period, Lieutenant," Lynn said. "We have too many contradictory accounts to plan out every move in detail. But by getting close to the center of power, and by providing modern arms and training to local units, it won't be long before the Bolshevik movement is put down. Then we have a stable Russia, probably under a democratic socialist government, in place of the Soviet state."

"Probably." Hunter frowned. "But we can't even be sure of that, can we?"

"Sure enough. Once the emergency was over, something resembling the pre-Red government would almost certainly have emerged. Democratic socialists, like Kerensky."

"And what happens in World War II? Will Russia still grind down Uncle Adolf for us?" Gomez shrugged. "Last time we went after the Commies, we had a plan to knock off Hitler too."

"It's possible that Hitler would never rise to power in Germany at all, without the Communist threat to get the right-wing reactionaries behind him."

"Suppose the Nazis did get in, though?" Hunter asked. "What then?"

"Sooner or later, Hitler would have been tempted by Russian resources . . . the Ukrainian farmlands, the oil fields in the Caucasus." She smiled. "There was no way Hitler could have conquered all of Russia. The country is just too big. So the outcome would have been the same, with Germany defeated."

"Come on, Hunter," Hendricks said irritably. "We've all

heard your sermons about Nazis before. The planning people have done their homework. Can't you give anybody credit for knowing their own business?''

Hunter studied the bearded man. ''I'd be happier if I could see that everybody *does* know his business, Captain. But so far I'm not even clear on what the two teams are supposed to be doing, much less on the whole Backlash scheme. And I'm getting damned sick of being kept in the dark.''

''Relax, man,'' Hendricks said with a casual smile. ''You've got the easy job . . . security. You guys keep these VBU people off our backs, and we'll do the rest.''

Hunter bit back an angry response. His arguments hadn't worked in over two months of Backlash planning and training. Why should they convince anyone now?

But that thought only made the misgivings he felt over the mission that much worse.

''I hear we have a target.''

''Yeah,'' Hunter replied. ''It's good to feel useful for something.''

The October wind whipped around the flanks of Mount Bannon, cutting like an icy knife through his heavy winter parka. He stood beside King on a spur overlooking the cliffs where Bravo Team was conducting a final exercise in mountaineering under Ranger supervision. The snow-shrouded, pine-studded mountain gave no outward sign of concealing the Chronos Complex.

''Where? When?''

''Not too far from a town called Buguruslan in South Russia . . . west of the Urals. October 28, 1918. Dr. Stein thinks the MSA was within a few miles of our snoop.''

The ''snoop'' was one of dozens of small, computer-controlled devices buried in different places and at different times in remote spots across the western and central areas of the Soviet Union. Each snoop was a simplified version of the recall beacons used to retrieve time travelers . . . a unit designed to detect what the Chronos Project technicians called a ''Magnetic Surge Anomaly.'' MSAs were the signatures of the operation of a VBU time gate; when a Soviet gate opened, the magnetic pulse was detected by the nearest snoops and a signal relayed across the years to monitors at Time Square.

It was vital to Backlash that Bravo Team know where and when VBU time-portal downlinks were operating. A careful survey of the latter part of 1918, however, seemed to indicate that there was only the one gate . . . and that it was operated infrequently. The consensus of the Chronos Project staff was that it was some kind of watch station or outpost, VBU agents monitoring important periods in Russia's history against the chance of intervention by a U.S. team.

Knock out that outpost and Bravo would have a free hand in carrying out Backlash.

"You think they can cut it?" King gestured down the slope toward where a long line of men in parkas and full packs were waiting their turn at rappeling down a sheer rock wall. "Seems like Hendricks and his boys don't care much for hard work."

Hunter shrugged. "He's supposed to be good. And Becker got him the FreeAm Medal after Berthoud Pass."

Inwardly, Hunter had his doubts about the captain, but he kept them to himself. Hendricks was competent enough, but there was a ruthless streak in the man that worried the Ranger. Could such a man exercise good judgment when it came to manipulating history? Would he ride roughshod over any obstacle, heedless of the consequences?

Or am I upset at having him replace me? Or at the thought of losing Rachel? The tumble of conflicting fears and emotions worried him. So much was at stake this time.

"What about your friend Simms?" Hunter asked. Master Sergeant John Simms, Bravo Team's senior NCO, had turned out to be an old acquaintance of King's. "Maybe we should judge Captain Hendricks by the company he keeps."

King pursed his lips. "Johnny was kind of wild . . . but a good kid. Saved my life in the Bronx Riots. But I haven't seen him since boot camp. A lot can happen to change a guy in fifteen years, Lieutenant."

Nodding, Hunter studied the climbers below. With Backlash scheduled to start in three more days, there wasn't time now for second guesses or recriminations. But he was worried. Hendricks and his people were cold, aloof with outsiders, and even after a month Hunter didn't feel he really knew any of them. Especially Hendricks, alternately easygoing and arrogant, competent and lax.

The mission ahead could spell victory or defeat for the United

States . . . life or death for generations around the world. A beginning, or more likely an end, to Hunter's life with Rachel Stein. And this time out it all rested in someone else's hands. An unknown quantity . . . Hendricks.

So much at stake . . .

Hendricks landed in the snow at the base of the cliff, stepped back, and squinted through tinted goggles against the sun dazzle on ice and snow. "Stop worrying, Johnny," he said. He unsnapped the line from his harness and waved that he was clear. Twenty meters above them, the next two of Bravo Team began their descent, dropping down the cliff in short, easy bounds, suspended from the ends of their lines. "We've got it made."

"You're sure they bought your story?" Master Sergeant John Simms looked worried.

"They bought it," Hendricks said cheerfully. "And Malloy and the other two will back up whatever I say now."

"I still can't believe they came through that . . . thing."

"Yeah." Hendricks grinned. "I thought all that time-travel crap was a fairy tale."

He considered Hunter, the man he'd killed back at Firebase Sierra. All through the training routines of the past month, he'd thought the Ranger looked familiar, but it wasn't until Malloy's arrival that Hendricks finally realized the truth. He wasn't certain he understood all the twists now, but several facts were clear enough. Travis Hunter—*a* Travis Hunter, he corrected himself—had arrived out of the future to win the battle at Berthoud Pass. That victory had changed the present Hendricks now occupied, a present where Denver was hailed as a great victory instead of as a stunning defeat.

It still made him uneasy to look at Hunter now. Hendricks remembered killing the man, remembered squeezing the trigger on his Colt and watching the .45 hole appear like a bloody third eye above the bridge of the Ranger's nose. The Stein girl had cleared Hendricks last doubts earlier that morning. *This* Lieutenant Hunter had never been to Firebase Sierra and knew nothing of events there. No one did, except Malloy and the other two refugees. And they could be trusted to keep their mouths shut.

Simms cleared his throat nervously. "Does this mean we're,

uh . . . going through with the mission, Swede? Going back in time?''

''Why not?'' Hendricks smiled again. ''We've traded on the hero bit long enough. I'm tired of playing one of Becker's little lambs . . . even though the duty's sure been soft.''

After Berthoud Pass, Bravo Company had been given the royal treatment for saving Becker's army at Denver. Then came the training for Backlash, five weeks off the battle lines in the comfort of the Chronos Project. Now it was time to move on.

Swede Hendricks had been moving on ever since the Occupation. Assigned to the Green Berets as part of a Special Forces expansion only a few weeks before Washington gave in to the Russians, Hendricks had found it wise to desert from his unit to avoid being rounded up by the Russian peacekeepers charged with ''demobilizing'' the Army. He laid low for a time in Georgia and Alabama, roping in other deserters and refugees to prey on collaborators and Russians alike. Eventually they headed for FREAM territory, where Army records were sparse and manpower was always welcome, and Hendricks's little band was accepted as a guerrilla unit organized by a Special Forces veteran in the wake of the Russian takeover. As Bravo Company, they'd managed to stay out of action, mostly, while still raiding for whatever supplies the Army itself couldn't provide.

Now was the time to move on again . . . to bigger and better things.

''You don't really think there's anything to this stuff about changing history and wiping out the Commies, do you, Swede?'' Simms asked him.

Hendricks shrugged. ''It doesn't matter to us, Johnny,'' he said. ''Look, this time-travel stuff is our ticket to . . . to whatever we want! If we can *really* go back in time, who cares about taking out Russkies or any of that shit?''

''Then what are we doing?''

''Hell, Johnny, anything we want! We'll have modern weapons. We'll know what's going to happen. And we can cooperate with the powers that be back there to get a slice of any pie we want. We could live like kings back there, man! *Be* kings!''

''Can we get away with it?''

''Why not? Once we go back there, we're on our own . . .

except for the Rangers. Maybe they'll join up. You said that guy King used to be a friend of yours.''

"Yeah . . . maybe.'' Simms didn't sound convinced.

"And if they get in the way . . .'' Hendricks paused, picturing Firebase Sierra again. He smiled. "Hell, I killed Hunter once. I'll do it again if I have to . . . and his buddies with him.''

Five

The steam locomotive chuffed and hissed where it squatted on the siding. It was an old Class S, a green-and-red-painted 2-6-2 engine parked alongside a water tower and a small mountain of coal. The primitive depot lay isolated by evergreens, a tiny outpost of 1918 technology in the middle of the Russian wilderness.

Although it was dark, 0400 by local time, Hunter's starlight scope turned night to greenish day as he observed the engine of the armored train. Sheets of metal hung nearly to the track like rust-streaked skirts, masking the locomotive's drivers. Little used before or after this particular period of history, armored trains like this one had seen extensive service with both sides on the vast, rolling steppes of Russia and Siberia during the Russian Civil War.

The engine was not in the usual place at the head of the train. Up front was a squat, ugly car, literally a rail-mobile fortress encased in steel, with hinged firing ports and a clumsy-looking turret. Behind that was a flatcar with sandbags piled up in barricades protecting heavy machine guns, then a brilliantly lit passenger car, a pair of armor-plated boxcars, and another sandbagged flatcar. Then came the engine and its coal

43

tender, where a line of ragged-looking men hauled coal under the watchful eyes of a double row of soldiers, working by the light of hanging lanterns. Behind the coal car was another flatcar, an open boxcar that appeared to be a rolling barracks for troops, and a last flatcar bristling with machine guns. Sleepy-looking sentries paced the ground beside the train.

"Good Lord, LT," Anderson said as he looked up from the eyepiece of his own night scope. "How does that thing even move?"

"Looks pretty heavy," Hunter agreed. "I imagine it's hard to stop once it gets rolling, though."

"I'll say." Anderson studied the train again. "You catch the guards' weapons?"

"Bolt-action," Hunter said, nodding. "Mosin-Nagants."

"So where are our VBU friends?"

"Check the boxcars . . . the two strung together. And have a look at that passenger car in front of them."

"Ah! Got it."

"I'd say we've found what we came for."

At first glance the railcars were just what they appeared to be, but a close inspection revealed anachronistic discrepancies. The two boxcars were linked to each other by a bundle of what looked like heavy power cables. Just ahead of the lead boxcar was a single passenger car. It, too, had power cables draped above the coupling mechanism, and a thin mast antennae extended above the car into the air.

Radio was not unknown in the year 1918, but its use aboard trains, even armored military trains in European Russia, was. And the generators capable of delivering power in the quantities suggested by those massive cables would not be in existence for another forty years or more.

"Whatcha think, LT?" Anderson asked. "A nuke power plant in one boxcar, the downlink in the other?"

"Almost certainly. Clever of the bastards, hiding it aboard a train."

"There are cables leading to that passenger car too."

"I see them. That'll be their headquarters. See the radio mast?"

"Lots of sentries," Anderson said. "But damned lax security."

Hunter nodded. The guards he could see were a scruffy-looking lot, wearing a variety of uniform parts. Some slumped against the side of the train they were guarding, while others sat or squatted nearby. Several were curled up against convenient trees or stacks of railroad ties, asleep.

"What're they here for?" Anderson went on. "Are they trying to change something?"

"Nah. Probably just keeping an eye on things," Hunter replied. "Trotsky is nearby, checking up on the local Red Army. The VBU is probably shadowing him, just to make sure their history goes the way it's supposed to."

Hunter studied the armored boxcars again. In past missions they'd found Russian time-portal equipment hidden in unlikely places—the turret of a castle in 1926 Germany, within one wing of a colonial house in 1777 Pennsylvania, even out in the middle of the woods in Revolutionary War New Jersey—but this was the first time the Soviets had used a mobile base. It made sense, though. If they were guarding important figures of the Russian Civil War, protecting them from U.S. Ranger intervention, it would be necessary to follow them across the endless expanses of Russia. The Russian Civil War had been fought and won by control of the railways, especially the great Trans-Siberian Railway, which stretched clear to Vladivostok on the Pacific coast. Having a time machine that could follow the rail lines across that vast country would be of vital importance to the VBU operating in this period.

"Whoa!" Hunter said. He adjusted his starlight scope, sharpening the focus. A door had opened on the end of the passenger car, and a soldier was stepping down a short ladder to the ground. He was dressed like the other troops around the train, in a greatcoat that hung to his ankles. His breath appeared as white puffs in the chill October air. As he set foot on the ground the sentries straightened up, though there was still a distinctly unmilitary look about them. One kept a cigarette in his mouth and his hands in his pockets as the soldier spoke to him. Hunter's attention was focused on the assault rifle slung muzzle-down over his shoulder. The lines of a Soviet AKM were unmistakable.

"VBU," Anderson said. "No doubt about it now. You think those laid-back fellas with the bolt-action rifles are time travelers too?"

"I doubt it, Roy. They're probably Red Army deserters,

rounded up and promised a bounty for doing a bit of sentry-go.''

''Makes sense. They wouldn't need as many VBU regulars for guard duty.''

''The Russian Civil War covers a lot of ground,'' Hunter said. ''And a lot of time. Even the VBU wouldn't have the resources to watch everything.''

''What about those ragged guys hauling coal?''

Hunter shifted his scope again. ''Prisoners, I'd say. Under close guard too.''

''White soldiers, maybe?''

''Probably. Can't tell from here.'' He began packing up the night scope. ''C'mon, Roy. Let's get back to the TLZ.''

The Ranger base camp was located not far from the Temporal Landing Zone, on wooded, gently rolling terrain bordering the vast, grassy steppes to the south. It took them an hour to track their way through the night across the three miles from the train depot to the camp. King, Gomez, and Walker were waiting for them when they arrived.

Quickly, Hunter filled them in on what the two Rangers had seen at the depot. King shook his head in mock despair. ''I can see it in your face, Lieutenant. You're thinking we can hit the train by ourselves.''

Hunter grinned. ''You have a better idea?''

The operational orders for Backlash called for the Rangers to be used strictly as a reconnaissance team, a decision that made good tactical sense. They'd come across other Soviet time-travel downlinks on other missions, and every one had been well protected and heavily guarded. Hunter's orders called for them to identify the Russian time base and report back to Time Square. Bravo Team would then return to take out the base . . . before proceeding with phase two of the plan.

Unfortunately, no one had expected the VBU to have a *mobile* downlink. American time-travel technology was not yet up to the point where the strike team could return to the precise place and time that the Rangers had just departed from, not unless they left their recall beacon here. If they did that, an hour spent briefing Hendricks in 2007 would mean an hour passing in 1918, and while the Rangers were reporting their find to Becker and Hendricks, the Russian train might leave.

A great deal of time and energy could be wasted pursuing the train with a force large enough to take it out.

The only alternative appeared to be for the five Rangers to attempt to take the Soviet base themselves, before the train had a chance to get under way.

"Hey, should be no problem, Chief," Gomez added. "We've only seen . . . what? Maybe twenty men around the train? Against the five of us . . ."

"We've only seen one we know is VBU, Eddie." Hunter said. "From the look of things, the VBU has some Red Army troops manning the machine guns on the train. Once we open up, I'm betting that most of those locals are going to hightail it for the woods."

"Sounds good," King said. "Their morale can't be good. When we hit 'em, their first thought is going to be to bug out."

"It's a gamble," Hunter said. "But I think it's worth a try. If we don't, that train'll be gone as soon as it's taken on fuel and water."

"Take 'em now," Anderson said. "I'd just as soon not chase them all over Russia."

"Right," Hunter agreed. He looked up. The sky was lightening in the east, above the distant black mounds of the southern Urals. "No telling when the train will be pulling out. We'll hit them now . . . before dawn. Now, here's how we'll do it. . . ."

Captain Oleg Fedorovich Rozhko climbed the ladder back into the light and warmth of the headquarters car, slipped the AKM from his shoulder, and replaced the weapon on its rack by the door. He sighed as removed his coat. The Red Army scum they'd collected to guard the train were an arrogant, insubordinate lot, hopeless as soldiers and dangerous to work with. Only the promise of gold and the demonstrated threat of the—to them—awesome firepower of modern assault rifles kept them in line.

But all seemed well so far.

Service with one of the *Vremya Ochrana Brigadi*—the Time Guard Units of the VBU—tended to be boring and primitively uncomfortable, but even with the danger of mutiny among the surly local recruits it was far safer than being assigned an active intervention mission. The *Ochrana* was typical of dozens of similar units scattered through Russian history at critical points and dates along the time line. Here in 1918, the VBU had agents with a number of people important to Russia's history— Lenin, Trotsky, Stalin, and others—and Rozhko's armored train provided the mobile link for those agents with the VBU's master base in 2007.

The VBU's higher-ups were not talking about recent losses in the continuing time war against the Americans, but there were rumors enough of serious reverses to the Plan in 1923 Germany and in 1777 America for Rozhko to draw his own conclusions. Soviet attempts to rewrite the past of the United States all had been failures, and the VBU had suffered heavy casualties, whatever the leaders might claim. Spending a year in the squalor and dirt and hardship of 1918 watching over key Bolshevik leaders and protecting them against the *possibility* of enemy intervention was certainly preferable to going up against the American time commandos head to head.

Fortunately, there was no indication at all that the Americans were interested in this particular place and year, not when they were being kept busy protecting the past of their own country by VBU missions elsewhere and elsewhen. Rozhko had resigned himself to the modest discomforts and inconveniences of his posting. In another two months, his tour here would be up, and he would say good-bye to the fleas, dirt, and—

Gunfire erupted in the early-morning darkness, the shrill, high-speed clatter of assault rifles. Autofire! That could mean only one thing. The Russian armies of 1918 were well acquainted with machine guns, but assault rifles were unknown. American time commandos were attacking!

He spat a Russian curse and bolted for the rear of the car. Two VBU technicians blinked owlishly at him from behind their consoles. "Comrade Captain!" one said. "All power leads from the reactor have been cut! An explosive charge, almost certainly—"

"Of course it was an explosive charge, idiot! Get out of my way!"

Rozhko reached past the technician and picked up a radio microphone. With the nuclear power out, the railcar's powerful shortwave radio would no longer be able to reach Vasilov and the other agents in Moscow, but emergency power would be sufficient to punch through to Obinin at Yarinsk.

He depressed the transmit key. "Obinin, this is Rozhko! Come in!"

It took several tries, but a moment later he heard Lieutenant Vadim Sergeivich Obinin's voice against the flutter of the short-wave static. *"Obinin here. Go ahead!"*

Obinin was in charge of the VBU party that was watching over Leon Trotsky. At the moment they were at Yarinsk, a tiny village forty miles to the north.

"Ch'yornee Ahgohn!" Rozhko said. The words were a code phrase meaning American time commandos were attacking. "I say again, Black Fire!"

There was a moment's pause. *"What are your orders, Comrade Captain?"*

"Alert Vasilov. Our power is out here. We cannot reach Moscow, and we cannot power up the downlink to alert Uralskiy. VBU Command Central must be warned."

"Da, Comrade Captain. Shall I dispatch troops to help you there?"

Rozhko considered a moment. It would take an hour for an armored train to cover the forty miles from Yarinsk . . . even assuming one had steam up and was ready to leave immediately. Another roar of gunfire just outside the coach decided him.

"No. It is imperative that headquarters knows what happened here. We shall set off the self-destruct charges if it appears we are about to be overrun."

"At your order, Comrade Captain."

"Rozhko out."

He replaced the microphone, listening to the chatter of gunfire from outside the train. In the distance, he heard the thunderous yammer of an American M-60 machine gun. There could be no hope that Obinin could get help here from Yarinsk in time to play a part in this firefight. If the battle was to be won, it would be won with the men and weapons at hand. But with the VBU resident agents in Moscow alerted, there would be time to counter the American threat.

Let the Americans try, he thought, smiling grimly. *In a war fought through time, there is always a second chance.*

Anderson hugged the shadows next to the coal car. A sharp blast echoed from farther down the train as one of the Rangers tossed a grenade into the sandbag barricades erected on a flat-car. The team's initial approach had been made in complete silence, with only the still forms of dead sentries sprawled in the darkness to mark their passage. Now gunfire spat and barked in the predawn twilight, as Russian soldiers died.

Settling his M-60 on its sling muzzle-down at his side, he sprinted forward to the iron rungs leading up to the locomotive cab, set his hands to the cool metal rails, and scrambled up. The engineer was in the cab, cowering wide-eyed against the complexity of pipes and valves and gauges at the front of the narrow space. Beside him, a soldier with an AKM brought his weapon up.

That Texan fired his Maremont from the hip, a short, precise burst at point-blank range that nearly tore the VBU agent in half. Blood splattered across the locomotive's firebox, hissing wildly as it drenched hot metal.

He swung to cover the engineer. *"Nyeh strelyat!"* the man shrieked. "Don't shoot!"

"On the deck!" Anderson yelled in Russian. "Face down!"

The engineer complied, and Anderson brought the butt of his M-60 down on the back of the man's head. He could take no chances with Russians—even harmless-seeming civilians—getting the drop on him when his back was turned.

Anderson stepped past the unconscious man to check the far side of the train. The Red guards had opened fire on their prisoners at the first shots, but the POWs had turned now and were overwhelming their captors in a wild rush. The Ranger saw one brawny prisoner, in the tattered rags of a uniform, hoist a lump of coal above his head and bash it down on the skull of a Red soldier, crushing the man's skull like a melon. Another POW was throttling a soldier from behind with the gasping man's own rifle. There was a roar from the crowd that drowned out the crackle of gunfire.

A ragged line of Red troops brought their rifles up, preparing to fire into the rioting prisoners again. Anderson swung his Maremont around and triggered a long, savage burst. Four of the soldiers spun, twisted, and fell in bloody heaps. The others took to their heels, throwing away their rifles and fleeing for the woods.

Anderson found himself looking down into the face of a blond, bearded giant.

"Mawtscraht dyekooyi!" the man said, grinning. *"Velmi rad vas vidim!"*

Anderson shook his head. *"Nyeh pahneemayoo,"* he replied in Russian. "I don't understand. *Gahvareeti lee vih pa Rooski?"*

The giant's broad grin transformed itself to a scowl and Anderson became worried. Had he just identified himself as an enemy?

"G'daw yste?" the man growled, one grimy forefinger prodding up at Anderson. *"Rooski?"*

"Ah . . . *Sprechen Sie Deutsch?"* Anderson tried, guessing at the man's blondness and piercing blue eyes. All of the Rangers spoke both Russian and German.

The former POW still looked suspicious. *"Ja! Ja, Deutsch . . . ein wenig!"*

A little German? Then who . . . ?

"Ich bin ein Amerikaner," Anderson said. He remembered Lynn Colby talking about the Western Allies intervening in Russia. Perhaps this man would assume he was one of them.

The giant brightened. *"Amerikaner!"* He slapped himself on his chest. *"Ich heiße Anton Dubcek!"* he declared in heavily accented German. *"Ich bin Tscheche!"*

Anderson blinked. Unless he'd misunderstood, the giant had just said he was Czechoslovakian. A fresh outburst of gunfire interrupted the conversation. A number of Red troops had been flushed from one of the railway cars, their hands raised in surrender.

They were met by Czech troops, armed now with rifles taken from their former captors. The surrender was not accepted.

Hunter triggered a burst from his Uzi that caught a Red soldier in the gut and tore him down, then ran for the side of the armored train. Grenade explosions shattered the night with noise and flame, and the confused shouts of running soldiers mingled with gunfire and the shrieks of the wounded.

There would be no time for finesse on this one. Eddie Gomez had snuck in past the sentries and set explosive charges on the cables linking three of the railcars, then withdrawn to the woods. Once the charges were set off, he'd begun laying down a steady barrage with his M-203 while the others rushed the train, each angling for a different target. Hunter's goal was the lit-up passenger car that almost certainly served as the VBU command post. Another soldier loomed out of the shadows between two cars, this one with an AK. Hunter shot him and moved on.

Greg King materialized from the gloom close by, his FN-FAL pointing high to cover sandbag barricades on a nearby flatcar, now abandoned. "Looks like they're on the run," he said as Hunter joined him.

"Right." Hunter pointed to the dead Russian with the AKM. "I've seen one VBU man. You?"

"Not a one. Maybe we got lucky, Lieutenant."

"It's about time."

"Think they already got a radio message out?"

"Almost certainly. I bet they have watchdog teams all over Russia . . . but there's not much any of them are going to be able to do. Not if *we've* got their time portal."

They sprang to the front of the passenger car, bracing themselves on the platform on either side of the door. This was a great time for grenades, but Hunter wanted to minimize damage to VBU equipment if he could. Already a fantastic realization was shaping itself in his mind.

He yanked the door open and King rolled through, his FN-FAL barking. Hunter followed close behind him. His Uzi snapped a trio of rounds into a Russian's body, punching him back through the door at the far end of the compartment. The Rangers charged forward through a plush and ornate sitting room, then banged through the door into what was obviously a radio room.

There were two men there. One, to the right in technician's coveralls, scrabbled for an AKM leaning against a console. King and Hunter fired together and the man crumpled as autofire tore into his back.

The Russian to the left had just flipped open a guard on an instrument panel, his hand reaching for the large red button underneath.

Hunter caught the movement as he fired into the technician. He swept his Uzi sharply to the left, his finger still clamped down on the trigger. Bullets pocked the far wall in a ragged line, then chopped into the second Russian, pitching him back from the console just as the magazine in Hunter's Uzi ran dry.

"Nice move, Lieutenant," King said.

Hunter silently pointed to the red button, and King's face went white. The VBU agent had been trying to set off a self-destruct.

Outside, the gunfire died away.

"Well, Greg," Hunter said, trying to control the shake in his voice. "Looks like we just captured ourselves a train."

Six

"Sehr erfreut, Herr Dubcek," Hunter said. "I am very pleased to meet you."

"And I, Lieutenant!" Captain Anton Dubcek's voice boomed in the still smoky interior of the captured passenger car. "I am happy to meet Americans at last!"

Communication between the Rangers and the rescued POWs was fragmentary at best. None of the Rangers spoke Czech, and none of the Czechs spoke English, but a mix of German and Russian was adequate for getting the message across.

Hunter knew from the Backlash briefings that a number of foreign nationals had become embroiled in the Russian Civil War, including the famous Czech Legion, but he'd not heard the full story before this. With broad sweeps of his arms, Dubcek filled Hunter and the other Rangers in on the Czech intervention in Russia.

In October 1918, there was not yet a nation called Czechoslovakia. The land that would soon take the name officially was part of the Austro-Hungarian Empire, and an ally of Germany in the world war that still engulfed Europe. Most Czechs favored independence and detested their Austro-Hungarian rulers. So many units felt that way that whole regiments surrendered intact to the Russians; one, the 1st Prague, had deserted en masse, marching through Czarist lines with their band playing at their head.

In February 1917, revolution toppled the Czar, and Aleksandr Kerensky established his provisional government. Czech nationalist Thomas Masaryk met with Kerensky in St. Petersburg soon afterwards urging him to recruit the thousands of Czech prisoners in Russia into an army corp to fight against Germany and Austria-Hungary.

"And we fight!" Dubcek declared, grinning broadly. "We fight at Zborov! When Russian Army run, Czechs only troops to stand and fight! Only army left in all Ukraine!"

"You were fighting for Russia, then," Hunter said. "What happened?"

"Bolsheviks happened!" Dubcek spat viciously. "October Revolution, and Kerensky is out. *Kaput!* Is beginning of Civil War, Reds against Whites, all across Russia! After big treaty, Czech Legion not allowed to fight anymore."

On March 3, 1918, the Treaty of Brest-Litovsk had ended Russia's part in World War I. Masaryk negotiated with the Bolsheviks to evacuate the Czech Legion, now stranded on Russian soil and forbidden to continue their fight against the Germans who occupied western Russia under the terms of the treaty. Masaryk's planned exodus was nothing short of incredible. The forty thousand men of the Czech Legion would cross Russia on the Trans-Siberian Railway, embark in Vladivostok for the United States, make their way across the U.S., and re-embark for Europe from New York. Once in France, they would continue their fight against Germany, this time in the trenches of the Western Front.

The movement began with the agreement of the Bolsheviks, in whose territory the Legion was operating, but the arrangement swiftly broke down as the Russians demanded that the Czechs disarm, and as Communist administrators attempted to use the foreigners for their own purposes. The final break came in May 1918; the Czech Legion would fight its way across Siberia to Vladivostok.

And it was that break which made the Allies decide to intervene in Russia.

Hunter knew more about the politics of that decision than Dubcek. The pre-mission background briefings back at Time

Square had described the desperation of the Allies as they sought a way to keep Russia in the war against Germany. After Brest-Litovsk, thousands of battle-hardened German troops had been freed in the east to fight in the west.

In March 1918, British troops had seized Murmansk and Archanglsk on the White Sea. They were swiftly joined by contingents of Americans, Canadians, and others. In the Far East, landings were made by American, British, and Japanese troops, who seized Vladivostok and moved west along the Trans-Siberian Railway. But there was no unity of purpose or agreed-upon goal among the Allied interventionalists. The British were attempting to strong-arm the Bolsheviks back into the war . . . or win the gratitude of a victorious White government that would take up the fight. The Japanese were more cynical, seeing in intervention a means for seizing large chunks of Siberia. The Americans, mistrustful of intervention but more mistrustful of the Western Allies, were there partly because President Wilson hoped the move would bring Allied support of his Fourteen Points and the League of Nations, and partly to block Japanese ambitions on mainland Asia. The politics of the situation were as murky as they were flawed.

Coming under the orders of the Allied Supreme War Council, the Czech Legion was seen as an interventionalist army already in place, and by the summer of 1918, they had seized most of the railway between Ekaterinburg in the Urals and Vladivostok on the Sea of Japan. The plan to evacuate the Czechs was abandoned, which was just as well, since the ships to transport forty thousand troops across the Pacific simply did not exist.

As of that evening, the Czech Legion—those of the troops who were not strung out along the five thousand miles of the Trans-Siberian Railway—was holding a line along the fringes of the Ural Mountains. If Dubcek was to be believed, they were the best fighting troops anywhere in all the Russias. Having talked to Anderson after the fight in the village, Hunter was inclined to believe the man's boast.

Dubcek was the senior officer of a band of Czechs who had been scouting behind the Red lines when they were trapped by a larger force and captured. The Czech was under no illusions about their eventual fate. After five months of fighting, he'd seen countless Red atrocities: slaughtered prisoners, POWs herded into railcars that were then set alight, tortures and butcheries that appeared to be second nature to peoples numbed by four years of constant, brutal war. "The Russians are strange people," Dubcek concluded. "They capture you, load you on train, transport you three thousand miles . . . then shoot you. For us, there was no hope. Then you come, set us free. How can we repay you?"

"I don't think repayment is necessary," Hunter said carefully. He did not want to offend this big, bluff soldier. "Will your people be able to reach Czech lines from here?"

"Is no problem, Lieutenant. Our lines are at Buguruslan, thirty miles east." His eyes narrowed, and he leaned forward, staring into Hunter's face. "We can be there in an hour or two with this train."

Hunter leaned back, considering. The capture of the train-mounted VBU time machine was a real coup . . . and an unexpected bonus in the time war raging between the Russians and the Americans. Once before, the Rangers had captured a Soviet downlink portal intact and had a chance to study it, but the study had been interrupted by the arrival of VBU troops from the future, and a battle that ended in the destruction of the equipment. They'd not planned on capturing this one; Hunter's orders were to locate the Soviet downlink base only, then bring in Hendricks and his team to take and destroy it.

But perhaps they wouldn't need to destroy it. Sooner or later VBU troops would come to find out what happened to their time-travel equipment, but Hunter now had the means to take that equipment elsewhere. It would be too dangerous to remain behind Red lines, but with the Czechs to help, there might be a chance.

He studied Dubcek thoughtfully. With the twenty-eight freed Czech soldiers to guide them through the lines, they just might pull it off.

"Okay, Captain," he said at last. "I think we might be able to work something out. This train has equipment that . . . friends of mine want to see. But to do it, I've got to get the train someplace safe."

"Safe? Safe? Lieutenant . . . Czech camp is safe . . . safest place in all the Russias! You take us there, you see! We welcome new American allies!"

Hunter thought about it a moment more, then stood suddenly and paced to the door of the coach. King was waiting outside, keeping a wary eye on the celebrating Czech troops. "Moving day, Greg! Round up the others and get them in here ASAP. Then find that engineer we rescued. I think Eddie's got him, back at the locomotive. Bring him too."

"Right, Lieutenant! Where we headed?"

Hunter looked back at Dubcek, who grinned at him from across the car. "East, Greg. We're heading east. Haven't you always wanted to visit Siberia?"

King's eyebrows hitched themselves higher on his forehead. "I'll tell the lads to pack their long johns." He hurried off into the night.

Vadim Sergeivich Obinin looked out the window of the coach at the passing scenery and scowled. It was frustrating—frustrating and infuriating—to be held at the mercy of local technology. There had been no train available to leave for Moscow immediately, and the telegraph lines between the front and the capital were down more often than they were up. It was fortunate indeed that Comrade Commissar Trotsky had been on his way to Moscow to deliver a speech, and that Obinin had been able to tag along.

Obinin had been one of the senior advisers to Commissar of War Leon Trotsky for nearly four months now, and could not help but admire the man. In that time Trotsky had traveled the length and breadth of Russia, organizing defenses, encouraging troops, exhorting the men to superhuman feats under the red banner of Communist ideology.

In an uncharacteristic departure from his Marxist-Leninist training, Obinin thought it a shame that the man was doomed. More internationalist in his outlook, he would run afoul of Stalin's narrowly interpreted nationalism after Lenin's death. Assassins would hunt him down at last in Mexico City in 1940.

Or would they? Obinin was only a lieutenant in the 1918 Time Guard Unit and was not privy to the long-range plans of the VBU's senior officers. But he'd heard rumors of future operations, hints and whispers of projects now being implemented that would transform history once and for all, eliminating the Americans and securing the blessings of world Communism for all men and all time. It was a glorious vision. Perhaps there would even be room in that new world for visionaries such as Lev Davidovich Bronstein, better known by his revolutionary name of Trotsky.

But first the American time commandos would have to be dealt with. Obinin's scouts had reported that the VBU train was gone. Bodies at the site suggested that most of its passengers, both local Red army troops and VBU agents, had been killed. That meant the Americans had taken the train . . . probably east, toward the Urals.

Fleeing wouldn't help them, of course. Once Obinin reached Moscow, they could send for reinforcements.

And then it would only be a matter of time.

Hunter and Anderson stood in the shadow of the crumbling wall of a medieval fortress. The city of Ufa stretched out below them, a long, narrow ramble of buildings on the heights of a narrow strip of land between the confluence of the Belaja and Ufa Rivers, not far from the front lines at Buguruslan. Dubcek had described Ufa as the ancient guardian of trade routes across the Urals. Now the Czechs guarded the city from the advancing Reds.

General Rudolph Gaida had welcomed them with open arms. The Czech officer was young for his rank, only twenty-seven, with piercing blue eyes above an aristocratic, aquiline nose. He'd been a lieutenant in the Austrian medical corps before deserting to the Russians. Gaida was enormously popular with his men, a dedicated, hard-driving man never satisfied with his own performance or that of others. Since his promotion to general in July, he had risen to become one of the senior officers in the entire Czech Legion.

Hunter had seen no reason to hide the fact that the Rangers were Americans. Russians and Czechs alike in the area were expecting the arrival of Americans with the interventionalist forces any day now, and admitting the fact avoided any embarrassing questions about differences in language, uniforms, and weapons. Hunter was wondering now if he'd done the right thing. The hours since their arrival had been one long celebration for the ragged-looking Czech troops who were now convinced that the newcomers were the vanguard of a long-promised American army.

The problem was, the White army for the most part was occupying the rear-echelon areas, leaving the fighting to the

Czechs. The promise of an international army intervening in the Russian War had been dangled before their weary eyes for months now. Only two days ago, Colonel Josef Svec, Gaida's chief of staff, had shot himself rather than lie again to the men about the arrival of outside help. The Legion's morale was at low ebb, the troops wavering and shaky. Gaida himself had all but given up on the chimerical promises of the British, American, and Japanese governments. Hunter wondered what would happen once they realized that the sum total of this new "American intervention" was fifty-odd men and a plan he still was not sure would work.

He did not have the heart to tell them that the *real* American army of intervention would get no closer than Murmansk and Archanglsk to the north, or cold, deep Lake Baikal far to the east.

On the ground at the Rangers' feet was their recall beacon. The spectral, blue auroral glow of an opening time portal danced and shifted in the air above it. By triggering the beacon, they'd given Time Square a target for their space- and time-twisting mechanisms. Greg King had vanished through the blue glow thirty minutes earlier, and they were awaiting his return.

Movement shimmered in the depths of the blue light.

King materialized from emptiness as he stepped through the portal and across a gulf of eighty-nine years.

"Welcome back, Greg," Hunter said. His eyes were already on the next figure solidifying in the glow. "Raye . . ." Then they were in each others' arms.

King grinned. "Better stand aside there, you two," he said as more shapes appeared in the light. Brian Fitzpatrick and Sarah Grant, arms laden with technical gear, stepped into the chill autumn air and looked around with wide-eyed curiosity.

Hunter had dispatched King back to 2007 with the news of their capture of the VBU time-portal apparatus. Evidently, that news was important enough for the American command to decide to take immediate action.

"General Thompson is quite excited about you've done," Sarah explained. "He rounded us up and told us to figure out what makes the Soviet time-portal equipment tick. We're to travel with you to Omsk."

"Omsk?" Hunter visualized a Russian map. Omsk was a fair-sized Siberian city on the Irtysh River some eight hundred miles east of Ufa. It was an important stop on the Trans-Siberian Railway, and the current capital of anti-Bolshevik forces in Russia.

"Captain Hendricks and his people will be arriving in Omsk in the next week or so," Rachel said. "That's where they'll be starting their training program for the Whites."

Hunter suppressed an uneasy qualm at Rachel's evident excitement. This, he knew, was what she'd been waiting for: the U.S. going on the offensive in the time war for the first time since the aborted attempt on Lenin's life. He looked back to King. "So we'll be staying in 1918?"

"Thompson thought it was important that we guard the VBU portal."

"This could give us our first clear look at Soviet temporal technology," Rachel explained. "Since it's on a train, we can study it while we're on the move."

Hunter nodded slowly. "It should work. We'll need permission from Gaida, one of the Czech leaders, but we're on good terms with him. The portal equipment hasn't been damaged . . . except for the power cables coming out of the reactor."

"Any trouble with locals messing with the high-tech stuff?" Fitzpatrick asked.

Hunter shook his head. "I've got Eddie and Walker down there keeping an eye on things, but the Czechs are more interested in us than in the train. Seems they think we're the American Expeditionary Force or something." He looked at each of the technicians in turn. "That's how we'll explain you people, by the way: Americans come to help the White cause. The Czechs are good soldiers, and they're friendly. We shouldn't have any trouble with them." He stooped and switched off the recall beacon. In a moment, the blue glow tattered and faded, leaving behind a lingering, sour taste of ozone. He picked up the beacon and replaced it in a rucksack. "Well, folks, let me show you your new home."

Hendricks stepped through the blue glow of the portal. If the coordinates back at the Chronos Project were accurate, this would be November 2, 1918. The air was chilly, and snow was falling from a leaden sky. He zipped up his field jacket, which he'd left hanging open in the warmth of Time Square.

He stood in an open field a mile from the outskirts of Omsk. The land was flat here, undulating gently for miles until it met the lowering sky at the distant horizon. To the east, he could see the white flecks of canvas tents, acres of them, where an army was gathering.

Other men stepped through out of the future . . . Simms with a sniper's rifle across his shoulders, Malloy with his M-16. Other men came through the swirling light in twos as they marched out of Time Square's portal platform. There was little of military order or formation to the group. Most of them needed shaves, and they wore a miscellany of forage caps, helmets, watchcaps, and other headgear, which gave them a motley look.

"So this is 1918 Siberia?" Simms said. "Doesn't look like much."

"Ah, don't think of it that way, Johnny," Hendricks replied, checking the recall beacon that hung from his combat webbing. "Think of it as opportunity!"

Simms gazed off toward the horizon, now fading into a gray murk as the snowfall intensified. "Looks more like a few million square miles of nothin'."

Hendricks chuckled. "Yeah. But it's gonna be all ours!"

Seven

"All I'm saying, Raye, is that this political intrigue could backfire," Hunter said angrily. "Hendricks could lose sight of the mission while he's busy playing big shot."

"The mission *is* political intrigue, Travis!" Rachel's reply was just as irritable. "How can the captain guide the Whites if he doesn't get in solid with the politicians?"

The argument had been going on for the better part of an hour, and Hunter was feeling tired and depressed. The pitching, swaying motion of the train wasn't helping his mood. Neither was the oppressive atmosphere of the coach, stuffy from the heat of a wood-burning stove.

I wish we could have traveled on the captured train, Hunter told himself. *Or that we didn't have to come at all. . . .*

They had left the VBU train and transferred to this one at the orders of Captain Hendricks, and Hunter still wasn't sure why. Nor was he sure why Hendricks and several of his men had left Omsk and met the Ranger team's train in the city of Ekaterinburg instead of sticking to the original plan of rendezvousing in the Siberian capital. All he knew was that this train was carrying the Provisional All-Russian Government's Minister of War, Admiral Aleksandr Kolchak, plus a contingent of British and Russian troops, on a tour of the front lines in the heart of the Ural Mountains. And Hendricks was spending most of his time closeted with Kolchak and Colonel Ward, the British senior officer, in the admiral's private car. Apparently Hendricks was already working to gain the confidence of the man who would soon be elevated to supreme power. It was November 10, 1918, and the coup that would make Kolchak Russia's ruler was only a week away now.

Just what was Hendricks saying to them up there? Was he claiming to be from the future and revealing Kolchak's destiny in advance? Hunter shuddered at the thought. The whole idea of tampering with history still made him queasy sometimes, and the thought of the damage Hendricks might do interacting with the locals—the unplanned, totally inadvertent damage— was frightening. The captain had insisted on having Hunter and Rachel on board, "in case I need advisers," as he put it. But so far their advice had not been necessary. Or wanted.

Meanwhile, though, Hunter's state of mind was making him moody, and it seemed like anything he or Rachel said only made things worse.

"When military and political goals start to get crossed, you only get into trouble," Hunter said at last. "Look at the muddle in Vietnam. Hell, look at the original Allied intervention in Russia, for God's sake. Everybody works at cross-purposes, and you end up pumping men and money into a no-win cause."

Rachel leaned forward. "Why can't you get behind the mission, Travis? Ever since this started, you've been against it."

"Because it's crazy," he replied flatly. "This sure as hell isn't the time or the place to try to pull this thing off."

"How can you say that?"

"The notion of helping the Whites topple the Reds looks great on paper," Hunter replied. "It's going to be a hell of a lot harder in real life. Woodrow Wilson tried to help the Whites, and he got exactly nowhere."

America's original intervention in Russia would never amount to much, Hunter knew: a few thousand men fighting under British command at Murmansk, and perhaps ten thousand more guarding supplies and keeping their collective eye on the Japanese at Vladivostok. But everyone—British, Russians, and Czechs—seemed convinced that a more substantial American force was expected anytime. And Hendricks had convinced the

British that those Americans had finally arrived.

He still wasn't sure why the Joint Chiefs, back in 2007, had elected to try a different form of intervention in Russia, an intervention through time. Several thousand American troops—plus thousands more Japanese, British, French, and other soldiers—had managed to do nothing in 1918 but bog themselves down in the blood and politics of the unknown war in Russia. Even with modern weapons and tactics, how could fifty men sent back through the time portal manage any better than those thousands of Allied troops?

"Okay! It didn't work before!" Rachel looked angry. "But this is our chance to wipe out Communism! Isn't that what we've been working toward all along?"

"What hope do fifty men from the future have to reshape the history of the whole damned Soviet Union? Russia is full of interventionalists right now. If they couldn't turn the tide against the Reds, what makes the Joint Chiefs think *we* will?"

Rachel looked away from him. "Is it your idea that we shouldn't do anything? That we shouldn't *try* anything?"

Hunter closed his eyes. It was the old argument, surfacing once again. Rachel had accused him more than once of not taking action for fear of doing the wrong thing in an imperfectly understood history. The thought that they might someday take a critical misstep due to insufficient or incomplete historical research still gave Hunter nightmares. They'd come close to taking that misstep several times already . . . and he'd thought that some of Rachel's experiences had brought her around to his way of thinking.

"Of course we have to do something," he said. "And we will. But I don't think the people in charge on this one know what the hell they're doing!"

"The Joint Chiefs wouldn't have authorized the plan if it wasn't sound."

"The first two things a soldier stops believing in are Santa Claus and the wisdom of the Joint Chiefs," Hunter said, forcing a grin. "Come on, Raye, face it. The brass don't know the details. They point to a spot on the map and say, 'Hey! There's a good spot to send some troops in!' Then they let somebody else work out the fussy details, usually the poor bastards they ordered to go."

"And what gives you such brilliant insight into their planning?" she flared.

"Maybe I just wonder how they can sit up there in their 2007 conference rooms and make their plans without being here . . . without seeing the blood and the mud and the horror for themselves! Hendricks is supposed to train and equip a cadre of Whites. Dammit, Rachel, they don't even seem to realize how many different White groups there are! It's not one army facing the Reds . . . it's dozens, and none of them seem to agree on anything!"

"They all hate the Bolsheviks."

"That's not enough. It wasn't enough before we started trying to tinker with time . . . and it won't be enough now."

Rachel was silent for a long time. When she finally responded, there was a quaver in her voice. "Can't you admit that you might be wrong, Travis? That even without your advice the mission could have been planned to work?"

"It's stupid to think they've worked everything out! Only an imbecile—"

She stood up suddenly, grabbing the edge of the seat to balance against the motion of the train. "Now I'm an imbecile! Dammit, Travis, you just can't accept the idea of Swede Hendricks running the show! Why don't you try working on the team instead of always playing solo!"

He started to protest, but she ignored him. Fighting the lurching movement of the railcar, Rachel left him. She slammed the door behind her, and Hunter was alone with his anger and his pain.

"Hey, buddy, how're ya doing?"

Greg King looked up from his newspaper, a German-language edition of the journal published by the Czech Legion. It was amazing what the Czechs could do, how much they had accomplished since taking up arms against the Bolsheviks. Trains in the Legion's service carried everything they needed to start a small city, from publishing facilities to a mobile bank. In the midst of the chaos in Russia, these exiles were a beacon of stability and civilization.

"Well enough, Johnny, considering the weather and all." It was November 10, two weeks after their arrival in the past, and it was bitterly cold. The extra winter clothing brought in by the Chronos technicians was not entirely successful in holding it at bay. Several inches of recent snow lay on the ground and on the roofs of Ekaterinburg's buildings. The onion-domes of Russian Orthodox churches rose above the town, catching the morning light. Far off to the west, against the gentle roll of the low, rocky Ural Mountains, were the smokestacks of several heavy industrial plants, deserted and silent now since the beginning of the country's suicide.

Master Sergeant Simms grinned. "Yeah, they weren't lying when they said Siberia was cold, huh?"

King looked at his old friend. It wasn't surprising to find Simms changed after fifteen years. One hell of a lot had happened since he'd last seen the man . . . to the country and to himself. If Simms seemed harder, more bitter now than when King had known him before, it could be that King himself was harder and more bitter as well. Ten years of war, of watching one's nation disintegrate, was enough to make anyone bitter.

But King sensed something more than bitterness, something disturbing enough to make King edgy. He wasn't looking forward to accompanying Simms back to Omsk, though he still wasn't sure what it was that bothered him.

"So how do you boys like it in 1918?" King asked.

"Not bad," Simms replied. He gave King a sideways look, and the corner of his mouth quirked upward in a half grin. "Not friggin' bad at all. Hey, you know, Greg . . ." He hesitated, as though debating whether or not to take King into his confidence.

"Yeah?"

"Oh . . . nothing. It's just . . . well, we've got a good thing going back here. If you ever feel like you want a change of pace from that Ranger shit, I could probably fix you up with us. Hendricks is a good sort."

King's eyes narrowed. The tone of what Simms had said, more than the words, suggested something more than a simple change of billet. Not that King would ever consider leaving Hunter's team.

"What the hell are you talking about, Johnny?"

"Never mind, Greg. You know me . . . the usual bullshit. Hey, what'd ya think of the big show this morning?"

"It was okay, I guess." King replied, happy to follow the other man's lead and change the subject. "If you like parades."

Earlier in the day a large, open field near the outskirts of town had been transformed into a parade ground for the review of eighteen thousand Czech soldiers. Thousands of Russian soldiers in greatcoats and fur hats ringed the field in an unprecedented display of White Army solidarity. The hastily erected review stand above the massed Czech troops had included a number of Allied representatives, mostly British. There had been endless speeches delivered to the assembled armies, and the British decorated some three hundred Czech men and officers for heroism. The Legion had received a national flag in recognition of Czechoslovakia's new status as an independent nation, and one Czech general, piratical-looking in a black eye patch, read a telegram from King George V, assuring his men of the British Empire's continued support. The White Minister of War had been there, too, accompanied by his staff. King had noticed that Swede Hendricks was never too far away from the man.

Admiral Kolchak was supposed to be the key to victory, but he hadn't impressed King much. Neither did Hendricks—or Simms, for that matter. The Bravo Team people worried him, but he couldn't quite define his concerns. They were easygoing, even lax . . . but the Rangers weren't exactly rigid themselves. So far, King had kept his unease to himself, but he was starting to wonder if he shouldn't bring it up with Hunter.

"Uh, look, Johnny," he said at last. Suddenly he felt uncomfortable with Simms watching him. It felt like his old friend wanted something King couldn't give. "I've gotta talk to Anderson and Gomez about guard details for the technical stuff."

"Sure, buddy," Simms said. His smile was a little forced, though, and he was studying King closely. "I'll see ya later, huh?"

Doubts would have to wait. Hunter and Rachel had been ordered to accompany Hendricks on Kolchak's private train on a quick inspection tour of the front lines. They'd be back in the evening. Then maybe King would talk to the lieutenant.

No, King thought. *It'll keep. But I wish to hell I knew what was going on with Hendricks and his people.*

Khungar Station was battered, pockmarked by bullets, with the masonry on one corner partly collapsed from an old explosion. The town was near the current White front line, on the route between Ekaterinburg and the key city of Perm to the west of the Urals. Czechs of Gaida's 1st Division had captured Ekaterinburg in the summer, but worsening weather and the increasing disaffection in the Legion's ranks had led to a stalemate on the northern front as autumn faded into winter.

Hunter left Kolchak's train with Rudolph Gaida. After Rachel's stormy departure from his coach, Hunter had sought out the dashing young Czech general and spent the remainder of the trip listening to stories of the Legion's exploits in Russia. The fascination of this firsthand view of history almost overcame Hunter's depression in the wake of the argument.

"Had we known that the Reds would be so brutal, we would have acted differently, of course," Gaida was saying in accented Russian. "But Czar Nicholas and his family were killed when the Bolsheviks realized we would soon liberate Ekaterinburg."

Hunter nodded. He knew that the last of the Romanovs had been butchered, together with his entire family and four trusted retainers, in the basement of the Dom Ipatiev, a long, rambling mansion on the crest of a low hill on the outskirts of the city of Ekaterinburg. The assassinations—and the romance always associated with deposed royalty—had spawned more than the usual number of tales about members of the czar's family being spirited away to the safety of the West.

"Could any of the royal family have escaped?" he asked.

Gaida shrugged. "I doubt it . . . but of course anything is possible. Reds and Whites in this country are all corrupt, and it would take little enough to bribe some official to look the other way." The disgusted look on the young general's face conveyed volumes about the feelings of the Czechs for the entire Russian nation.

A loud, hearty voice greeted them in Russian as they rounded a corner. It was Hendricks. "General! And our own Lieutenant Hunter! Join us, won't you?"

Bravo Team's commander was standing in the middle of a tight knot of staff officers and soldiers. Beside him were two men Hunter had seen earlier from a distance, but had not actually met.

Admiral Aleksandr Vasilievich Kolchak was a grim-featured, saturnine man with cold eyes and a proud, stiff-backed bearing. The hair visible under the hood of the admiral's parka was worn short, exposing a high forehead that seemed permanently set in a grim frown. The other man was Colonel John Ward, commander of the 25th Battalion of the Middlesex Regiment, Great Britain's token commitment to the White cause in Siberia. Ward was a bluff, thickset man, the very image of the classic "John Bull" . . . or, Hunter thought, Colonel Blimp. The smile he gave Hunter and Gaida was fatuous.

"Well, gentlemen, bit of a cold day, eh?" he began cheerfully in English. "I must say this temperature is quite impossible for our lads. Don't really see how anyone can expect to fight in this sort of weather."

A staff officer translated his words into Russian. When he responded, Gaida's eyes were as icy as the chill wind. "My people have fought in this kind of weather since autumn set in, Colonel."

"Hmmph. Yes. Well, of course my lads aren't used to this climate yet, don'tcha know. Most difficult to adjust to all this."

"Nor are they likely to do so," Kolchak added gruffly. There was an undercurrent of hostility there, only poorly hidden. "Not until your government releases them for front-line duty."

"Now, Admiral . . . Minister . . . you know that isn't my province at all," Ward said placatingly. "I'm sure that more aid will be forthcoming once the Russian government has demonstrated its ability to field an effective fighting force. After all, sir, you cannot expect to have foreigners defeat the Reds for you. You must win back your country through your own efforts—with our assistance, perhaps, but still through your own efforts."

"The Legion feels the same way," Gaida said bitterly. "Russian troops must take over more of the burden of fighting. Our men are at the limit of their endurance."

"Indeed." Kolchak surveyed Gaida coldly. "Czech troops have already refused to go into battle several times. Perhaps it truly is time for a change."

"Gentlemen, gentlemen," Hendricks said. "Come, we must act together if we're to stop the Reds. I think we can guarantee some changes soon, General Gaida. Isn't that right, Colonel?"

"Hmm . . . yes." Ward smiled broadly, glancing at Kolchak. "If only we had a stronger White government, I'm sure we would see some sweeping changes."

Hunter glanced from one to the other. Since his arrival at

Omsk, Hendricks had spent most of his time winning the confidence of these and other prominent men. By maintaining the pretense of being the representative of a new, more vigorous American interventionalist effort, the captain was slowly building a solid power base for himself. He was smooth, diplomatic . . . Perhaps he really was on the verge of getting these disparate personalities and interests to work together.

Maybe Backlash can work after all, he told himself. *Maybe.*

Farther up the street, a military band started playing a tinny rendition of ''Colonel Bogey.'' The officers began to walk up the street toward the soldiers—Britishers from the Middlesex Regiment, it seemed—with Hunter trailing behind. Conversation had turned to less controversial matters, but Hunter couldn't help feeling that the music only underscored the point Kolchak and Gaida had been making. Great Britain had sent no more than a hundred fighting men and a regimental band into Siberia; the Whites seemed largely content to let the Czechs fight their battles for them. And the Czechs wanted exactly what they had sought at the beginning of this confused war: the chance to go home.

The band shifted to a new tune, ''It's a Long Way to Tipperary'' this time, as the officers reached the open field where they were drawn up. Hunter scanned the landscape beyond the outskirts of the town, where soldiers, mostly Czechs, were crouched in trenches or huddled around small fires trying to keep warm. What did they think of this inane performance by their British allies?

A deep, throaty sound, like the rumble of a train, made the chill air tremble. An explosion blossomed from a field beyond the parade ground and train tracks. The crash sounded moments later. The British band crashed to the close of their number, and Colonel Ward shouted orders to his subordinates. The formation wheeled about and began marching toward the railroad station and the waiting train. Red artillery fire continued to rain down on Khungar, all of it exploding harmlessly in the forest.

Czech troops took cover as the shelling increased in tempo. The last of the British soldiers filed through town, with Kolchak, his entourage, and Hunter following. Unhurriedly, British bandsmen and Russian staff officers boarded their train, and with a screech of its whistle, the locomotive began chugging out of the depot, heading east. Meanwhile the Czechs appeared to be organizing skirmish lines, moving off across the fields toward the north and the source of the shell fire. There were already several dark clumps on the snowy fields, marking where the random fire had cut soldiers down as they dispersed from their close-ranked unit formations.

The episode was representative, Hunter thought, of the original Allied intervention in Russia. So far as he knew, the Middlesex Regiment never got any closer to combat in Siberia than they had that afternoon, as their train steamed out of the town amid the crashing thunder of Bolshevik shell fire. The sum total of their assistance to the Whites had been the promises, the speeches, the medals . . . and the band's rendition of the British marching songs provoking an artillery barrage. Perhaps the strangest aspect of it all was the fact that World War I was due to end on the following day . . . at 11 A.M. GMT on November 11, 1918. With the Armistice, any reason the Allies might have had for trying to force Russia back into the war would end, and yet the intervention would continue for several months yet, with none of the participants entirely sure what it was they were trying to accomplish. The plans made for Operation Backlash seemed no clearer . . . and no more likely to succeed.

It was, Hunter reflected, one hell of a way to fight a war.

Eight

The captured train bearing the Rangers and Dubcek's Czechs left Ekaterinburg the following day, following Kolchak's train. Omsk was twenty hours away by rail, but the trip took considerably longer. The Trans-Siberian Railway's tracks were deteriorating in places, and movement across bridges and around curves was carried out at a snail's pace.

They arrived outside of Omsk early on the morning of November 16. Omsk was Siberia's second-largest city, long the capital of the western part of that region and once the place of exile for no less a personage than Dostoyevski. It was built at the confluence of the Om and Irtysh Rivers, and even in 1918, it was something of an industrial center. Hunter could smell the city's tanneries long before Omsk itself came into view. In another few decades, Hunter knew, it would be the center of one of the most important industrial regions in the U.S.S.R. In the latter part of 1918, it was the capital of the anti-Bolshevik Russian forces, ruled by a coalition Directory that styled itself the All-Russian Provisional Government.

As the train slowed to approach the station at Kulomzino, a small railway town across the Irtysh River from Omsk proper, Hunter stepped onto the rear platform of the passenger car.

King was already there, leaning against the iron railing with his hands folded in front of him. Something was troubling the master sergeant, Hunter knew, but he'd not yet learned what it was.

Shit, Hunter thought. *We've all got problems*. He'd been thinking more and more about the argument with Rachel and about pulling out of time-travel ops entirely. *Let someone else do it, someone like Hendricks*.

He was about to ask King what was bothering him when the master sergeant stiffened. Hunter looked past him and saw what had caused the reaction.

A gallows had been erected along the railway embankment, a kind of display rack for trains coming from the west or departing for the east. It consisted of two upright poles fifty feet apart, with a slender beam stretched between them. At least twenty bodies had been suspended from the crosspiece. Protruding tongues and blackened faces showed that their executioners had not tied the knots to break the victims' necks cleanly, but that death for each had been a long and agonizing process. The passage of the train set the bodies swaying and twirling slowly, a parody of life. Notes had been pinned to some of the corpses. Hunter managed to read one, the crude Cyrillic letters proclaiming the man to be *Bolshevyestskii shpion*, a Bolshevik spy. The Whites had been at work here.

Whatever he'd been about to say was forgotten in the silent horror of those bloody, staring eyes. Hunter had seen photographs of such scenes—partisans hung by Nazis—in histories of World War II, but those images had been distant, antiseptic, and made remote by the passage of years. The smell of the corpses mingled with the sharp odor of the tanneries, emphasizing the reality of a starkly unrealistic scene.

The train rumbled past, and King turned slowly to look into Hunter's eyes. "What in the bloody hell are we getting into here, Lieutenant?"

Hunter was unable to answer him.

Rachel couldn't sleep. The argument she'd had with Hunter on the train ride to Khungar still gnawed at her. If Backlash went as it should, she would not have much more time to spend with Travis, and the feeling that they were wasting precious moments when they could be together lay like a massive weight across her shoulders.

Rachel wasn't sure what time it was. Was it still late on the night of November 17, or early on the eighteenth? Restless, she climbed out of the narrow bed, taking care not to wake Sarah, who was asleep in the bunk above her. Since their arrival in 1918, the two women had shared a sleeping compartment in the armored train's passenger car. It had once served as sleeping quarters for the VBU officers who had run and guarded the mobile downlink. Quietly, she dressed in army fatigues, boots, and a heavy coat.

The platform on the coach car was a good place to stand and think, although the wind was bitterly cold. Leaning on the railing, Rachel studied the dark, silent streets of Kulomzino. Street lanterns cast isolated pools of liquid light on the snow. Near the train, trash and wood had been stuffed into an open fifty-gallon drum and lit, and a trio of Czech guards warmed their hands over the flames.

"Anything I can help with, *Fraulein?*" a voice asked in German behind her.

Rachel turned, saw another Czech guard watching her from the shadows of the platform. The Czechs accepted her as one of the Americans, and she'd become friendly with several who spoke German, despite her own broken knowledge of the language.

"*Nein, Herr Sergeant Fryscak,*" she replied. "*Danke.*"

Somewhere, the scratchy sound of a violin wavered through the night air. The Czechs in the rail yard lifted their voices in a song. Though she couldn't understand the language, Rachel could feel the sadness, the bitterness behind the words.

Sergeant Fryscak seemed to read her mind. "A song from home," he said softly. "Home . . ."

The isolation these men must feel, she thought. Until six days ago, they'd still been set on continuing the fight against Germany and her allies. Since the Armistice, all they really wanted was to return to the new homeland created for them out of the ashes of the dead Austro-Hungarian Empire.

But the Czech Legion, as far as the intervening Allied nations were concerned, was too useful where it was. While the various foreign armies continued to get bogged down in a confusion of goals, policies, and politics as thick as Russia's mud, the

Czech Legion already held almost the entire length of the Trans-Siberian Railroad. Those four thousand miles of tracks were the key to Siberia, Rachel knew, the only means of transport across the vast and still untamed length of Asia. The Allies—particularly the Allied Supreme War Council—were not about to let so valuable an asset as the Czech Legion go home . . . not yet. The promise of going home was being used to win the cooperation and allegiance of what was arguably the finest army in Russia.

The Czechs themselves referred to it as "swinging." Rachel knew they even had a newspaper that, in a twist of gallows' humor, was called *Swings* . . . and their discontent was growing. How long the Czechs would allow themselves to be "swung" by the Allied commanders, she didn't know. The exact sequence of events in the Civil War were still fuzzy to her, although she knew there was a crisis of some sort coming up.

It's one tiny part of what we're trying to change, she thought. If Backlash could engineer a clear-cut victory over the Bolsheviks, the Czechs could go home.

Off in the distance, over the ragged singing, she heard a clatter of hooves on cobblestones, shouts. A rifle shot rang loud in the darkness.

Tonight a Cossack regiment was mounting a bloodless coup in Omsk. Orders from Hendricks had been issued restricting the technical team and the Rangers to the train depot for security purposes. Bravo Team was in town, apparently ready to ensure that the coup would go as it was supposed to. By morning, the government would be in disarray, ready for an unopposed takeover by Admiral Kolchak. When that happened, Backlash would be one step closer to completion, with Captain Hendricks in a position to cooperate with a friendly government. Then, as the opportunity presented itself, the interventions in history could begin, and the Communists driven out of power. History would be changed; her mother would never have died. . . .

And in that new history Rachel Stein would be another person, with new memories, a whole new life. Perhaps that version of herself would never fall in love with Travis Hunter at all.

She knew it bothered Hunter to think of losing her. Every person involved with Chronos lived every day with the knowledge that they were working toward what amounted to voluntary suicide. They could kid themselves with the idea that ''they'' would still exist in the new version of history—in some other form, perhaps, but still alive to enjoy peace and freedom in an America, indeed a world, without Communist oppression. But when the Transformation Wave they generated by changing the past reached 2007, they would all be replaced . . . no longer the same people at all. As good as dead.

And everything brought about by the war against Communism would be different too. Even little things, like the love that had sprung up between a technician and an Army Ranger drawn together by the Chronos Project.

They'd discussed the possibility once of using the time portal to escape the effects of the Transformation Wave, going into voluntary exile in a past time. But could they condemn themselves to living out the rest of their lives in a strange time and place? Could they live knowing that, as outsiders, something they did or said could generate new, unexpected changes that would wipe out the future they'd struggled to create? And where would they draw the line when it came to saving certain people from the effects of the Wave? If Rachel and Travis settled down, safe in the past, what about the rest of the team? The rest of the Chronos staff? And what about the millions of people who would never even know that their past was being changed?

Rachel shook her head sadly. It was one thing to think about escaping their own handiwork, quite another to actually do it. She had made her own peace with herself a long time ago. Her love for Hunter against a whole world made new again . . .

But perhaps Travis was having more trouble accepting it. Maybe that explained the way he was dragging his heels over Backlash.

She thought of her angry words on Kolchak's train. Rachel didn't really believe that Hunter was jealous of Hendricks. But this operation was no place to allow personal doubts to cloud the judgments the commander of the mission *had* to make, and so far the captain's actions had been swift, decisive, and competent. It hurt to realize that, in this instance at least, Hunter may well have been replaced by a better man.

Her fists, inside her greatcoat pockets, clenched. She loved Travis Hunter . . . needed him. But it seemed that Operation Backlash, the whole Chronos Project, was now an obstacle

between them that they could not break down.
And there's not much time left even to try....

The streets of Omsk were deathly silent, with a brooding air of tense expectation pervading the entire city. It was the morning of November 18, 1918, and the Siberian capital was grim in the aftermath of the bloodless but unexpected coup that had swept the White government from power overnight. No one knew yet what would replace it ... except for a handful of strangers whose knowledge came from history books.

Captain Hendricks leaned back in his chair, a satisfied smile playing over his face. Everything was going according to plan—*his* plan—as well as the plan framed by General Becker and the Joint Chiefs of Staff eighty-nine years in the future. For now the plans still coincided, but that would change. Someday, when Hendricks no longer needed the Chronos Project's resources ...

That won't be long now, he told himself. Across the city of Omsk from the crumbling edifice of the *Dvoretz Gasteeneetsa,* the hotel where Hendricks maintained his new HQ, the remnants of the All-Russian Provisional Government were meeting in the old Governor's Residence to grant Aleksandr Kolchak supreme power. Kolchak would listen to Hendricks now, with the success of the coup the American had helped to plan.

And another useful man was with Hendricks now, a man the captain knew he would have need for in the months ahead. Brian Fitzpatrick was an awkward, foolish young man, even easier to manipulate than Kolchak or Colonel Ward. Certainly he was the weak link on the Chronos technical team, the ideal agent to help Hendricks unlock the secrets of time travel for Bravo Team.

"We know we can operate the downlink independently from the Russian portal in 2007," Fitzpatrick was saying. He pushed his glasses higher on the bridge of his nose. "And we can tune the shift vectors to keep them from locking on."

"Meaning?" Lynn Colby asked, her eyebrows arching.

Fitzpatrick grinned. "Meaning the VBU can't send troops into our downlink."

Hendricks rubbed his chin. "Could we tie into their equipment? Tune it or whatever, so we could drop in on them?"

"Maybe," Fitzpatrick said. "If they didn't change their

codes. It would take some study.'' He paused. ''There's another thing, Captain. Raye . . . uh, Miss Stein thinks the machine might actually be a time portal in its own right.''

''But this is wonderful!'' Colby said. ''We could go anywhere we want . . . any*when* we want, even after we lose touch with Chronos.''

''That's the idea, baby,'' Hendricks said. ''That's the idea.''

He considered her happily. Colby was another useful dupe, a bit on the plain side, but entertaining enough in bed and a useful source of information on Kolchak's Russia. He enjoyed manipulating her a lot more than Kolchak or Fitzpatrick, at least.

And if we've got us a time machine of our own, there's nothing to stop us from doing whatever we please, Hendricks told himself. *Russia will just be the start!*

There was a knock on the door, and Malloy poked his head inside. ''Sorry to bother you, Swede, but we've just had word. Kolchak's in . . . he just accepted the dictatorship.''

''Great! We can start moving now.'' Hendricks turned to Fitzpatrick. ''All right, Brian, thanks. Now, I want you to keep me informed about your research. And try to spend a lot of time with Miss Stein. I'd like to know what she's coming up with, but I hate to wade through all the reports.''

Fitzpatrick smiled eagerly. ''Sure, uh, sure, Swede. Captain.''

''Swede to my friends, Brian. And I want you as a friend.'' Hendricks knew that Fitzpatrick wanted the Stein girl, but more than that, he was sure, the technician wanted acceptance. He was a lot like Colby that way, easy to control. Easy to use.

''What about us?'' Simms asked. ''Any orders?''

''Yeah. We've got to solidify our power base with Kolchak. Have the boys get ready unless anybody else gets the same idea. I've got to see the admiral . . . and start taking some steps to get the Brits out of the way.''

Hendricks stood up, still smiling. ''Things are falling into place. All we have to do now is go with the flow.''

Things are falling into place. And pretty soon no one will be able to stop us.

''There was nothing more that could be done, Grigor Grigorevich,'' Obinin said. He slumped back in his seat and took another sip of the strong Russian tea Vasilov had given him. "Not without launching a major assault against the entire Czech force."

"You believe Captain Rozhko to be dead, then?"

Obinin frowned. "There is no proof, one way or the other. He is dead . . . or he is a prisoner of the Americans. They may, of course, have kept our people alive to help them understand our time-travel technology."

"The situation is quite serious, then," Vasilov said. "Deadly, in fact."

Lieutenant Obinin nodded agreement. Outside the frost-encrusted windows of Vasilov's office, snowflakes danced above the gray streets of Moscow. In the distance, the clustered, onion-dome towers of St. Basil's rose against a dark and forbidding sky close by the walls of the Kremlin.

Moscow, in the closing months of 1918, was a grim and claustrophobic city, Obinin thought, a city of death and dying. Bolshevik militias roamed everywhere, arresting and shooting civilians for offenses ranging from gathering wood for fires to suspicion of antirevolutionary activity. Terror gripped the city in bloody claws. Only three months before, a woman named Doris Kaplan had fired two bullets into Lenin's brain. The god of the Bolshevik Revolution had survived, thanks in part to a team of VBU surgeons brought in from 2007, but history had destined Lenin's recovery to be a slow and incomplete one. He would not be back in the public eye until the next spring. In the meantime the Red Terror stalked Moscow like some horrible, medieval plague.

It was ironic, Obinin thought. The VBU *Ochrana* team was there to guarantee the success of the revolution, to make certain that American time commandos did not interfere with Russia's destiny. But it was the Bolsheviks themselves who were the *Ochrana*'s biggest problem. Red Guards were everywhere . . . searching, prying, questioning. Several VBU agents had been killed already, shot on the spot or dragged off to unknown fates in the Lubyanka on suspicion of antirevolutionary activity.

For that reason, there was no time machine in Moscow, only Lieutenant Vasilov and the handful of KGB guards assigned to keep watch over Lenin. It had been felt that the mobile time machine offered better security for the VBU portal gear, an assumption that was obviously mistaken.

"The situation is desperate," Obinin said. "But we still have our *dubok*." The Russian word literally meant "little oak" but had come to mean any message drop used by KGB or GRU agents. Time operations had given a whole new dimension to the concept of drops.

Vasilov scowled. "It could mean our deaths, Comrade. . . ."

"Perhaps, though the responsibility was Rozhko's. Consider the alternative, however . . . should the Americans succeed in changing the outcome of the Civil War. We have our duty, whatever the consequences."

"*Da*. Of course." Vasilov passed his hand over his eyes. "How long will it take?"

Obinin shrugged. "A week for the message to reach our people uptime. After that . . . as long as it takes to find us through the 2007 gate. It depends on their accuracy."

"A week?"

"It is a big war, Comrade Vasilov. I doubt that the Americans can make much of an impression on events in that short a period. Time, it appears, is on *our* side for once."

Vasilov's face split in an uneasy grin. "Which is how it should be." He reached into a drawer of his desk, producing a pair of glasses and a bottle of vodka. "Shall we drink to the future, Vadim Sergeivich?"

"To 2007, Grigor Grigorevich." He watched as Vasilov poured the liquor. "And to our victory over the Americans."

"*Zah pahbeda!*" Vasilov agreed as he raised his glass. "To victory!"

Nine

Hunter leaned back in his seat, studying the profile of Swede Hendricks against the morning light flooding through the hotel room's narrow window. All of the Rangers were there, along with Rachel and the other two Chronos Project technicians. Lynn Colby was there as well, her tiny frame dwarfed by the captain, with Sergeants Malloy and Simms flanking them.

Hendricks had called this meeting to tell them about the coup.

With first light that morning, Hunter had been awakened in the railway van he and his men were using as a barracks by a roar that literally shook the car. The roar had continued, a throbbing, pounding thunder coming from the center of Omsk and which Hunter only gradually realized was the sound of tens of thousands of wildly cheering people. It was November 19, and the capital was thronged with crowds eager to pay tribute to Aleksandr Vasilievich Kolchak, newly proclaimed Supreme Ruler of All the Russias.

It was a startling contrast to the brooding silence in the streets the day before. Then there had been too many doubts, too much uncertainty at the outcome of the coup on the night of the seventeenth. Details were still sketchy. Cossacks under the command of an Ataman named Krasilnikov had arrested three socialist members of the Directory, but they hadn't taken any other steps, nor did they suggest what their coup was supposed to accomplish besides the removal of the left-wing leaders from the government. It was only after an all-day session of the remaining members of the Directory that the decision was made to proclaim a dictatorship . . . and to make Kolchak the dictator.

"So far history is on track," the blond historian said. "We know that Krasilnikov made his move on the night of November 17. And Kolchak stepped in the next day."

Hendricks chuckled. "Yeah . . . but they wouldn't have done it without me and my boys. It went down smooth."

Hunter frowned. The man's smug self-assurance grated at him. "Just what was your part in the affair, Captain?"

"Hell, we just put the whole coup together, that's all. It was *my* idea to use that Brit colonel, Ward, and his men to control the city . . . to make sure Krasilnikov's men weren't interfered with." He reached out and patted Lynn Colby on the shoulder. "Have to hand it to you, Lynn. You put it right on the money! I got an intro to Kolchak through Ward, just like you said we could. Ward is really hot on the guy . . . figures he's just what the Whites need to get them pulling in the same direction."

"It really is remarkable," the girl said. "No one has ever known for sure just who put the coup together. Colonel Ward was always a prime suspect, of course, because he liked Kolchak. Certainly it looked like he ordered the Middlesex Regiment to support the coup. But now it turns out that it was *us*, using Ward and his troops!"

"Anyway," Hendricks continued, "my boys helped Ward's men, setting up machine guns, laying out fields of fire. We made sure Krasilnikov's Cossacks got through without being challenged. Pulled it off too. Not a single shot fired! Like I said . . . smooth."

"Where do the Cossacks come into all this?" Hunter asked.

"Oh, they're just some new acquaintances of mine," Hendricks replied easily. "Splendid soldiers, among the best in the world. They'll be providing Backlash with the majority of its new recruits."

Hunter chewed on the implications of that. He still knew next to nothing about the details of Backlash and felt as though he were trying to thread his way through a maze blindfolded.

The Rangers' orders called for them to maintain their electronic watch for signs of VBU time-travel activity, and to engage in "such operations as the commanding officer may from time to time direct them to carry out." But a deliberate effort had been made to keep him and his men in the dark. Security was one thing, but Hendricks's hints and isolated tidbits of information no longer constituted security. It seemed more a way of proving that he was in command.

That was a game Hunter didn't care for at all. "You know, it would help things considerably if you would let us in on your planning, Captain," he said. "Keeping us in the dark isn't going to help your mission . . . and if my people put their foot in it because we don't know what the hell's going on, it could jeopardize everything."

"I suppose there's no harm in your knowing," Hendricks said. He spoke with an irritating condescension. "In the past few days, I have managed to win Admiral Kolchak's complete trust. My team will begin immediately to train a cadre of picked locals. We'll be starting with volunteers from among Krasilnikov's boys."

"Train them?" Gomez asked. "In what?"

"In modern tactics. In elite commando and assault operations. In modern weapons. We are forming an army, gentlemen—the *B'yelee Smert*, the White Death. With their help we'll make sure Kolchak wins, and crush the Reds once and for all."

"The single obstacle to a White victory was a lack of common purpose," Lynn added. "Kolchak provided that purpose historically, but by the time he took command, the Reds were on the offensive and the Whites were unable to form an effective single front against them. Swede's White Death Commandos will win Kolchak the victories he needs to consolidate the anti-Red Russians behind him. Those victories will convince the British to send substantial aid to the Whites . . . and that will be our turning point."

"All of Russia's been looking for someone with a strong hand," Hendricks said smugly. "Someone able to stand up to the Bolsheviks. Now they have him. And he's ours."

"He could still turn on you," Hunter said softly.

"Then we get rid of him. But right now I control the Supreme Ruler of All the Russias." The captain smiled at Hunter.

"Everything is going exactly according to plan."

Maybe so, Hunter thought bitterly. *But so many things could still go wrong.*

Major Sergei Sergeivich Andryanov suppressed his irritation as he showed his clearance papers to the KGB guard. The soldier's eyes widened as he saw Andryanov's authorization code . . . and widened still further as he read the signature and countersignature on the papers. *"Da, Tovarisch Mayar!"* He saluted stiffly. "You may pass!"

"I should think so," Andryanov replied dryly. He pocketed the ID and authorization and strode past the guard. He knew it was useless to take out his frustrations on a KGB man who was simply carrying out his duty, but it was impossible not to feel bitter. The VBU's High Command was using him as a messenger boy. Andryanov had no doubt whatsoever that his current assignment was punishment for the failure of his part of the operation in 1777 North America—mild punishment, to be sure, but punishment nonetheless. Ever since his return to the Soviet Union of 2007, they'd been using him for minor make-work tasks such as this one.

Damn the Americans anyway, he thought. *But for them . . .*

He entered the Tainitsky Gardens, an ever-surprising maze of pathways and green enclosed within the Kremlin's walls, south of the Presidium, where the Soviet Union's rulers deliberated, and the museum-churches that dominated Cathedral Square. He passed Pintsuk's statue of a seated Lenin, strewn now with flowers left by the faithful. Ahead, beyond the gardens, the massive, red-stone south wall of the Kremlin bulked against the sky. The Moscow River lay out of sight beyond that imposing barrier, but he could see the skyscrapers of the *Zemlyanoy Gorod* district to the south.

The Moscow of 2007 was a grim, gray, claustrophobic place, Andryanov thought, even here in the Kremlin Garden. For all that the city was master of nine tenths of the surface of the Earth, the Soviet Union's rulers had never yet learned to master their own people without the apparatus of the police state.

Perhaps, once the VBU was victorious, once the United States was eliminated from history and their damned time commandos tracked down and destroyed, perhaps then Mother Russia could afford to relax the discipline that circumstances had forced her to impose upon her children.

He approached the Kremlin's south wall. Towers reared against the sky at intervals, towers with names bearing arcane histories: Water Tower, Annunciation Tower, the First and Second Nameless Towers. Andryanov's destination was a squat, peak-roofed structure between the Annunciation Tower and the First Nameless Tower. It was called, fittingly enough, the Secret Tower.

The name came from a legendary, secret underground passage leading from the Kremlin during Czarist times. It had been a gate tower until 1930, when it was walled up by government officials seeking to limit access to the seat of Stalin's government. The secret it bore now was far stranger than anything ever imagined by any Czar.

"Stoy!" A pair of soldiers with the green shoulder boards of the KGB blocked his way. *"Pakahjiteh vashee boomahgee!"*

Andryanov surrendered his papers once again and stood motionless while one of the guards studied them. The other remained several paces back, his AKM trained on the major's chest.

They were taking no chances. The first KGB guard summoned a captain from a nearby guardhouse and showed the papers to him.

As he waited, Andryanov studied the outline of the old gateway in the base of the tower, now filled in with bricks. To one side, recent excavation had cut a door-sized opening in the barrier. The passage beyond, closed since Stalin's time, was cave-black.

"Thank you, sir," the captain said, returning his papers. He unclipped a flashlight from his belt and extended it to Andryanov. "You will need this."

"Spaseebah, kapitahn." He accepted the light and flicked it on. "I will return momentarily."

The papers specified that he alone enter the Secret Tower itself.

Inside, brick dust and mustiness lay heavy on every surface. He knew where he was going and approximately what he would find. The tower had been opened up by VBU archaeologists several years before, when it was decided that the Kremlin wall itself would provide an excellent emergency *dubok* for time-guard units in trouble in Russia's past.

The possibility of electronic or mechanical failure in a VBU downlink was always present, as was the possibility of an attack by American commandos. The VBU command had allowed for such mishaps by arranging message drops like this walled-up corridor in the Secret Tower, which personnel in the past could use to send emergency reports to 2007. Some VBU operative had placed a sealed canister bearing a message there decades ago. A small radio transponder inside was keyed to broadcast a simple come-get-me message after the passage of a certain number of years and months.

He swept the flashlight beam across brickwork and cement. The archaeologists had already loosened some stones in one wall. Momentarily, he wondered at the paradox. Why hadn't the archaeologists removed the message container when they opened up the wall in the first place? He wasn't sure he understood the scientists' explanation. According to them, an agent placing a message cylinder in its drop actually created a new universe, identical to the old except for the presence of the message. Looked at that way, it was possible that opening the niche too soon would reveal no message, since the events and decisions that led to its placement had not yet been made. After that, the explanation devolved to discussions of quantum mechanics and how an event could both *be* and *not be* . . . and from there Andryanov lost the thread of reasoning entirely.

Behind the bricks was a small lead cylinder. Whatever the physics of the thing, the message drop had worked.

Andryanov did not have the code to open it, of course. That privilege was reserved for the bosses back at Uralskiy. He slipped the container into his coat pocket, drew his Skorpion machine pistol, checked it, and slipped it back into its shoulder holster.

What year was the message from? The VBU maintained many guard outposts in many years, and this container could be from any of them. He knew a quickening of his pulse as he considered it, however. The surest way to get back on the good side of the VBU command structure was to get into action.

This message from the past, whatever it was, might well be his ticket back to official favor.

Ten

"So you see, Captain, we've got a real problem here." Hunter tapped the map of Siberia spread out on the desk in Hendricks's office. "A magnetic surge can only mean we've got company . . . VBU company."

Hendricks frowned as he studied the pencil marks slashed across the map. "Can't you narrow it down closer than that?"

Rachel shrugged. "That's as close as it is possible to come, Swede. The surge was a long one, but the equipment we have with us here doesn't show much more than direction. There was no time for a triangulation. Judging by the strength of the signal, it was a long way away. At least a thousand miles. Maybe as much as fifteen hundred."

Hendricks shook his head and tapped the map with his forefinger. "That could be anywhere between Bratsk and Chita. Half the width of the continental United States. How are we supposed to find them?"

After almost two months of watching, the team's MSA monitors had registered an event . . . a powerful magnetic pulse that almost certainly marked the opening of a Soviet time portal. It could only mean that the VBU had sent reinforcements to 1918, and that they had deposited them somewhere in central

Siberia. Rachel had brought the news to Hunter that morning, and together they had made their way to Hendricks's HQ in Omsk to bring him into the picture. If the VBU was sending a new force into Russia, maybe even building a new downlink base, it could throw the whole Backlash project into jeopardy.

But why set up so far from Omsk? Possibly they were shooting blind, but Rachel had assured him that the downlink they were studying was capable of better accuracy than that. It could hit a target to within, say, twenty miles. If they landed in the middle of Siberia, they must have been *aiming* for the middle of Siberia. Why? The only thing Hunter could think of was that they knew it would be next to impossible to track them in so much wilderness.

"We're going to have to go hunt for them," Hunter said at last.

Hendricks lifted his eyebrows. "Hunt for them? In the middle of all that?"

"Unless they've brought their own transportation, they're going to be stuck with the rail lines," Hunter said. "Same as us."

The others nodded. The railways were the only form of long-range transport across Siberia in 1918. That one fact was central to the conduct of the war.

"We'll take MSA snoops," he continued. "And RDFs, in case they use radios."

"It's a long shot," the captain said slowly. "We'd need more than just your Ranger team to track them down. Five men in all that . . ."

"So? Couldn't some of your men help us out?"

Hendricks shook his head. "No way, Lieutenant. The training program for the *B'yelee Smert* is just getting off the ground. I can't spare anyone at this stage of the game."

"Even to save the whole op?" Hunter had trouble keeping the exasperation out of his voice. When Hendricks didn't answer, he continued. "All right, Captain, how about this? I'll send up to General Thompson for some more security people. We could get enough manpower to track down the VBU. With Dubcek's Czechs, maybe some of your White Death people, too, we could handle them."

"The answer's still no, Lieutenant. It just won't work."

This time Hunter didn't bother hiding his reaction. "Come

on, Hendricks! If the VBU is out there, we've got to go after them! Our whole job is to keep them off your backs . . . but we can't do it unless you let us get some help."

"Your job is whatever I say it is," Hendricks said. "Nothing else. Right, Johnny?"

Master Sergeant Simms looked uncomfortable. "Uh . . . right, Swede. Captain."

"But . . ." Hunter shook his head. How was he supposed to get *anything* done?

"Travis, I think Swede's right," Rachel said. Her casual use of the captain's nickname grated on Hunter. "There's no way to be sure you'd be able to find their base, or to make sure you got them all even if you did find it. What if some of them got through to us in the meantime?" She shivered. "We need you to help protect the technical team."

"Better to pull your people out, then, Raye," Hunter said. "If there's a danger—"

"We can't leave now!" She looked from Hunter to Hendricks, then back again. "We've had a breakthrough on the VBU downlink. We're learning so much!"

"That doesn't change anything!" Hunter said angrily.

"But it does! There are so many things we can learn . . . things that could revolutionize the whole project." Rachel's words tumbled out in an excited rush. "We need more time to study the equipment. Don't send us away now, Swede!"

"I didn't intend to," Hendricks said, smiling. "No, Hunter, the lady's right. You're more valuable here than off chasing VBU phantoms in Siberia. And that's final."

Hunter looked down at the map. He wanted to argue, wanted to convince Hendricks, but the captain had clearly made his decision. There'd be no changing his mind now. *I never thought I'd hear Rachel arguing against taking action, though*, he told himself bitterly. Since their argument in Ekaterinburg they had drifted so far apart.

"Right," he said at last. "We'll play it your way, Captain."

Hendricks smiled again. "Good. Ah . . . Miss Stein, I need to talk to the lieutenant about some other matters. Military decisions, y'know."

"Certainly," Rachel replied, glancing at Hunter again with an unreadable expression. She gathered up the map. "I'll get back to the train. We've got tests scheduled this afternoon to see if we can tune the VBU downlink to our recall beacons."

After she was gone, there was a long silence. Finally Hendricks leaned back in his chair, studying Hunter with an unnerving intensity. "I hope you understand, Hunter, how difficult some of my decisions are. This Siberian thing . . . it just wouldn't work out. Anyway, we're getting close to moving into the next phase on Backlash, and we can't let ourselves be distracted now." Hendricks hesitated, then reached across to his desk and picked up a folder. "What is your assessment of the Czechs?"

"The Czechs?" Hunter was confused by the sudden turn of the conversation. "They're good soldiers. Disciplined. Loyal to their own leaders. Now that the war in Europe is over and they have their own country, most of them just want to go home."

"Lynn Colby says that won't be possible for quite a while. It's occurred to me that we could make use of them. Do you think they could be brought around to support the admiral?"

"I don't know. I doubt it. They weren't too happy when they heard Kolchak had taken over. I thought they were all pulling out for the east."

On November 21, the Czech National Council in Ekaterinburg—the organization that passed as a government for the Czech soldiers in their Russian exile—had condemned the Kolchak coup and ordered them to withdraw from the Urals. A few—General Rudolph Gaida was one—hated the Bolsheviks enough that they were continuing to fight alongside the Whites, but most were content to maintain their control over the Trans-Siberian Railway and remain aloof from local politics.

That, Hunter reflected, was probably the smartest move they could make.

"That could change," Hendricks said. "Lynn thinks there is an excellent chance that the Czechs would support Kolchak . . . if they were properly motivated."

"What kind of motivation?" Hunter asked.

"A martyr."

The word chilled Hunter. "I don't think I follow you."

"There is a particular Czech officer . . . quite popular with his men. According to Lynn's history books, he's going to make quite a bit of trouble for Admiral Kolchak next year. It occurred to me that we could kill two birds with one Czech.

If that man were to die, if the Czech Legion thought the Reds had killed him, they'd fall all over themselves trying to get back in the fight. And Kolchak's authority won't be challenged by this guy later on.''

"Who are you talking about?"

"Gaida."

Hunter's eyes widened. "Are you seriously thinking of assassinating General Gaida? The man is one of the Legion's heroes. He also happens to be a decent man."

Hendricks's smile widened. "Read your history, Hunter. Rudolph Gaida is destined to become a Czech Fascist in the years before World War II. Your 'decent man' will be in Hitler's pocket one day. Dead, though, he could rally the Czech Legion to Kolchak's cause . . . when they learn he's been killed by the Reds. And we would have dedicated, professional military volunteers for the White Death commandos."

"God*damn* it, Hendricks! You can't be serious!"

Hendricks gave a slight shrug. "It's only an idea we've been toying with here. We have to look at all possibilities, you understand. I gather you're opposed to the idea?"

Hunter felt a hard twisting in his stomach. "You're damned right I oppose it!"

"Because you feel he's a 'decent man'?"

Hunter struggled to order his thoughts. The problem was that he *did* think the Czech general was a good man . . . and a good soldier. The man's political views mattered less to Hunter at the moment than did Hendricks's cold-blooded manipulation of the Czechs, but that was not a point he could argue with the man. There was another tack he could try, however. "Hell, I don't care if Gaida turns out to be Jack the Ripper! You're playing cowboy here . . . shooting from the hip. This wasn't part of the original Backlash plan, was it?"

"My operational orders give me considerable latitude, *Lieutenant*." He stressed Hunter's rank. The tone was hard, cold. "They call for me to make such alterations to the plan along the way as I see fit."

"My God . . ."

"We are fighting world Communism, Hunter. If one man's death helps us—"

"Dammit! You have no idea what effect Gaida's death will have on history!"

"Lynn thinks she knows."

"This whole op stinks, Hendricks. From first to last, it stinks to high heaven! You want to murder a man to trick eighty thousand men out of going home. It's sick!"

"That will be all, Lieutenant!"

Hunter felt momentarily light-headed. He reached out to support himself on the corner of the table. "Sir," he said. It took an effort to control his voice. "I respectfully submit that you should re-open the portal to Time Square. I have had some experience with time ops, and it is my opinion that you are playing with something very dangerous. Dangerous to us . . . and to our history, our world. I think we should review your idea with your CO—with the Joint Chiefs, if necessary—before trying to implement it."

"Your suggestion is noted. Dismissed."

"Sir—"

"Dis*missed!*"

Hunter began to say something more, then thought better of it. He executed a precise salute, turned on his heel, and strode from the room.

He could feel Hendricks's eyes hard on his back as he stepped through the door.

Master Sergeant Simms waited for the door to close behind Hunter before speaking. "He's gonna be a problem, Swede," he said softly.

Hendricks laughed. "We'll keep him out of trouble, Johnny. He's a good little soldier who listens to his superior officer." He paused, looking thoughtful. "Just in case, though, we'd better keep closer tabs on him. Get that kid Fitzpatrick to sweet-talk the Stein girl into moving the Rangers' recall beacon from the train to one of the warehouses near our barracks. Say we're making more room for the technicians to work on the train. That way Hunter won't be able to slip uptime without our permission. Not that he will . . . we've got him under control."

"What about our own beacon?" Simms asked.

"I'll keep that here." Hendricks smiled broadly. "It always pays to keep an ace in the hole, right?"

"Yeah." Simms rubbed his chin. "But are you sure we shouldn't do something about those Russkie time travelers?

That landing in Siberia could be serious. Why didn't you let Hunter go look for them?''

"I'm not sending anyone from Bravo out there, Johnny. And we can't afford to have anybody from Chronos snooping around here. Hunter and his team are bad enough. We can keep an eye on them, but we can't let Becker catch on to us too soon. Not until we're ready to make our move."

"And the VBU?"

"If they cause any problems, Hunter can get his wish. The Rangers and those so-called commandos of ours can deal with the Russkies . . . or they can buy us enough time to get the hell out of here to someplace safe. Or somewhen safe." Hendricks chuckled. "Anyway, if things got *really* rough, we could always cut a deal with 'em."

"A deal?" Simms frowned. "With the Commies?"

"Why not? We've got one of their time machines. They're probably anxious to take out Hunter's bunch, and we can help. We could even hand over the Stein girl . . . she'd be a prize, with everything she knows about Chronos and her daddy's work."

"Could we trust them?"

"If we had to. But look, Johnny, the VBU isn't going to be a problem. When we finally change history, we'll wipe away the whole future, Chronos and the Soviets and all. Until then, all we have to do is keep our friend the lieutenant out of our way."

Simms shook his head. "This long-hair stuff gives me a headache, Swede."

"Me too," Hendricks admitted with a grin. "But with that little nerd Fitzpatrick to help us with the time machine, and Lynn ready to hand us all the history stuff we need, we've got it made. Bravo's never had it so good, Johnny."

"I just hope Hunter doesn't get in our way, Swede. He could still cause trouble."

"Maybe so . . . in fact, I kinda hope he *does*. He'll never know what hit him."

It had taken Andryanov nearly forty-eight hours to find Obinin and Vasilov in 1918 Moscow. He'd stepped through the temporal gate and emerged in a snowbank, somewhere among the low, wooded hills forty kilometers west of Moscow that would one day shelter the *dacha* hideaways of the Soviet elite.

Without a downlink to aim for, there was always an element of uncertainty. Andryanov had heard of early time travelers missing their targets in such blind, crosstime transfers by thousands of kilometers and tens of years; this time the accuracy was quite good. The bemused Red militiamen who examined Andryanov's carefully forged travel papers and given him a ride into Moscow aboard their battered truck told him the date: December 10. He'd been aiming for the fifth.

He'd lost one day getting into Moscow through snow- and mud-blocked roads and a second trying to find his VBU contacts once he got there. There were drops and signals to use in such a case, but the Bolsheviks were suspicious and watchful, and it was difficult to locate the two agents . . . or any of the handful of other VBU men stationed in the city.

Finally, though, he'd found what he was looking for, an inconspicuous chalk mark on the stone wall enclosing the weirdly striped and colored towers of St. Basil's Cathedral, just off Red Square. The mark led to a *dubok*—a message drop—underneath a green-painted bench along the Kremlin Wall, not far from where Lenin's Tomb would one day be built. The message thumbtacked to the bottom of the bench directed him to an address a few blocks away, and he met Obinin and Vasilov at last.

"I am alone," he told them as he removed his heavy overcoat and fur hat. Their office was cramped but warm from the blaze in a cast-iron stove against one wall. For all their problems with the local authorities, the VBU agents had pull enough to secure plenty of firewood and food. Obinin even produced a rare bottle of vodka to toast the meeting with.

"Alone!" Obinin gaped. "What are they thinking of, sending one man? I mean no disrespect, Comrade Major, but . . ."

"Oh, reinforcements are coming, Lieutenant. They are simply not coming *here*."

"Where, then?"

"Your message gave Uralskiy a succinct understanding of the situation." Andryanov's mouth twisted with the memory of his superior's consternation upon learning that the 1918 downlink had been captured. "It was obvious that our train was taken through the White lines, that it must, by now, be somewhere east of the Urals . . . in Siberia.''

"Da." Vasilov nodded mournfully. "That was our assessment."

"The probability, then, is that the Americans are studying the downlink somewhere safe . . . somewhere along the Trans-Siberian Railway, since they have no way of taking it elsewhere." He accepted a glass of vodka from Obinin. *"Spaseebah, tovarisch. Nahzdrovia!"* He tossed the drink down, savoring the white fire. "It could take considerable time to locate them. Siberia is a rather large region, after all . . . even if we limit our search to the railway. The danger, Comrades, is that the Americans could tamper with our history before we find them . . . that they could wipe out Uralskiy and the entire structure of the VBU in 2007 before we can locate and destroy them.''

"What is to be done then, Comrade Major?"

"It has already been done." Andryanov smiled and gestured for a refill with his glass. "When Uralskiy got your message, they assembled a highly skilled VBU team through the main portal. Their destination was not Moscow, but a downlink already established . . . and many years in the past."

"Before 1918? But why?"

"So that if the Americans *do* succeed in changing history, they will not touch the force sent to stop them. The Transformation Wave caused by their tampering will sweep forward from 1918. All of history after this year will be changed, but we now have our base of operation safe and secure long before this year. The downlinks, you understand, can operate as limited-range time machines in their own right. In fact, I came here from the base. I was dispatched here to Moscow to alert you . . . and to put part of our plan into motion."

"Then our reinforcements are coming from the past, not the future!" Obinin chuckled. "A neat solution."

Andryanov shrugged. "It guarantees our success. It gives us time to hunt down the Americans, even if they have already altered history. It also gives us time to trace what they have done and undo it."

"Restoring our history before it is changed. *Very* neat."

"In any case," Andryanov continued, "sixty spetsnaz commandos under the command of Colonel Zamiatin will emerge near Irkutsk sometime within the next few days. They will find and capture one of the armored trains the Czech bandits are using on the Trans-Siberian Railway at this point in the war and make their way west, searching for the Americans. Uralskiy believes the enemy will have established himself near Omsk. That was the capital of the White movement, after all, and would give them access to Kolchak and his government.''

"That makes sense." Vasilov nodded. "What are our orders, Comrade Major?"

Andryanov looked away, toward the large windows and their view of the Kremlin. "We are to coordinate our actions with the spetsnaz." He struggled to control his expression. The VBU was the joint project of two organs of Soviet intelligence: the KGB and the military GRU. The spetsnaz, the dreaded *Spetsialnoye Nazhacheniye,* was an arm of the GRU. Andryanov had served with the spetsnaz on previous missions and had no reason to be fond of them. They tended to blunder straight into a situation without recourse to the more subtle—and less obvious—approach favored by the KGB.

Still, the current situation seemed to call for a direct approach, and perhaps this time the *vashti* back in Uralskiy knew what they were doing. But at least he had his own opportunity to take action against the Americans.

After a moment, he went on. "We are to penetrate the White lines and investigate Omsk." He patted his coat's hidden pocket. "I am carrying documents that should enable us to move unchallenged. Once we are in place, we locate the train and report to the colonel."

Obinin looked uncertain. "Is there not a risk of the Americans tracking us by our transmissions, Comrade Major?"

Andryanov nodded. "The possibility has been considered. It is one reason why the spetsnaz team is entering 1918 somewhere in all that vastness to the east." He shrugged. "We will maintain radio silence except when communications are essential. No, Comrades, the Americans will be quite unable to prepare for our attack. The advantage, this time, is overwhelmingly with us!"

Vasilov smiled and poured another round of drinks. "If we are to sit the fight out as observers, then at least we have something good to watch. Shall we toast victory?"

Andryanov took the glass and nodded solemnly. He would soon have the satisfaction of seeing his American enemies taken or killed . . . and full redemption in the eyes of his superiors. *"Da! Pahbeda!"*

Eleven

Travis Hunter slapped a magazine into his Uzi, chambered a round, and cursed. "Looks like we've got a riot out there, Greg," he said. "Let's saddle up."

"Yeah." King nodded grimly. "I've called the men out already. Where the hell is Kazanov, anyway?"

"In town somewhere. We'd better find him."

Their orders, delivered that morning, were to stay with the train. Vladimir Leonidovich Kazanov had been sent with those orders by Hendricks himself—*Gospodin* Hendricks, as the *B'yelee Smert* major called him—but something in the stocky, muscular Cossack's manner had convinced Hunter that the man knew more than he was telling.

Could Hendricks have known about this rising before it began?

The captured train was an island of calm in the midst of chaos and confusion. Firelight illuminated the streets of Kulomzino, turning the sleepy railroad town into a scene out of a nightmare. Crackling flames mingled with the rumbling murmur of mob noises, interspersed with occasional gunshots, screams, and shouts. Through the coach windows, Hunter and the other Rangers could make out the scurrying figures of men, women, and children fleeing the terror through the deep banks of snow. Other shapes moved more purposefully, soldiers of the White Army deploying to guard key positions. The spearheads of the rising appeared to be groups of armed railway workers that had rushed into the streets earlier that evening. Hunter still remembered the shrill voice of one speech maker, calling for the overthrow of Kolchak and his bloody-handed thugs.

The area around the rail depot was largely controlled by White troops now, the worker gangs dispersed by shouted commands and by gunfire. The sounds of fighting continued to rise above other parts of Kolchak's capital and its environs.

Orders to stay put or not, Hunter had to know what was going on. Hendricks was in Omsk, a very large place to search if he was not at his headquarters, but Kazanov ought to be somewhere close by, in the town of Kulomzino. With King close behind, Hunter hastened through the door of the railway carriage. Anderson, Gomez, and Walker waited on the platform, weapons ready.

It was the first night of winter. The chill December wind carried the smells of smoke and blood, and Hunter's shiver was not entirely due to the cold. He knew the pattern of coup and countercoup, bloodshed and reprisal, all too well. Kolchak had been in power barely a month now, and already the first flush of enthusiasm was wearing off, dimming the prospects of a White victory. The admiral's government was already being perceived as too corrupt, too concerned with the trappings of power, and not close enough to the people it ruled. Hunter knew from the Backlash briefings that it was just a loss of confidence that had led to the ultimate failure of the White cause.

But the briefings never mentioned this rising. No overt changes had been introduced so far, so it must have been a part of the original Chronos history . . . a failed part of that history, since Kolchak had stayed in power. *If they knew it was going to happen, why wasn't it mentioned? Why not work to shore up Kolchak's position instead of letting his government make the same mistakes?*

A White soldier shifted in a vague approximation of attention as the Rangers passed the rearmost car of the train. Hunter found himself wishing that Dubcek and the other Czechs were still in Kulomzino, but they had left two days before. General Gaida, now commanding one of Kolchak's armies, had offered Dubcek a place on his personal staff. So White Death troopers stood guard on the captured downlink now, another reminder of how Hendricks was extending his personal control over every aspect of Backlash.

Hunter glanced at Anderson. "I want you to stay here, Roy. Keep an eye on things."

"Good idea, LT." The Texan grinned. "These old boys need somebody to show 'em how to wipe their noses."

"Stay with the train," Hunter ordered. "Don't fire on anyone unless you're attacked . . . and keep Rachel and the other technicians from leaving."

"You got it, LT," Anderson said cheerfully.

Hunter turned away, the other Rangers fanning out around him. They moved slowly through the streets of Kulomzino, working their way past crowds of civilian refugees fleeing the fighting in the heart of town. Twice they passed knots of White soldiers, unarmed and obviously panic-stricken.

"Gutless wonders," King commented. "Makes you wonder how they're supposed to stand up to the Reds at all."

"They're not exactly the cream of the crop," Gomez agreed.

Confused shouts erupted from the next street corner. A moment later, a number of men in rough worker's clothes spilled from a side street and surged toward the Rangers. A few waved handguns or bolt-action rifles. Most clutched picks, shovels, and pry bars. "*Vot!* There are some of the bastards!"

Hunter's Uzi subgun bucked in his hands, but he kept the muzzle sharply depressed. Clods of dirt, snow, and mud spit and geysered from the unpaved street between the Rangers and the mob.

The workers in front skidded to a halt, unwilling to face automatic fire at point-blank range. Hunter brought his Uzi up to his shoulder, aiming squarely for the leader.

Most of the men appeared to be railway workers or laborers—civilians, all of them. The conflict that had been building in Hunter's mind for weeks now reached its climax. To support Kolchak, to change history against the Reds, he was expected to fire into a crowd of rioting civilians. He found that if it was necessary to save his life and the lives of his men, he was ready to fire, but to randomly kill these people . . .

"Disperse!" he yelled in Russian. He sensed movement at either side as the other Rangers shifted their weapons, covering the crowd. "Go home!"

"Comrades!" a voice shrilled from the back of the mob. "These are the foreign oppressors . . . the hirelings of Kolchak and his gang! Kill them!"

The mob edged forward and Hunter fired a second warning burst, closer this time. Someone screamed as a bullet fragment shrieked off stone and stung his leg.

The crowd broke then, scattering. Hunter searched for the Red agent who had been spurring the mob on but couldn't tell who it was.

They hurried on. Sounds of gunfire ahead were sporadic now, but the sharp cracks of volleyed rifle fire could be heard from the direction of the center of town.

Walker cocked his head, listening. "What's happening over there?"

"Firing squads," Hunter said grimly. "The executions have already begun."

They turned a corner, entering a narrow plaza. A line of White soldiers stood there, their backs to the Rangers. Others dragged two people through the trampled snow toward a blood-splattered section of wall. By the wavering light of a burning house down the street, Hunter saw bodies already sprawled in the snow, twisted, broken, arms still tied behind their backs. The soldiers shoved the next two bound victims in front of the wall. Neither prisoner wore a coat, and both looked bruised and bloodied from their rough handling. One of them was a young woman, her dress hanging in tatters from one shoulder.

Gomez clutched his M-16 tighter in his hands. "I don't like this, Chief. That sort of thing isn't part of my job description."

"I thought we were fighting the Communists," Walker added. "Not civilians . . ."

Hunter said nothing, but he had to agree. Turning the military tide against the Reds by training White commandos and winning battles was one thing, but this was something else entirely. The man fell to his knees, sobbing. The woman stood beside him trembling, looking around wildly, obviously dazed.

A White officer raised his hand. *"Gotovyee!"* The line of White soldiers stiffened, their rifles snapping up in front of their faces.

The officer turned his head and Hunter saw his features. "Kazanov!" he shouted. "What the hell are you doing?"

"Pretsyeleevat' sya!" The rifles dropped into line, aiming at the two prisoners.

"Dammit, Major! *Stoy!*"

"Strelyat!"

The line of rifles barked as one. The two victims were jerked back against the wall as small, bloody explosions snapped from their chests.

Hunter strode across the square, elbowing through the line of soldiers. Kazanov turned to face him, his pale, icy-blue eyes mild under his peaked hat with its skull insignia of the *B'yelee Smert*.

"Do not interfere, Lieutenant," the Cossack told him in the same even tones he had used to give the orders to fire. "As you can see, matters here are well in hand."

"By whose authority are you shooting these people?" Hunter demanded.

"Does it bother you, Lieutenant?" Kazanov smiled. At the wall, the woman twisted, her feet aimlessly kicking at the snow. A low, bubbling moan escaped her lips.

The White Death major drew a heavy revolver from its holster, strode across the snow, and stood above the woman. Something unpleasant glittered in his eye as he pointed the weapon at the woman's head.

"Major, stop! You can't just shoot these people!"

Kazanov's finger tightened on the trigger. The pistol's explosion was startlingly loud, echoing from the walls of the buildings around them. The woman's legs thrashed once and were still. The major fired again. "They are rebels." He spat at the bodies at his feet. "Traitors. Probably Bolshevik agents."

"Probably . . . ?"

"It is war, Lieutenant." The Cossack gave a careless shrug. "Terrible things happen in war."

Hunter was keenly aware of the sullen looks from the line of waiting soldiers. He did not have the authority to give Kazanov orders and they knew it.

The major hesitated, eyeing Hunter coldly, then continued. "You asked for my authority? My orders come from your own Captain Hendricks, of course . . . countersigned by Admiral

Kolchak himself! It was *Gospodin* Hendricks who warned us that this little demonstration was going to occur tonight."

"What . . . ?"

"An impressive demonstration of the abilities of the *B'yelee Smert*, don't you think?" He nudged the dead woman's bare leg with the toe of his boot. "My orders are to suppress this . . . this rabble with whatever force I consider necessary, and nowhere do they say that I am to check my actions with you!" He holstered the pistol. "I suggest you return to your train, Lieutenant. Stay there. We have matters here completely under control, and we do not need your . . . *help*." The sour, sarcastic inflection on the final word ended the conversation.

Hunter turned and stalked from the square, feeling the dark stares of the firing squad against his back as he left. *If we support atrocities like this*, he thought, *we're as bad as they are! I've got to get to Hendricks . . . got to talk to him! We should be curbing Kolchak's bloody-mindedness . . . not cheering him on!*

But he knew that there was scant chance of winning that kind of support from the Bravo Team leader. If Hendricks had known about this rising, he should have prevented it, not used it as a showcase for his precious White Death Commandos!

Behind him, soldiers prodded two more civilians into line in front of the wall. Hunter gathered the other Rangers and led them back toward the train as Kazanov's commands again rose above the bloody streets.

King found Rachel in the rail coach with Brian Fitzpatrick and Sarah Grant. He stamped the snow from his boots as he entered, shutting the door against the bitter wind outside. Chill winter sunlight spilled through the car's windows. It was December 22, the day after the attempted coup. There was little sign now of the fighting that had raged through the streets of Omsk and Kulomzino . . . or of the executions.

"Rachel," he said, "thank God you're here. Can you come with me into Omsk?"

"Can it wait?" She shook her head, her brow knitted with impatience. "These equations are important."

King knew the Backlash technical team had made important breakthroughs in understanding the Soviet downlink, that they were in the middle of determining how the VBU time-portal gear could be turned to American recall beacons. There were exciting possibilities there, but . . .

He shook his head. "No, Rachel, it can't. The lieutenant needs you."

"Why? What's happened?" She looked alarmed. "Is he okay?"

"He's gone to Bravo's HQ to pull Hendricks's cork."

Fitzpatrick's eyes widened. "What do you mean, Master Sergeant? I thought everything was going quite smoothly!"

King looked at the slight technician as though seeing him for the first time. He remembered Fitzpatrick from the Chronos facility, but had rarely spoken with him and knew him only slightly. "What happened last night wasn't my idea of 'smooth,' son. It was a damned bloody massacre. The lieutenant's fed up with supporting that kind of thing . . . and I, for one, don't blame him!"

"We've been hearing stories," Sarah said. "Nothing definite. Something about mass executions?"

King nodded. "The Whites captured well over a hundred prisoners last night. There's talk of shooting them, yeah."

"Bolsheviks," Fitzpatrick said. "Swede—" He stopped, suddenly hesitant. "I heard they were Bolshevik agitators."

"Aw, come on! All of them? Looks to me like Kolchak rounded up whoever was handy, and now he's going to shoot them." He turned to Rachel. "The lieutenant might need your support, Rachel. He's going to be pushing Hendricks to suspend operations until we can check with Time Square."

"But why?" Rachel seemed genuinely puzzled. "What good would that do? Swede's pretty much on his own with Backlash, and once a major change is made to history, well . . ." She shrugged. "One week later and we get a new 2007, anyway, when the Transformation Wave hits."

Yeah, King thought. *A 2007 without Communists . . . and no Chronos Project. But what's it going to have instead?* "I think the lieutenant is concerned about what we're replacing it with," he said aloud. "Right now, the Whites are no better than the Reds."

"It was that way to begin with," Rachel replied. "Changing it is going to take time. You don't expect Swede to remake the entire population of Russia in a month, do you?"

So it's "Swede," is it? King frowned. He knew Rachel and

Hunter disagreed over the fundamental aspects of Backlash. Was Rachel falling for Hendricks's rugged good looks and easy manner? *I suppose girls might go for that type,* he thought. *But I thought Rachel had a thing for the lieutenant.*

"Rachel, you ought to go," Sarah said. She closed her eyes. "I saw them out there this morning hauling bodies away in trucks, stacked up like frozen cordwood . . ."

The other girl shook her head. "Don't you see? Those things are a part of this history! We haven't done anything to change things yet. When we do . . . well, we'll hope it'll be better. But I don't see what Swede could be doing differently!"

"Hendricks's White Death helped suppress that uprising last night," King said angrily. "I'd say he's helping Kolchak quite a bit, even if he hasn't actually changed things yet. The lieutenant is just questioning what we're doing back here if all we're doing is helping Kolchak kill people!"

"That was the whole idea, wasn't it?" Rachel snapped. "Help the Whites win? Doesn't that mean killing people?"

"That's right," Fitzpatrick put in. "You can't make an omelet—"

"Don't say that!" Sarah looked horrified. "The ends never justify the means!"

Rachel sagged, looking very tired. "Maybe they do when history is going to change, anyway. Swede has to protect Kolchak long enough to find the right opening."

"Don't give me that!" King's anger surfaced now. He remembered the dazed look on the face of that woman in front of the firing squad the night before. She hadn't looked much like a Red agitator . . . hadn't looked much like any kind of a threat at all.

"I don't like the killing any more than you do!" Rachel was on her feet now, her fists clenched, her face chalk-white. "Dammit, there's nothing we can do! We just have to go along until Swede can find the right time and place to get Kolchak under control!"

"Yeah. And what if he can't be controlled? Or if Hendricks doesn't know what the hell he's doing? I think he's been running off half cocked since the mission began! No plan! No direction except helping a bloody two-bit dictator stay in power."

"Well, it's not your place to judge, is it?"

King felt himself go cold. "No, ma'am, it isn't." *She's with Hendricks*, he thought. *She's so convinced that slimy bastard's got it right.* "Sorry I bothered you."

He slammed the door behind him and hurried through the cold toward Omsk.

Twelve

Raucous laughter greeted Hunter as he entered the hotel. Just off of the front lobby of the *Dvoretz Gasteeneetsa* a party was in full swing in the large, richly ornamented ballroom. The room was packed with Hendricks's men, high-ranking officials of Kolchak's government, and White Army officers resplendent in gaudy uniforms heavy with medals and braid. Most of the White officers wore massive spurs that rattled like marbles in a tin can as they walked. From the atmosphere of gaiety and easygoing fellowship, it was hard to believe that any of the soldiers had spent much time at the front. The somber, wartime spirit that pervaded the rest of the city was absent here.

"Tovarisch Ahotnik!" Hunter blinked at the improbable Russification of his name and turned. Major Kazanov weaved toward him, hoisting a glass in salute. Vodka was in short supply after four years of prohibition, but there was no shortage of *samogan*, the harsh, home-distilled brew favored by the Russians when there was nothing better. "Comrade Hunter! *Kahk pahjeevaheetee, tovarisch?"*

There was no sign that the Cossack officer even remembered their last encounter. *"Harashaw,"* Hunter lied. "Fine, thank you. Where is Captain Hendricks?"

"Captain Hendricks! Ah, you do not know? It is General Hendricks now! Admiral Kolchak himself bestowed on him this honor only this morning!"

"General . . . ?"

"It is the admiral's opinion that *Gospodin* Hendricks's warning was instrumental in stopping the attempted coup last night! He has been promoted to general and elevated to a permanent position on the Supreme Ruler's personal staff! This gathering is in celebration of that honor . . . and of the splendid victory of last night!"

Hunter frowned. Hendricks's information could not have been crucial to that "splendid victory" since, as far as Hunter could determine, the coup had been crushed without Hendricks's help in history's original version. However, if Kolchak *thought* the information vital, he must be very grateful indeed.

And Hendricks had taken the first large step toward a major change in history. The influence an unknown American captain could bring to bear on Russian events was very small, but a general on Kolchak's advisory staff . . .

"I must see the . . . general. Where is he?"

Kazanov pointed unsteadily across the room. Hunter could see Hendricks reclining on a low, raised platform. Malloy was with him, together with a bevy of local girls, but Master Sergeant Simms, surprisingly, was nowhere in sight. Somewhere a small orchestra was playing very badly, while officers and civilian women danced or snuggled and kissed. The scene held the promise of a developing orgy, Hunter thought. The room, in Russian custom, was uncomfortably stuffy and hot, and many of the girls had already started relieving themselves of excess clothing.

"So, Lieutenant," Hendricks said as Hunter approached the platform. A hint of a smile played across his features. "I understand you and your men were out late last night. Such . . . *devotion* is commendable, but it wasn't necessary, you know. My people had the situation under control."

"So I was told." Hunter looked at the man's uniform with distaste, a gaudy affair heavy with gold braid and medals, and gold-encrusted epaulets that lay on his shoulders like wings. A half dozen of his troops lined the wall behind him, startlingly out of place in their combat fatigues, with M-16s gripped at port arms in front of them.

Bodyguards . . .

"In case you didn't know, *General*, there are firing squads shooting prisoners in the streets out there." Hunter spoke English so that the women curled up on the cushions by his side would not understand. One—a black-haired, bare-breasted girl with dark almond eyes—giggled at his unintelligible speech. "You knew about the coup ahead of time."

Hendricks looked puzzled by Hunter's outburst. "Of course I did. Lynn is most useful in her capacity as a . . . ah . . . trusted adviser."

"Goddammit, man! If you knew the coup was going to happen, why couldn't you help Kolchak by *preventing* it instead of letting it go ahead?"

"Why should we want to prevent it?" The Bravo Team commander sipped *samogan* from a glass, grimacing at the liquid's bite. "We had quite a few of the leaders picked up before it started, but we made certain the coup went on, as scheduled."

Hunter was appalled. "In the name of God, why?"

"Oh, come now, Lieutenant. Don't be naïve! By ruthlessly crushing the rebellion, the admiral's position is stronger than ever! There will be no challenge to his rule now."

"I thought the enemies were the Bolsheviks."

"Our enemies are *anyone* who stands between the Whites and victory! Between *me* and victory!" He touched the dark-haired girl's shoulder, stroking the bare skin. "You know, Hunter, there's a great future for you with us . . . if you can demonstrate that you are a team player." He chuckled at his own joke. "A great *future* . . . get it?"

Hunter looked at him coldly. "I suggest, sir, that we contact Chronos."

"Eh? What do they have to do with it?"

"Somehow I don't think Operation Backlash ever envisioned anything like this! Victory over the Reds is one thing. Slaughtering civilians is something else entirely!"

"Relax, Lieutenant. Everything is under control." He gestured with his glass at the crowded room. "Why don't you join the party?"

Hunter's fists closed at his side. "I have my duties to perform, *General*."

"Nonsense! Nonsense!" Hendricks slipped back into Russian, addressing the dark-eyed girl at his side. "Here, Tanya. Go with the lieutenant. Show him a good time."

Hunter's fury surfaced. "What in the hell are you playing at, Hendricks?" His outburst shocked the room to silence and made the bodyguards stir uncomfortably. Tanya stepped to his side and took his arm, pressing it against her breast, but he jerked away angrily. "This mission isn't a goddamn party!"

An unreadable mask dropped across Hendricks's features. "You are addressing a general of the White Army, Lieutenant," he said in Russian.

"I am addressing an officer of the United States Army," Hunter replied in English. "Or have you forgotten that?"

"I have forgotten nothing." Color was rising in Hendricks's face now. "Nothing!"

"You'd better pray that's so, because you're gambling a universe on the toss of your dice!" Stiffly, Hunter saluted the captain and spun on his heel, stalking from the crowded room in a torment of thought and anger.

There was nothing more to be accomplished here. The recall beacon was being kept near Bravo Team's assigned barracks building in Omsk—a ploy by Hendricks, Hunter decided, to keep it under guard. If they moved fast, though, the Rangers could find the beacon there and use it to get back to Time Square. Then perhaps they could do something about "General" Swede Hendricks.

Hendricks watched the Ranger push through the laughing throng. "Danny!"

Malloy straightened up beside him, leaning close to hear Hendricks's orders. "Hunter is going to be trouble," Hendricks said. "I'll bet a screw with Tanya here that he's heading for the recall beacon."

"He looked pretty pissed off," Malloy replied. "And his men'll back him up too. Could be a real bitch if he decides he doesn't want to play."

"Yeah." Hendricks touched Malloy's shoulder. For a moment, he wished Simms was in Omsk to handle Hunter, but the master sergeant was already on his way to Perm with a mission . . . a very important mission. "Danny, tell Chuck and Solly to round up some of the boys and get them over to Number 12."

"The warehouse?"

"Right. I have a feeling our friend's heading there. I want him dead. Now."

"Yes, General. You want me to go with them?"

Hendricks frowned, thinking. "No . . . no, the boys can handle it. I want you to head for the downlink. Grab Fitzpatrick and have him warm it up . . . then hang around, just in case. I may need you to take a little trip for me. I'll call you on the radio if I do."

"Yes, General," Malloy said again. The soldier rose from the platform, made his way through the cluster of Russian girls, and hurried from the room.

Hendricks put an arm around Tanya and drew her close with a satisfied smile. Travis Hunter had interfered with his plans for the last time.

Hunter met King in the snow-swept street outside the hotel.

"She won't help us," King said, answering Hunter's questioning look. "Whose side is she on, anyway?"

He thrust aside the mingled pain and fear King's words stirred. "C'mon, Greg," Hunter said quietly. "This way." ·

"What's happened?"

"Trouble. Hendricks is going off the deep end. Calls himself general now . . . and the way he's acting, I think he's gone into business for himself!"

"Oh, God."

"We've got to get back to Time Square. Go round up the men. Bring them over to Number 12 Reenok Ooleetsah. I'll be there, warming up the recall beacon."

King looked grim. "What about the technicians?"

Damn! He didn't want to leave them with Hendricks, but . . . "We have to leave them," he decided. "Hendricks may try to stop us, and we have to move fast. They should be okay where they are, and we won't be gone long."

"What do you figure to do about him?"

Hunter looked away. "I don't know. We'll tell General Thompson what we know. Maybe we can get Becker to suspend the mission until Hendricks explains himself."

"We're going way, way outside chain of command on this one, Lieutenant."

"Yeah. Mutiny anyone?" He shook his head. "The damnable part is, we can't point to anything Hendricks has done wrong. But that guy scares me. I want to bring in Thompson.''

King nodded. "I'm with you, Lieutenant. I'll get the lads. See you at Number 12.''

Ten minutes later Hunter entered the large, run-down warehouse located on the Reenok Ooleetsah, Market Street. The interior was musty and only dimly lit by sunlight slanting through the tall, filth-encrusted windows that decorated one long wall. Pine crates and boxes were stacked in dusty disarray. One end of the building had been reserved for extra equipment brought into 1918 by Bravo Team and the technicians.

One of Hendricks's men stood guard there . . . or rather, he *slouched* guard. His back to Hunter, his M-16 leaning nearby, he was perched on one of the crates and was nursing a large glass jar filled with a pungent-smelling clear liquid. He was, Hunter decided, less than happy about being left out of the party at the hotel and had decided to do a bit of private partying on his own.

A guard on the time travelers' supplies was necessary, for theft and the black market were by this time basic to the economy of Omsk . . . and there was no telling what members of the city's underworld would make of—say—one of the magnetic surge detector units, or of the team's temporal recall beacon. This soldier, however, was less interested in the warehouse's contents than he was in the contents of the bottle. He leaned back, tipping the wide-mouthed jar to chug down the last swallow. Hunter drew his .45—he had left his Uzi at the Rangers' barracks—took five swift and silent steps forward, and brought the butt of the pistol down on the base of the guard's skull. The man toppled to the side, the empty jar smashing on the floor in a spray of glass shards. Hunter eased the body off the crate and rolled it aside, checking first to make certain the man was still breathing.

The recall beacon was stored on a makeshift shelf against the warehouse wall. Hunter took the small device, switched it on, and positioned it on the floor. They now had approximately twenty minutes to wait before Time Square received the signal, powered up, and opened the portal between 2007 and 1918. King and the others would be here by then.

A door banged open at the far end of the warehouse. "Bicksley! It's us!" Hunter whirled at the shout, crouching behind a crate. He saw shapes moving toward him, three . . . no, four men, all of them carrying M-16s. "Hey, Bicksley! Where the hell are ya?"

Four of Hendricks's men, carrying assault rifles and showing up here now, could only mean that Hendricks had decided to act before Hunter could get away to the future. The Ranger snaked out one hand, snatching up the guard's M-16 and thumbing the bolt latch to chamber a round.

The men froze at the sound, their rifles coming up in alarm. "It's him!" one shouted. "The Ranger! Get him!"

Gunfire spat and snapped, chopping into the crate with 5.56 mm NATO rounds. Splinters whirled past Hunter's face as he crouched low, seeking shelter.

He didn't want to fire at American soldiers, but it was obvious they had no such compunctions regarding him. "What the hell are you people doing?" he bellowed. Perhaps he could win time by bargaining . . . or by bluffing—

Automatic fire crackled in response, smashing into the wall at Hunter's back, chopping into the ruined crate, gouging chunks of rot-soft wood from the floor.

Okay, so they don't want to chat. He swung around the side of the crate, his weapon level, squeezing off a sharp, short burst. The attackers scrambled for cover as Hunter's fire cracked above their heads.

He looked from side to side, gauging angles and fields of fire. Determined men could work their way up among the crates, moving from cover to cover and nailing him in a crossfire in the end. And he couldn't move the beacon, not if the technicians in 2007 were to be able to lock on to it and hold a solid fix on its time-space coordinates.

"You don't have a chance, Hunter," someone yelled from across the room. "Make it easy on yourself and come on out!"

"You want to talk about the penalties for killing a superior officer?" Hunter yelled back. "This won't look real good in your service records!"

He heard a laughing "Aw, shit" and someone's muttered, "Is this guy for real?" Hunter took advantage of the pause to shift to the right, slipping behind another stack of crates from which he had a better view of the warehouse's central aisle.

Someone shouted from the other side of the room. "Hey, Lieutenant! Let's talk!"

Hunter frowned. By launching their attack, Hendricks's men had left little to talk about. The attempt could only be a diversion. Hunter looked away from the direction of the voice, scanning the shadows between the stacks of crates. If they were trying to sneak up on him . . . there! Movement flitted through the shadows. Hunter shifted his position, covering this new threat. "What do you want to talk about?" *Keep them talking* . . . .

"We figure you don't understand your situation, Lieutenant! Y'know, you'd be playin' it real smart if you were to join up with Swede and the rest of us! You could—"

The shadow burst from cover, sprinting toward Hunter's position. He triggered the M-16, the muzzle flash blazing in the dying light. The running man flung his arms wide and fell backward over a crate, his rifle clattering on the wooden floor.

"Christ, Chuck! He popped Dal!"

"Get the bastard!"

Gunfire cracked and rattled. Hunter hugged the floor as rounds sizzled overhead or buried themselves in wood.

Then he lifted his head. There were new sounds now, rolling volleys of autofire coming from outside. The gunfire directed at Hunter abruptly ceased. When Hunter peered over the top of the crate he was sheltering behind, he saw his attackers racing for the warehouse door. The sounds of gunfire in the street grew in intensity.

Then Anderson burst in, followed closely by Gomez, King, and Dark Walker.

"Hey, Chief!" Gomez snapped. "Where are you?"

"Back here!"

"That was quite a reception out there," Anderson observed. "There are at least five men covering the front of the warehouse . . . and more around the side."

"Yeah," King said. "We had to make a dash for the door. I think we got one—"

"Two," Dark Walker corrected him. The Dakota snapped a fresh magazine into his Galil.

"Okay," Hunter said. He checked his watch. "The beacon is counting down. We have about twelve minutes. Eddie, Greg, cover the door. Roy, Walker . . . stay with me. Watch the windows. They'll rush us again in a minute. They'll *have* to—"

The attack came as Hunter predicted it, a half-spirited rush against the warehouse door. When they withdrew, they left two more bodies in the snowy street outside.

Moments later the shifting auroral light of an open portal shimmered above the beacon. "Time," Hunter called. "Portal's open! Walker! Roy! Go through!"

"On our way, LT," Anderson called. "See you on the other side!"

The two men stepped through the light and vanished. The three remaining Rangers backed toward the beacon, keeping their weapons trained on the door and windows. "Now," Hunter said. "Greg, Eddie . . ."

Both men stepped into the light—

An explosion shattered the doors, tearing one off its hinges and twisting the other savagely aside. Two men appeared in the smoke before the echo ceased, firing their assault rifles in long, sweeping bursts from the hip. Bullets snapped and whined close above Hunter's head. He fired a reply, his M-16 chattering as he hosed lead into the half-glimpsed figures pouring through the door. Something hot plucked at his sleeve.

Still firing, he stepped backward into the light . . .

. . . and stumbled onto the raised platform, blinking as his eyes adjusted to the sudden brilliance of Time Square's fluorescent lighting. King and Anderson caught him by the elbow, steadying him. Relief welled up inside as he looked around, a little wildly. They'd made it. *Now we'll bring that maniac to heel*.

The Chronos complex control room was the same as when he'd left it, over two long months before. The same time would have passed here, of course. A month's passing in the past was a month's passing in the present, unless portals were opened to more than one time. He saw the familiar, spare figure of General Thompson standing by a console, hands clasped behind his back. Dr. Stein stood nearby, his face creased in a worried frown.

"General!" Hunter started forward. "General Thompson!"

"Hold it right there, young man," another voice commanded.

Hunter's head snapped around to face the speaker. "General Becker . . ." His eyes widened. Just behind Becker were a pair of armed security guards and another figure, tall and lean, still wearing an army parka dripping with melting snow. "Sergeant Malloy! What the blue blazes . . ."

"Lieutenant," Becker said. "All of you are under arrest. Take them, men."

Rifles at the ready, the guards closed in.

Thirteen

"With respect, General, you're nuts." Hunter stood at attention in front of Becker, his eyes focused on an imaginary spot on the wall behind the general's left shoulder. "Hendricks has gone into business for himself. He tried to kill us. When he missed, he sent Malloy through the downlink to beat us here and . . . destroy our credibility."

"As far as I'm concerned, Lieutenant, you *have* no credibility." Becker's face was creased by a bulldog's frown, which gave him an almost mournful look. He leaned back behind General Thompson's desk, which he had appropriated for this interview, and laced his fingers across his belly. "You abandoned your post at a critical point in the mission. According to Sergeant Malloy, VBU agents were in the area and threatening Operation Backlash. That could be construed, Lieutenant, as desertion in the face of the enemy."

It was nearly forty-eight hours after the Rangers had stepped through into the Chronos base. The five of them were not under arrest—not quite—but they were confined to quarters, and an MP posted in the passageway outside ensured that they would be going nowhere on the base without an escort. Only General

Thompson's intervention had kept them all from being thrown into a detention cell at Becker's command.

"That's nonsense, General, and you know it!" General Thompson sat in a chair at Hunter's left, his arms folded across his crumpled tunic. Disgust and anger put a raw edge to his voice. "I know this man. He wouldn't have returned unless he felt it was necessary."

"Maybe, Alex," Becker replied. "That's *your* story, and I respect you for standing up for your men. But Swede Hendricks is a goddamn hero! The hero of Berthoud Pass."

"Maybe we should examine that hero's credentials a little more closely!"

Hunter remained silent as the two generals exchanged verbal fire. In the past two days, all five of the Rangers had been through debriefings that amounted to interrogations. Malloy's testimony had been damning; the Rangers, he'd insisted, had never supported Hendricks, had been guilty of drunken and disorderly conduct, and—when the technicians picked up evidence that a VBU force was approaching—had refused to investigate but insisted on returning to 2007.

Hunter could almost admire Hendricks for his use of the technology. Rachel and the technicians had made impressive strides in understanding how the Soviet equipment worked, to the point that they'd been able to send Malloy forward in time to a point only a few hours before the Rangers arrived at Time Square via the recall beacon. After seeing Hunter and his men arrested, he'd returned to 1918 using the Chronos portal and the open gate to the warehouse.

It was convenient, of course, since Malloy was no longer around to reply to Hunter's charges. Meanwhile the hours dragged on. Since time passed at the same rate at both ends of an open portal, it would be December 24, 1918 . . . Christmas Eve. What was happening to Rachel? What had Hendricks told her about the disappearance of the Rangers?

If she was working with Hendricks now, as King suggested, did she even care?

"You know, sir, there's only one way to be certain who is telling the truth," Thompson said, continuing the debate with Becker. "Send someone back . . . people you trust. Get a second viewpoint."

Becker looked uncomfortable. "I don't want to do that,

Alex. You heard Malloy. Things are delicate back there right now. If I send in a bunch of new people, it could interfere with whatever Hendricks is up to right now!''

''Bullshit, General! Send a couple of your aides! All they need to do is look around . . . ask some questions!''

Becker looked thoughtful. ''I could send Major Landry, I suppose.''

''With respect, sir,'' Hunter said, ''I suggest you send more than one staff officer. Hendricks tried to *murder* me and my men. What makes you think he won't happily shoot anyone who threatens him or his plans?''

''And you say *I'm* nuts, Lieutenant? What would Hendricks stand to gain killing my staff officers? That would be an admission of guilt . . . and I'd go in and shut him down!''

''Maybe, sir. But remember, once he makes a major change to history, we've got something like one week before the Transformation Wave hits us up here. So far he hasn't done anything major, but sooner or later he will. Once that happens, we'll be rewritten right out of history, and he'll still be back in 1918, living like a king!''

''And that, Lieutenant, is precisely why he's back there. To rewrite history.''

''Yes, sir. I just hope that the new world we get is better than this one.''

Becker's lips compressed into a thin line. ''If we eliminate Communism, Lieutenant, Operation Backlash will have achieved one hundred percent success. The United States will be safe and free! World War III will never have happened! That, Lieutenant, is worth just about anything we can pay . . . including our lives!''

''If you say so, General.'' Hunter hesitated, then added words he'd never expected to use. ''But there could be worse futures than one dominated by Communism!''

Simms squinted through the Leatherwood ranging sight mounted on his M-21 sniper's rifle. Slowly, very slowly, he tracked across a sea of faces.

The city of Perm was shaking to the crash of artillery, the insistent yammer of machine-gun fire. It was Christmas Day, 1918, and Perm was under an all-out assault by Kolchak's

Northern Army, under the command of General Rudolph
Gaida.

Admiral Kolchak had narrowly been stopped from disarming
all of the Czechs when he learned that the Czech Legion was
refusing to support his coup. Simms knew, because he'd been
there when Hendricks had talked him out of it. Some of the
Czechs had been willing enough to keep fighting the Reds, and
Gaida was one of them. Kolchak had been impressed enough
with the man to give him command of one of three armies
stretching from Samara to Ekaterinburg. Of the three, Gaida's
had been the most successful, thrusting forward and seizing
Perm after a sharp fight, taking thousands of prisoners and vast
stores of weapons and supplies.

Now Gaida had one more service to perform for the White
cause.

Master Sergeant Simms had left Omsk on the train that carried Dubcek and his men to the front. Their eight-hundred-mile
journey through the low, snow-smothered Urals had taken almost three full days. They had arrived outside of Perm on
December 23. Once the fighting was under way, it had not
been hard for them to separate themselves from the others, find
a secure spot at a slit window in an onion-domed Orthodox
Church tower, and wait for the battle to burn itself out. It was
late in the afternoon and the Bolsheviks were in full retreat
when General Gaida and his staff entered the heart of Perm.

"C'mon Sarge," one of the soldiers with him said, shifting
restlessly. "Nail the son of a bitch and let's clear out!"

"Patience, Slick," Simms replied. "Patience. Just a little
. . . ah!"

The telescopic sight encompassed Rudolph Gaida's face, the
cross hairs bisecting his forehead. The range was six hundred
yards. With the silencer affixed to the M-21's muzzle, the
Czechs would have no idea where the shot came from.

Simms knew a moment's heart-pounding excitement mingled
with terror. Up until now, Bravo Team's interference in the
past had been minimal . . . minor changes that would have af-
fected the world and the history of 2007 very little, if at all.
The pretty black-haired girl from the Chronos Complex had
explained it to him the week before in a session in Swede's
office. What was her name? Rachel Stein . . . yeah.

This would be different, though. In the history Simms and

Hendricks knew, Rudolph Gaida had not died until the end of World War II. If he died now, that would be a change that would rewrite history completely. There'd be no going back after this.

As his finger tightened on the trigger, Simms found himself hoping Swede knew what he was doing.

The harsh *phut* of the silenced rifle could not have been heard for more than a few yards beyond the church tower. Six hundred yards away, General Rudolph Gaida opened his mouth to give an order to one of his staff officers. The 7.62mm round smashed through bone and tissue just below the Czech's left eye, blasting from the rear of the man's skull in a gory spray of blood and brains.

In the tower, Simms smiled. He had just changed history, and the knowledge gave him a tremendous sense of power.

Now Swede's plan could really get into full swing!

"Well, sir," Hunter said as he and the other Rangers stood. "This is a surprise."

Thompson stepped through the door to their quarters and nodded bleakly, Hunter thought. It had been nine days since their return to 2007. *Something more has happened. What?*

"As you were, men," Thompson said. "I . . . ah . . . have some news."

"Word from Major Landry?" Hunter guessed. "What did he have to say?"

"Nothing. He still hasn't come back."

Hunter frowned. That meant that Becker's staff officer had been gone for five days now. What would the date be in 1918 now? December 31, he decided. The last day of 1918. "Hendricks has him," Hunter suggested. "Or he's dead."

"In fact, we've lost contact with 1918," Thompson said. "I'm worried."

"Yes, sir. I would be too."

"There's more. The general decided not to wait for Landry any longer. He's gone too."

"What?"

"Said he had to talk to Hendricks himself . . . and that he would get word back to us within three hours. It's been almost six hours now, and still no word."

"Hendricks has changed something," Hunter said flatly.

"He's pulled something big . . . and is just marking time now until the Transformation Wave hits us. He can afford to kill anyone we send back to check up on him, because he knows that seven days after he makes his change in 1918 . . ." Hunter snapped his fingers. "*Fft!* We're gone!"

"I'm afraid you're right." His mouth worked against some unspoken emotion. "Damn it all, we should have listened to you from the start!"

"It wasn't your fault, sir. You tried."

"I tried . . . but it wasn't enough." Thompson paused. "I checked up on Hendricks."

"Oh? Find out anything interesting?"

"He's not Special Forces, for one thing. He was in their training program but dropped out about the time the U.N. occupation forces arrived. That got me suspicious. I radioed the Denver area command. Seems Hendricks's men have a long history of offenses against local civilians."

"Eh?"

"Looting. Rape. Variants of the old protection racket. No proof that Hendricks himself was ever involved, but—"

"But it doesn't sound like Bravo was everything it was made out to be," King said.

Thompson gave a half smile. "Good help is so hard to find these days."

"Did you tell Becker?"

"I tried. He didn't want to believe it at first, but I think that was what finally got him worried enough to go check things out for himself. He . . . he has a lot of political baggage riding on Hendricks, you know."

"His protégé," Gomez said. "The guy he recommended for the FreeAm Medal."

"That's right."

"Okay," Hunter said. "So what do we do now?"

"I want you to get back there, and fast! Find out what Hendricks is doing . . . what he's done to Landry and Becker and what he's trying to do with history."

"It's been nine days, General. If he's done something big enough to rewrite history during that time . . ."

"We could vanish at any moment. I know."

Dark Walker rubbed his chin. "Is it possible to send us back to . . . say, December twenty-second? Maybe right after we left

Omsk? We know he hadn't changed anything in a big way at that point. If he _did_ change anything after that point, we could go back and stop him before it happened.''

Thompson shook his head. "Nice thought, Corporal, but we're just not up to it. The fact that you men and Sergeant Malloy were shuttling back and forth through time on the twenty-second makes things fuzzy for several days in both directions . . . hard to pin down.''

"We're shooting for the twenty-first, then?''

"That's the simplest. We have solid time coordinates that should bring you out pretty close to that date.''

"Can't we just follow Becker back through the warehouse portal?'' Anderson asked.

"That portal closed just after he went through. Anyway, even if it was open, we'd have to assume that Hendricks would be waiting for you. If he was responsible for the disappearances of Landry and Becker . . .''

"It means he's posted guards with orders to capture or kill everyone coming through from 2007,'' Hunter said. "Not healthy. Do you think you could shift the spatial coordinates a bit, General? Maybe set us down outside of town someplace?''

Thompson nodded. "Dr. Stein's already working it.''

"Good. That'll let us move in on Omsk without letting anyone know we're back.''

"I'm sending another recall beacon back with you,'' Thompson said. "As soon as you're in 1918 and can set it up, trigger the beacon. We'll lock a new portal open on your signal. You . . . might need help.''

"Hey,'' Gomez said cheerfully, "there's five of us, and only forty or fifty men with Hendricks. No problem!''

"There are his White Death Commandos,'' Walker reminded him.

Gomez made a face. "I'm not counting them.''

"You'd better,'' Thompson said. He held Hunter's gaze with his own. "I'll round up a strike force and have them ready to come through when we get your signal. I think you can count on a couple of platoons to deal with Captain Hendricks, if you need them.''

Hunter nodded. "And meanwhile we can be pulling a fast recon and learn what he's been up to.''

And we'll also be safely out of the reach of a Transformation Wave . . . just in case the bastard's already managed to change history somehow. If he did something on . . . what would it be? The twenty-fifth? If Hendricks changed history on Christmas Day in 1918, the Wave could hit us here at any moment!

Thompson studied each of the Rangers in turn. He seemed to be reading Hunter's mind. "I don't have any orders I can give you, men. You'll have to play it as you see it. But I trust you . . . trust your judgment. If you think Hendricks needs stopping, it'll be up to you to stop him. Any way you can!"

"We'll get the son of a bitch, General." He was thinking about Rachel. How was she? If Hendricks had harmed her, or any of the technicians . . . "Count on it."

"I'm counting on *you*, Travis," Thompson said quietly. "God help us, we all are."

Together they made their way through the corridor toward the elevator that would take them to the portal chamber.

Fourteen

Hunter swung his pistol to cover the figure that materialized out of the driving snow, then relaxed as he recognized Dark Walker.

"No guards, Lieutenant," Walker said with a smile. "Apparently the White Death has no great affinity for snow."

"I'm with them," Gomez said. "San Diego was never like this."

The Rangers were crouched behind a snow-covered platform in the rail yard at Kulomzino. The captured VBU train was a bulky shape half visible through the blizzard. Behind them, the town was silent, brooding. By Hunter's best estimate it was New Year's Day, 1919. Five hours had passed since their arrival on a windswept plain north of Omsk.

Hunter shivered, and not just from the bitter cold of the Siberian morning. Since passing through the blue glow of the time portal, the Rangers had lost all contact with the Chronos Project. When they had set up their beacon and switched it on to call for General Thompson's promised reinforcements, it had not functioned at all. After an hour of waiting . . . nothing. No sign that Time Square had latched on to the beacon's transtemporal signal. They were cut off.

A breakdown, Hunter thought. *Please, God, let it be a breakdown.*

But it might not be a malfunction at all. If Hendricks had changed history somehow and the Transformation Wave had already reached 2007, Time Square could be gone now, edited out of existence in a new version of history that didn't include an American time-travel project.

They had to know for sure before they acted.

"Right," he said. "We need intel, and we need to get the beacon checked out. Let's get out of the weather."

They moved carefully toward the train, alert for any challenge. It was vital that the Rangers avoid contact with Hendricks and his men, even with the *B'yelee Smert,* until they were ready for a showdown. Contacting the technical train was enough of a risk without having some zealous sentry reporting that Hunter's team was back.

Or carrying out Hendricks's orders to kill them.

Reaching the rail coach, Hunter tried the door. It was locked. Impatiently he pounded against the glass with his gloved fist. The door opened a crack, and Sarah Grant's face peered from the lighted interior.

"Where's Rachel?"

"She's not here!" The slender, auburn-haired technician smiled. "God, she'll be glad to find out you're back from your mission. Did you find the VBU?"

VBU? Hunter frowned. Hendricks must have decided to keep the technical team in the dark. A story about sending the Rangers to look for VBU agents would be plausible; everyone knew that Hunter had been pushing for action since they had picked up that magnetic surge out in the Siberian wastes. Yes . . . Rachel and the others would accept the story, until it was too late.

"Let us in," Hunter told the girl. "Please. We've got to talk with you."

Sarah hesitated, then nodded, stepping back to allow the Rangers to file inside. Warmth and light replaced frigid darkness. "What's the matter, Lieutenant?" she asked. "Has something gone wrong?"

"Everything's gone wrong," Anderson said, stripping off his bulky parka. "Starting with that nut Hendricks."

"Where did Rachel go?" Hunter asked.

"Downtown. She went to see the captain, I think." She paused. "What's going on?"

"Trouble, Miss Grant," King said softly. "One helluva lot of trouble."

Rachel Stein left Hendricks's office in the Dvoretz Gasteeneetsa feeling frustrated and angry. *I wish he'd let me see Father* . . . .

For days now the captain had been interfering with the technical team's schedule of tests for the captured downlink equipment . . . ever since the day Travis had left Omsk, in fact. The threat of having the VBU discover the location of the equipment and track down the Backlash operation was a valid one, of course, and she'd been willing to go along with postponing any long-running experiments that might cause a magnetic surge. But why wouldn't he authorize a trip to 2007, so she could go over their findings with her father? Was Operation Backlash in that much danger?

If only she could talk to Travis . . .

It hurt that he had left Omsk without even saying good-bye. She thought of King's visit on the morning after the failed coup attempt. Travis must have been upset that she hadn't wanted to get involved in his quarrel with Hendricks. Was *that* why he'd not come to see her?

She closed her eyes and leaned back against the wall of the hotel corridor. Travis had always held such grave doubts about Operation Backlash . . . and about how the brass was keeping him and his men in the dark. Rachel was beginning to know exactly how he felt; Hendricks was telling the Chronos technical staff nothing about his operations, his plans, or even when and how Backlash was supposed to alter history. He refused to tell her when Travis was coming back from his extended patrol—or even where he'd gone, exactly. And now he was refusing to let her talk to Time Square.

Rachel hated being kept in the dark. It left her feeling so helpless.

"Hi, Rachel!"

She opened her eyes. Brian Fitzpatrick was there, holding out her parka. "Heading back for the downlink?"

"Hello, Brian. Not quite yet. I have to pick up some equipment at Number 12."

A plan, half formed and ragged, was wavering at the edge of her consciousness. Hendricks had a recall beacon, but he kept it in his office, closely guarded. That left the one stored at Number 12. Suppose she went ahead and triggered it . . . signaled for a portal from 2007 and went through? What could they do to her . . . lock her up for desertion? She was a civilian, for all that she worked for a military project, and they could scarcely discipline her for going back to see her father one last time. There was a guard at the warehouse, she knew, but she should be able to talk her way past him.

At least she could go check out the possibility. Hendricks's high-handed tactics during the past week or two had her on edge. What if there was something to Travis's suspicions? Maybe she could get some answers from General Thompson.

"What's the problem, Rachel?" Fitzpatrick asked. He held her parka for her as she slipped it on. "Getting static from the general?"

" 'General.' " She mouthed the word unpleasantly. "Yeah. How are we supposed to finish our research if no one will tell us what's going on . . . and they won't even let us talk to 2007? Damn right I'm getting static. Static of the brain, trying to get *anything* done!"

"Well, hey. I could put in a word with the general. He has me in for conferences all the time . . . to brief him on the technical stuff, y'know. What did you want?"

"A chance to get back to Time Square. We've taken things as far as we can here . . . especially now that we can tune the Russian gear to work with our beacons. What I need now is access to the mainframe computers at Time Square."

"Uh." He looked thoughtful. "That could be tough. I know the general doesn't want to violate security right now."

"What security? It's not like the VBU doesn't already know we're here! It's not like we have to keep the portal shut down for fear of giving ourselves away!"

Fitzpatrick slipped one arm around Rachel's waist, standing so close that his side pressed against her. "I'll talk to him and see what I can do, Rachel. Uh . . . meanwhile, maybe you and me could go over some of my notes together. Maybe later tonight?"

She twisted away from Fitzpatrick. "Brian, please!"

"Huh? What . . . ?"

Rachel knew that Fitzpatrick was attracted to her. He'd suggested working late on more than one occasion and tried to crowd her personal space closer than she liked when they were alone. He was nice enough, but his familiarity only made her more sharply aware of how much she missed Travis.

"No, Brian. Just . . . no. Leave me alone." She turned and walked toward the hotel lobby, leaving him standing in the hallway behind her.

"So history has been changed somehow," Hunter said. The words hung, heavy and irrefutable, in the silence of the railway coach.

Sarah looked up from the recall beacon. "Everything checks out perfect in the diagnostics, Lieutenant. If you can't reach Time Square . . ."

"It's because there is no Time Square."

"Good God, LT!" Anderson's face was chalk white. "The Transformation Wave must've hit 2007 right after we left! We just missed getting caught."

"Yeah. It also means that Hendricks changed things somehow . . . what, Sarah, about a week ago?"

The technician nodded. "The exact time lag, past to present, varies with the nature of the change . . . but a week would be about right."

"Yeah. When we were in 1923, it took six days for things to reconfigure all the way uptime. So . . . whatever Hendricks did, it would be . . . when? December twenty-fourth? The twenty-fifth?"

"Have you heard *anything*, Miss Grant?" King asked. "Something important, happening a week ago?"

"Not much. They've been keeping us in the dark, really." She hesitated, a frown creasing her forehead. "There was a lot of excitement over a big victory on Christmas Day. A battle at some city west of here . . . Perm, I think it was. I'm afraid I didn't pay much attention at the time."

"How about it, Chief?" Gomez asked. "Was Perm supposed to be a defeat? Was that the change?"

Hunter shook his head. "No, Perm was one of Kolchak's biggest victories. That's not it, though the timing's right." He looked at Sarah. "You're sure it was a victory you heard about, and not a defeat?"

"Oh, yes! I'm sure of that. I heard some of the sentries talking about it. The White Army commander was killed, you see . . . and I remember thinking it was a shame he'd died even though he'd won such an important victory."

"What?" Hunter sat bolt upright. "What commander? Who was killed?"

"I don't remember the name. Wait. Geeda? No, Gaida."

"Gaida? Rudolph Gaida?"

"That sounds right."

"What is it, Lieutenant?" King asked. "Gaida?"

"Got to be. Remember? He was a Czech . . . and one of Kolchak's best generals. And the way I heard it, he survived until World War II. He certainly did *not* die in 1918!" He was remembering an earlier conversation with Hendricks. "That son of a bitch probably had some of his men shoot Gaida during the battle! *That's* the change! It has to be!"

"Hey, LT, did you see Simms around at all before we headed uptime?" Anderson asked.

Hunter tried to remember. "He wasn't at that party . . . and I didn't see him for a couple of days before. But I wasn't really looking for him."

"Simms . . ." King looked thoughtful. "I didn't see him at all after that train left with Dubcek and the other Czechs. Do you think . . . ?"

"I'll bet it was," Hunter replied. "He probably took some other Bravo people with him. They killed Gaida, and that changed everything."

"Yeah, but what changed?" Gomez looked puzzled. "I mean, what did Gaida do—or not do—to wipe out Time Square?"

"I don't know," Hunter said. "Hendricks told me once that Gaida was slated to cause problems for Kolchak. Maybe . . ." Hunter felt an uneasy crawling sensation in his stomach. "Maybe Gaida's death ended with a victory for the Whites— a *big* victory for the Whites. If the Bolsheviks were destroyed . . ."

"Y'know," Anderson said with a trace of wonder in his voice, "old Hendricks just might have pulled off what we were aiming for. The end of Communism!"

"Is it possible, Chief?" Gomez asked. "We've *won* . . . just like that?"

"It could be." Hunter's eyes narrowed as he thought. If the Communist movement was defeated and rooted out by the Whites, there would be no Communist menace after World War II, no Cold War, no World War III or global humiliation of the United States, no occupation by a Soviet-directed United Nations.

There would be no secret Chronos Project in the mountains of Wyoming, and no response when they triggered their recall beacon, *here*, in 1918.

Dark Walker shook his head. "All we know with certainty, Friend Eddie, is that the change has cut us off from 2007. Probably by eliminating the Chronos facility. What we do not know is what kind of world has replaced the one you knew."

Hunter noticed Walker's use of the word *you*. The Amerind had already lost his universe, a world where the British Empire had beaten the rebellious American colonies in the 1770s. In that reality with its strangely twisted past, the Soviets had still dominated the world. Walker was reminding them that there were many possible realities, many possible outcomes to tamperings with the past.

"You know, people," Hunter said reluctantly, "the Soviets don't hold a monopoly on evil."

King tugged at an earlobe. "You mean we might have got rid of the Reds and brought in something worse?"

"I don't know," Hunter said. "Maybe."

"Maybe everything worked out the way it was supposed to," Anderson said. "I mean, Hendricks might have got it right despite everything, and won the whole damned war for us!" He grinned, but it was halfhearted, and his voice carried an edge of worry to it. "General Thompson and the rest of them up in 2007 might be living in a real golden age now, compliments of Swede Hendricks and the White Death Commandos!"

"We've got to know." Hunter wanted to believe the scenario but could not. There were so many uncertainties. "We've got to know! Has our intervention brought on a golden age . . . ?"

King finished the thought. "Yeah. Or a new kind of hell."

"Mankind has a marvelous facility for creating new and wonderful hells for himself," Walker observed.

"What can we do about it?" Gomez asked.

"We can check it out." Hunter looked at Sarah. "Will you help us?"

"What, me? How?"

"Can you run the VBU downlink? Send us uptime?"

Her eyes grew large. "You're going to the new future. The new 2007."

"Not quite." He was thinking of the Exclusion Principle. If there was a Travis Hunter in the new universe, he could never travel all the way uptime. Time travel might allow them to double up on themselves in the past but not in the present, defined by the time machine at the Chronos facility. "I figure we could shoot for some time short of 2007 and avoid the Exclusion Principle that way. We could visit 1980 . . . 1990, maybe. That'll give us an idea of how things have been changed."

King rubbed his jaw. "We've blundered into some alternate worlds accidentally, Lieutenant. Now you're figuring on trying to find one on purpose."

"We've got to, Greg! It's the only way to know whether we've got to fight Hendricks . . . or help him!"

"You know," Anderson said. "There's a line in the Bible 'bout tellin' the good guys from the bad. 'By their fruits ye shall know them.' Seems like that's what we're fixin' to do."

"It's a long way to go to sample a fruit tree, Roy," Hunter said. "It'll be dangerous. Volunteers only."

"Shoot. Always did like climbin' the neighbor's fence to get peaches from his orchard, back when I was a kid!"

"Greg?"

"Oh, I'm with you, Lieutenant," King told him. "You know that. No matter how scatterbrained the plan is . . ." Gomez and Walker nodded their assent.

Hunter grinned and turned to Sarah. "We'll need someone to operate the downlink, help us set coordinates."

"Of course, Lieutenant." She nodded toward the recall device. "I can set the pickup frequency on the beacon so I can track you through the Soviet equipment. It'll be a lot more accurate dropping you in that way, and we'll be sure we can get you back."

"Good." Hunter felt a small, inner pang. *I'd rather have Rachel running the controls on something like this. But she's been supporting Hendricks all along. We can't risk trying to bring her in on this . . . and we damn well can't take the time*.

His eyes locked with King's. The master sergeant seemed to read his mind. "Best this way, Lieutenant," King murmured.

Hunter nodded. Would any of them be able to trust Rachel again? The thought burned, and he thrust it aside. "Can you cover yourself if Hendricks's people come by while we're gone?" he asked the girl.

"That's easy enough. I'll tell them I'm running calibration tests, and they won't know the difference. As long as they don't know you're back . . ."

"Right. And I want to keep it that way." Now that the decision was made, it was easier. "I want to leave as quickly as possible. With the downlink locked on to our recall beacon, an hour uptime will be an hour here, right?"

Sarah nodded.

"Good. We'll plan to stay . . . two hours should do it. Is that okay with you, Sarah? Can you hold the fort that long?"

"No problem." She grinned. "If any of them are hanging around the downlink when you signal, I may have to delay things a few minutes before I reel you in."

"Just so you *do* reel us in," Hunter said. "We have to find out what this new future is like, and I'm afraid that when we get there, we're not going to want to stay!"

Brian Fitzpatrick leaned into the cold wind as he made his way back toward the armored train. He was not particularly upset by Rachel's sharp rebuff at the hotel. She was probably feeling lost and lonely now, thinking that Hunter had deserted her. It wouldn't be long before she would come around.

Fitzpatrick alone, of all the Chronos technicians, knew that Hunter and the Rangers would not be coming back. Hendricks had shared the secret with him over a week before. The Bravo Team leader had wanted to know just how a change in the past would affect people trapped by it in the future . . . and finally had admitted that it had been necessary to send the Rangers back uptime in the hope of marooning them there.

By this time, the 2007 that Fitzpatrick knew was gone, but that suited him fine. General Hendricks had carved a powerful place for himself in the past and had told Fitzpatrick many times that he was relying on him for the success of his plans.

And now that Hunter was permanently out of the way, well
. . . who else did Rachel Stein have to turn to? Fitzpatrick
smiled in the darkness, despite the cold stinging his cheeks.

Ahead, light spilled from the rail coach as the door opened.
Fitzpatrick stopped, watching a procession of shadowy figures
alight from the car and make their way toward the boxcar that
housed the Soviet downlink. He recognized Sarah Grant, but
who—

Fitzpatrick stiffened, drawing back into the deeper shadows
that clung to the walls of the Kulomzino depot. Those five
men, the weapons they carried . . . it was not possible! One of
the figures looked up in the light of a street lamp, and Fitzpatrick
recognized the lean features of Sergeant Roy Anderson.

The Rangers were back!

The technician drew back further, watching as the six figures
entered the downlink boxcar. Swede would have to know about
this . . . and fast!

Fifteen

The town was gray and crumbling, and though people walked everywhere, it managed to convey an impression of lifelessness, as though the spirit of its inhabitants had long since been crushed and buried. Police—Hunter assumed they were police—haunted every corner in massive, visored helmets and dark blue uniforms, with submachine guns or shotguns cradled carelessly in their arms. The streets were cluttered with trash, the facades of the stone buildings worn and drab, eroded by decay and neglect.

Hunter looked past the buildings at the saw-toothed ruggedness of mountains rising abruptly from the blue waters of the lake to the west. People pressed past the two Rangers, most ignoring them, some looking at them with outright suspicion.

"See anything you recognize?" Hunter asked. He kept his voice low, his manner matter-of-fact. He felt conspicuous in his Army fatigues and naked without a weapon.

Beside him, Anderson shook his head warily. "I must've walked these streets a million times, LT. But this ain't the same town."

Despite familiar landscape and remembered street names, it was difficult to recognize Moran, Wyoming.

They had two hours to explore this new world, but Hunter felt as though the mission were already complete. In the darkness shrouding the depot in Omsk, they had waited until the guards were withdrawn from the VBU downlink, then entered the boxcar. It had taken only a few minutes for Sarah to power up the device and to lock its scan frequency to the recall beacon King carried in a rucksack on his back. "Two hours," Hunter had told Sarah. "We shouldn't need any longer than that to check it out. Then we'll send the signal and you can retrieve us."

Sarah had grinned and given him the thumbs-up before opening the gate.

Travel through the Russian machine into the future had been much the same as with American equipment—a swirl of blue, auroral light, the harsh tang of ozone in the air, and an abrupt transition from the musty interior of the boxcar to broad daylight, along the shores of Jackson Lake.

They'd chosen Jackson Hole, Wyoming, as a target because all of the Rangers were familiar with the area. The Chronos Project base was hidden under the slopes of Mt. Bannon, a few miles to the southwest, and in 2007, the region was the headquarters for Free America's Central Command Armed Forces.

They'd settled on 1990 as their target year . . . close enough to their own time to be recognizable, distant enough that the Exclusion Principle would not be a factor.

It felt like late spring, though they couldn't be certain of the month. There was snow on the mountain peaks around them, but flowers were in full bloom and the air was warm in the sunlight. They could see the outskirts of Moran from the glade where they emerged from the portal. Hunter and Anderson had left King, Walker, and Gomez with the recall beacon, their weapons, and their now unnecessary winter parkas, and hiked the two miles up the road to town.

Hunter looked across the street to see a pair of policemen eyeing the two Rangers and wondered if this hastily planned recon had been such a good idea. "I think we're attracting unwanted attention, Roy," he murmured.

"I see 'em, LT. Think it's the clothes?"

Hunter shook his head. "We didn't have much choice." Their Army fatigues were all they had for this expedition.

They'd decided back at Omsk that Army uniforms would not seem too out of place in a small, western town, so long as they didn't carry weapons openly. But this place had an atmosphere close and heavy with mistrust and fear, where anything out of the ordinary was instantly suspect.

Anderson nudged Hunter in the side. "Look down there. Looks like a newsstand . . . and we can get off the street. Let's check there."

The Moran Village Bookstall was part newsstand, part bookstore and tobacco shop, a small, dimly lit establishment with creaking wooden floors and narrow aisles. An overweight woman with silver hair and a grandmother's frown watched them coldly from behind the counter but said nothing as they browsed through the clutter. The air was pungent with the mingled odors of tobacco and alcohol.

"We might find a paperback atlas here," Hunter said, his voice low as he scanned the racks of books. The selection seemed rather sparse, the titles of most meaningless to them.

"Better yet," Roy said. His hand closed on a thick book and plucked it from the rack. Hunter read the title: *The 1980 World Almanac and Gazetteer*. Inside the front cover, a prominent imprint declared that the book had been approved for publication by the National Information Council and cleared by the Official Censor's Bureau in Washington, D.C. Hunter's growing unease focused on the warnings, and he felt a chill along his spine.

Quickly he thumbed through the book. A crudely printed world atlas was at once familiar and alien. The vast sprawl of the Soviet Union was still there, and Hunter felt a moment's desperation. *We failed. Russia is still intact.*

But there were changes, ominous ones.

The National Socialist People's Republic of Greater Germany sprawled from Poland to the Atlantic. The Empire of Japan embraced the eastern Pacific, from China to the north Australian coast. Iran and India and the cluster of Arab states from Arabia to Pakistan belonged to the National Socialist Federation of Russia.

Hunter blinked and read it again. The N.S.F.R.?

"Good Lord, Roy! America lost World War II! Or else it was never fought."

He checked the almanac's table of contents, then leafed

through the history section. A superficial reading suggested that a lot of the history from *before* 1919 had been deliberately rewritten, not by time travel but by government censors. What was he to make, for instance, of the blunt statement that the American Civil War was fought to put down a slave rebellion in the South? Such obvious distortions called everything into question, but the broad outline of how history had changed after 1919 seemed clear enough.

There was no mention of the Communists . . . or of a Bolshevik government in Moscow. The Russian Revolution of 1917 ended with a socialist government under Aleksandr Kolchak, Savior of All the Russias. At some point within the next few years, the country's democratic socialism had shifted to national socialism . . . and a Fascist dictatorship. Hunter read on. World War II had capped Hitler's rise to power with success upon success; evidently Germany had never made the mistake of turning against Russia. Instead, Germany, Japan, and Russia had joined in subjugating the decadent and decaying body of the British Empire. The almanac gave the date for Hitler's invasion of Britain as September 19, 1940. The war was over by 1943, for the United States remained isolationist and neutral.

National Socialism had proven to be the wave of the future. There was no clear indication of how America had succumbed at last to the Nazi tide. Reading between the lines, Hunter guessed that the U.S. had never pulled free of the Depression, that unemployment and poverty had reached the point in the early 1950s where discontent boiled over among the voters and the Nazi Party's nominee was elected president.

The American Nazi Party, it seemed, had run the country ever since.

Dawning horror gripped Hunter as he continued to page through the book. Every nation on Earth was ruled by some version of the National Socialist Party—the Nazis—with the exception of the Empire of Japan. It was hard to believe. Had Hendricks's presence in 1919 Russia made such a difference?

This stems from the death of Rudolph Gaida, Hunter reminded himself. Gaida's resistance to Kolchak must have made the difference. How?

"You two going to buy something?" the woman at the counter asked. "This ain't the State Library."

"Uh . . . sorry." Regretfully Hunter replaced the book. He

would have given anything to be able to take it with him, to study it in detail later, but they had no money. The Rangers were always careful not to take coins or bills into the past; denominations with minting dates of 2007 could cause unfortunate incidents. "C'mon Greg."

"Just a minute, you two," the woman demanded. "You can't just come in here and read my stuff without buying nothing! You read that book, you pay for it."

"We were just leaving, ma'am," King said.

"No, you weren't. You were reading my stock and not paying for it! Maybe I should call the Enforcers in for a chat, huh?"

"That's not necessary."

"Don't tell me what's necessary, youngster! Who are you two, anyway? Don't know you . . . ain't seen you around, and you're dressed queer." Her voice was rising in pitch and volume. Hunter glanced toward the dirt-smeared window and saw the two policemen he'd noticed earlier crossing the street toward the shop.

Rachel was thoroughly scared when she turned the last corner on the road back toward the rail depot. She had never even gotten inside the Market Street warehouse; there were five Bravo Team soldiers standing guard on the street outside the door alone, and evidence of more troops within. As she approached, a corporal had demanded to see a pass from Hendricks. When she couldn't produce one, he'd told her that even the technical team was denied access to the stored equipment "unless the general says so."

Hendricks had converted the place into a fortress, and he was making certain that he maintained control over the recall beacon. Why?

She badly needed to sit down and sort things out. Hendricks's strong-willed, no-nonsense approach had attracted her at first, but she was feeling shaken now. *Suppose Travis was right?*

The armored train rested on its siding just ahead. She followed the beaten-down path through the snow toward the railcar, hurrying now to get out of the arctic cold.

She heard a shout, followed by a stream of unintelligible but angry-sounding words. She paused, following the sounds to their source, the downlink boxcar.

The heavy door slid back, spilling light from the boxcar's interior across the snow. Men leapt out, Bravo team soldiers and White Death Commandos both, clutching their weapons as they dropped to the snow. Rachel stopped in her tracks, crouching down on the path, hoping that she would not be seen in the darkness. Hendricks's men were everywhere around the railcar. What was going on?

Rachel stifled a small gasp as Sarah was hauled bodily from the boxcar. The girl kicked and struggled until one of the soldiers hit her, hard, a solid blow to her face. She slumped then, and the man hoisted her across his shoulder like a sack of grain and started off toward town. Two of the soldiers remained beside the boxcar, while the rest followed the man with Sarah. She heard their laughter, harsh against the cold night.

"Stop! You two, stop!"

Hunter glanced back over his shoulder at the two Enforcers. They wore military-looking uniforms with blue-and-white arm bands: a swastika superimposed on a five-pointed star. "Run for it, Roy!"

Conversation would be pointless. They had no papers, no IDs that would mean anything in this universe.

A piercing whistle sounded behind them. They rounded a corner, their boots pounding on the cement sidewalk, and ran headlong into a third policeman.

The collision sent both Hunter and the third Enforcer sprawling on the ground. Anderson hesitated, but Hunter waved him on. "Keep going!" The policeman dragged his pistol from his holster, but Hunter knocked the weapon aside before he could aim it at the fleeing Anderson. They grappled, Hunter struggling to get back on his feet.

Then the two pursuing Enforcers were there, pulling Hunter off their comrade. Something struck Hunter behind his left ear, sending him sprawling to the pavement.

Rachel hid in a broom closet until the laughing voices and the click of boot heels on wooden floors receded into the distance. She had followed the soldiers back from the train, determined to learn where they were taking Sarah Grant . . . and why. She'd halfway expected them to carry the unconscious girl back to Omsk and Captain Hendricks's HQ, but the journey was much shorter than that—an abandoned and decrepit shipping office close by the Kulomzino depot. They'd taken her inside; Rachel had been able to track their movements by their raucous voices and by the light that suddenly shone from the windows of what might have once been an office.

She knew Sarah was awake. The girl's scream had cut shrill and cold above the laughter as Rachel picked her way into the building. Rachel had no clear idea of what she could do, but she *wouldn't* abandon her friend.

The closet had offered a quickly accessed hiding place when she heard the clump of booted feet outside the door behind her. For the better part of half an hour, Rachel crouched in the darkness among ancient, mildewed mops and rusty buckets, tears streaming down her cheeks as she listened to them beat Sarah in the room next door. Only when the soldiers left did she emerge. ''Take good care of her, Lenny,'' one called over his shoulder.

She glanced up and down the deserted hallway, desperately wishing she hadn't left her Beretta automatic aboard the train, stowed with her other things in the coach. A floorboard creaked under her foot and she froze. What if the guard heard?

There was no sound but the muffled sounds of a girl's sobbing. Rachel moved silently to the door, testing the knob.

It was open.

The guard was there, a big, husky man, but he had little interest in keeping watch. His back was to the open door and his M-16 was leaning against a chair. His trousers were gathered around his ankles as he leaned over the brass four-poster bed, his full attention on the girl spread-eagled on the mattress.

A white fury consumed Rachel, driving her forward. She took three swift steps, scooping up the rifle by its barrel. The guard turned at the sound—or tried to. His pants tangled his legs and he fell, sitting down hard on the edge of the bed.

There was no time to turn the weapon around to fire, no thought that the noise might summon help. Rachel swung the rifle in a whistling arc, catching the soldier squarely on his left temple. The expression of stark surprise on his pug face was transformed to a blank and empty look as the rifle butt crunched bone. His eyes rolled up in their sockets and he collapsed to the floor, an ungainly sprawl of bare flesh and disarrayed clothing.

Rachel was at Sarah's side. Her wrists and ankles were handcuffed. *Handcuffed!* Tears of frustration and rage coursed down Rachel's cheeks. She turned away and began pawing through the guard's pockets.

"They're not there, Rachel," Sarah said, her voice breaking. "One of the others . . . has the keys—"

"Sarah!" Rachel had thought the girl unconscious. "What did they do to you?"

Sarah rolled her head back and forth on the bare mattress. Her face and breasts and stomach were bruised, livid black and blue marks showing where they'd hit her. There was blood on her mouth.

"Never mind me, Rachel. They . . . know I helped . . . Lieutenant Hunter."

"Travis! Here?"

"He's here. Just got here." In short, gasping breaths, Sarah told Rachel about the Rangers' arrival and of their hurried scouting trip to the future. "They must be trying to get back by now."

"I've got to get you out of here!"

"No. Don't have . . . keys. Leave me."

Rachel looked at the body on the floor. "I think I killed him. If they find him . . ."

The girl attempted a smile. "They can't think I did it. I'll tell them Whites did it. You . . . you've got to help Travis."

Rachel raced out of the building and into the cold night, hating herself as she fled. There was nothing she could do for Sarah now, and yet . . .

The memory of what Hendricks's soldiers had done to Sarah Grant burned in Rachel's mind, seething, storming. She had to retrieve Travis . . . had to. Once he was back, perhaps then they could rescue Sarah, do *something*.

It wasn't until she drew near to the armored train that she remembered the guards in front of the downlink boxcar.

"Who are you? Talk!" The prod reached out from behind the glare yet again and stroked along his jaw. There was a crackle of current, and pain exploded anew in a burning strip from his nose to his ear. His back arched against his bonds, a wrenching of mind and muscles that dragged a trembling scream from a throat already gone raw. He tasted the salty tang of blood, felt its warm stickiness on his face.

He had no idea how long he had been here . . . had no idea of where "here" was. He'd decided that the second policeman, the one he'd been able to bluff, had clipped him behind the ear with his weapon while Hunter was dealing with his partner. Consciousness had returned slowly, through a red-shot haze of pain. He was naked and strapped to a straight-backed chair that was bolted to the floor, the only light the arc-bright glare of a lamp directed squarely into his eyes. He could sense his interrogators in the darkness behind the light and elsewhere in the room, but he couldn't see them. They numbered, he decided, more than two. He could distinguish at least three different voices as they bombarded him with questions, accompanying each with jolts of current administered from heavily taped and padded electric prods.

"What is your name?"

"Where are you from?"

"What is your block?"

"Who is with you?"

"Why are you here?"

Hunter shook his head, trying to clear it. He was aware of questions and more questions . . . and of unrelenting pain. How long had it been? He'd told him his name any number of times. *For all the good it'll do them.*

The prod touched the bare skin of his thigh. *Pain!* Hunter screamed again. His body arched sharply, held to the chair only by wrists and ankles. When he slumped back into its embrace, he was only hazily aware of a voice.

"We can keep this up for a long, long time, Travis. You know that, don't you?" A prod hovered before his eyes, then descended, lightly touching his chest, but without current, without pain. Slowly the prod scraped down across his belly. "We could also play . . . even more interesting games. We've barely started to work on you, Travis. How long do you think you can hold out? Why don't you tell us what we want to know and save yourself a lot of . . . unpleasantness?"

"Wouldn't . . . believe me . . . if I told you." It was agony to get the words out. Blood dribbled from his mouth. *Must've bitten my tongue . . .*

"Oh, I don't know about that. Why don't you try us?"

"Okay, I'm . . . time traveler . . ."

He heard chuckles in the darkness. "A time traveler? That's a new one! Here from the future, are you?"

Raw pain geysered between his legs, leaving him gasping and sobbing. "Perhaps we've been too gentle with you, Travis. Perhaps you need to know we mean business."

Sixteen

Hunter heard the explosion but could not immediately react to it. The pain, the shock, had dulled his thoughts, leaving him fuzzy-headed, unthinking when the far-off rumble made the lamp sway and flicker. A moment later the lamp winked out. At first Hunter thought he'd gone blind, but the sudden consternation among his questioners made it clear that the power had failed.

"Hey! What happened to the lights?"

"Never mind that! What was that blast?"

"Dunno. Sounded like—"

The voice was never able to describe what it sounded like, for at that moment a door burst open and gunfire spat clattering death. Hunter's eyes, accustomed to the brilliance of the lamp, could see very little, but he was aware of light spilling through the door, of shadowy figures moving against it. Gunfire cracked again, and something heavy brushed Hunter's shoulder as it collapsed next to him with a grunt of pain.

The silence that followed was as startling as the sudden noise.

"*Madre de Dios!* Chief, are you okay?"

"Eh? What?" That was Gomez! He felt hands tugging at the straps on his wrists.

151

"Hey, Greg!" He heard Anderson's voice from the doorway. "He's in here!"

The details of his rescue were a bit blurry, but he was able to sort it out in the next few minutes. His delaying tactics with the police had worked, and Anderson had been able to get back to the others . . . but not before he was able to see where they were taking Hunter. Moran was not a large town, and the squat, gray-walled police station was easily located. The Texan had led the others back into town, using an appropriated car as a means for getting there without attracting attention. A 40mm grenade from Gomez's M-203 had obliterated the front door of the building, along with much of the surrounding wall, and the Rangers had rushed in and overpowered the handful of policemen there while the plaster was still spilling from the blast-cracked ceilings.

"LT?" Anderson peered into Hunter's face. "You okay? What'd they do to you?"

"I'm—okay." His voice cracked. His throat was dry, his hands shaking so hard, he could not control them. He felt wildly, sickeningly dizzy as he tried to stand. "Just give me a moment."

Daylight dimly lit the interrogation room, filtering through dust and drifting smoke as it filled the open door. Dark Walker handed Hunter his clothes, retrieved from an outer office. "Can he travel?" he asked Anderson. "Others will be here soon."

King appeared against the light, the recall beacon in his hand. "I think we'll be best off if we just sit tight," he said. "I don't think they'll be too eager to come in after us."

Hunter watched as King set the beacon on the floor and switched it on. With the new settings, Sarah should be able to read the signal back in 1919. Escape—and safety—was only twenty minutes away.

If all was going well at the Soviet downlink in 1919.

"But why not?" Rachel did her best to sound bewildered. It was not difficult to do. She was bewildered by this sudden shift in the situation. Or rather, she corrected herself savagely, by the change in her *perception* of the situation. Hendricks had been a rat all along. She knew that now. Poor Sarah . . .

"Sorry, miss." The guard shook his head. "General's orders. No one goes inside."

She turned away from the railcar. According to Sarah, the Rangers were way overdue for retrieval. They might be waiting around their beacon now—if "now" had any meaning across over sixty years—waiting for pickup. And if they were in trouble . . .

She *had* to get inside! But how?

"More company," Walker said, peering across the ruins.

Hunter looked up, trying to focus on the Amerind. "What?"

Gomez, Walker, and Hunter were crouched in the wreckage of what had been the front office of the Moran police station while King and Anderson watched the back. The beacon rested on the floor nearby, maddeningly quiescent now, with no hint at all if their signal had been received. It had been nearly forty minutes.

Hunter looked up. "What?" His voice was still raw.

"Tanks . . . APCs. Looks like they called in the Army."

"Hey, Chief," Gomez said, concern in his voice. "You okay?"

"I'm fine, Eddie." Hunter held out one hand, studying it. The trembling had nearly ceased. "Just a little woozy, is all."

"You had us pretty worried there for a while."

"It had me worried too." He managed to grin. "I'm just glad you found me."

Or would it have been better if they hadn't? If they hadn't come back for me, they could have waited it out up in the hills someplace, instead of getting trapped here.

Hunter suppressed a shudder. If they *hadn't* come back . . .

The torture did not seem to have left any permanent damage, though there were some painful burns on his thigh and stomach, fiery now when he moved and his clothing scraped them.

There was no time for might-have-beens now. His men had returned, and now they were surrounded by heavily armed Enforcers and elements of the United States Army. The grim swastika-on-star that had replaced the familiar American flag fluttered above a barricade fifty yards away.

"You in there!" An amplified voice boomed across the street. *"You are completely surrounded! Release your hostages! Throw down your weapons and come out with your hands behind your heads! If you do exactly as we say, you will not be harmed!"*

"No way!" Gomez yelled back. "Take one step toward us and the hostages die!"

"You cannot escape. Surrender now and we will guarantee your safety. You have our promise!"

"Somehow I don't quite trust them," Walker said.

"Yeah." Gomez jerked a thumb toward a uniformed body lying nearby. "Especially when the 'hostages' are already dead."

The ruse—drawing the names of several dead Enforcers from their ID cards and claiming that they were holding them hostage—had bought them time, but the trick would not work for long.

"These guys don't impress me as the type who are all that concerned about their buddies," Hunter observed. "They want *us*."

"It was worth a try," Walker said. "Miss Grant may still open the portal."

"Let's hope so." Hunter flexed his fingers around the grip of his Uzi, enjoying the heft of the weapon. *Whatever happens,* he thought, *they're not going to get a chance to question me again.*

"But what's it all about, Brian?" Rachel snuggled closer to Fitzpatrick as they walked, taking his arm in both of hers. "Why are there guards on the downlink car?"

"Oh, the general's probably just worried about Red saboteurs. That shouldn't affect *you*." He patted her arm affectionately.

"I wanted to run some checks on the alpha carrier transpositions," she said. "But they looked like they weren't letting anyone in. Will you come with me, Brian? Please?"

"Why, of course I will, honey! You just leave everything to me!"

Rachel grimaced inwardly. She didn't like playacting for Brian, didn't like the slimy feel of manipulating him with unspoken promises of sex. She could see the glitter in the technician's eye, could almost hear the gears click into place in his mind as he anticipated an evening of "working late," alone with Rachel, in the downlink car.

But Rachel could think of no other way of getting past those guards short of shooting them. She didn't know if they would have let her in or not, but she was very sure that her presence would be reported to Hendricks. It would *have* to be, now that Sarah had been caught using the downlink to help Travis. Better, Rachel thought, that Brian be the one to insist on going inside. Perhaps if he was as solidly in with Hendricks as he liked to claim, their presence wouldn't even be reported. If it was, perhaps Hendricks trusted Fitzpatrick not to help the Rangers. The Chronos technician's feelings for Rachel—and his dislike of Hunter—were obvious enough to anyone who knew him.

The guards stopped them outside the railcar. "Sorry, Brian," one of them said. "General's orders. No one goes inside."

Fitzpatrick drew himself up to his full five-foot-eight height. "Aw, come off it, George! Those orders certainly didn't apply to me, did they? Was I named in them?"

"Well, no, but . . ."

"I'm General Hendricks's chief technical adviser, for God's sake! How am I supposed to finish my research for him if I can't get into the damned car?"

"Uh . . . I'll have to check, Brian."

"Do that! And hurry up, will ya? It's freezing out here!"

"Huh. Don't I know it."

The guard turned away, pulling a small radio out of his parka and speaking into it for a moment. Rachel remained silent and tried to look inconspicuous. If she had tried this on her own, once they found the dead soldier in the freight office they would immediately suspect her. But there should be nothing to make them question Brian's presence here.

She hoped.

The guard put the radio away, then signaled to the other sentry to slide open the door. "They say it's okay, Brian," he said. "Just don't turn the damned thing on, okay?"

"We weren't planning on it."

Rachel caught Fitzpatrick's broad, suggestive wink at the guard out of the corner of her eye and saw the soldier's reply, a leering grin. She felt unclean somehow during this, but at least they were not likely to be disturbed.

The interior of the boxcar was crammed with electronic gear, with massive power conduits and busbars focused on a tiny stage. A control panel at one end of the narrow car carried the switches, verniers, and console screens necessary for operating the portal . . . a much cruder affair than the Chronos time machine, but sufficient for the task. A switch inside the door turned on the overhead lights, naked bulbs screwed into porcelain sockets.

"Well, here we are." Fitzpatrick grinned as the heavy, corrugated steel door slid shut on rumbling tracks and boomed hollowly as it closed.

"Why don't you go boot up the computer?" She tried to keep her voice low and sexy, suppressing the quaver she felt in her throat.

Fitzpatrick looked blank. "Why . . . ah . . . I thought . . ." He turned away.

The fire extinguisher was a small, red-painted cylinder clipped to a bracket on the wall. Rachel pulled it down, raised it high above her head in both hands, and brought it down on Fitzpatrick's head as hard as she could. The technician crumpled without so much as a groan, collapsing at her feet.

She dropped the fire extinguisher beside him and hurried to the computer console. She switched it on, waited for the program to load, then entered Sarah's access code. Time-space coordinates spilled across the screen. Good. Sarah had managed to save the data for her lock on the Rangers before Hendricks's men had found her.

Improvised caps bearing English equivalents to the Cyrillic letters were printed on the console keys. Rachel's fingers felt like lead as they moved over the keyboard, entering commands to activate the portal. Cursing, she cleared an error and forced herself to concentrate. She looked over her shoulder once as she gated power from the reactor to the downlink. The power-up operation was largely automatic, but it took time . . . *time . . . !*

How much time did she have?

"No more games," the megaphone voice boomed. *"Surrender now or we come in after you!"*

"They mean it," King said. He stayed low, lest a sniper glimpse him long enough to chance a shot. "They've got fifty . . . maybe sixty men set to rush us back there."

"They've been revving their tank engines out front," Hunter said. "Probably to make noise and cover their moves."

He looked at his wristwatch for the thousandth time. It was now nearly an hour and a half since they'd switched on the beacon . . . and a good four hours since their agreed-upon two-hour stay in this alternate reality should have been up. There was no avoiding it any longer. Something had gone wrong back in 1919, and they were trapped here.

Damn! He felt weary . . . and crushed. *This is one hell of a universe we're sticking the world with.*

Then blue light shimmered into dancing glory above the beacon. Gunfire crashed from the rear of the building in the same moment. "Move!" King bellowed. "Move! Move!"

There was no time to think, no time to retrieve the beacon. The Rangers plunged forward into the blue light.

"Travis!"

Rachel's exclamation was a shriek of joy and relief. She fell into his arms as he stepped off the platform, clinging to him as the other Rangers came through. All of them were filthy, their parkas coated with plaster dust, and there was an ugly, beet-red welt on the side of Hunter's face.

"Where's Sarah?" King asked sharply. "What happened?"

In halting, urgent phrases, Rachel told them about Sarah's capture . . . and of how she had found the girl chained and beaten in the freight office.

Hunter slumped to the floor of the boxcar, his back against one wall. With the six of them—plus Fitzpatrick's inert form— it was crowded to the point of claustrophobia.

"What are we going to do, LT?" Anderson asked. He looked toward the boxcar door and licked his lips nervously. "Five of us can't take on all of Hendricks's men . . . and the White Death too!"

"What would be the point?" King said. "It's too late. The future's been changed . . . and we know what it looks like now."

Rachel raised her eyebrows. They told her what they'd seen of 1980, torture and the stifling atmosphere of a brutal police state, in a North American Fascist dictatorship. "It's hard to believe such a large change came from one man's life."

"I gather one man's life had quite a large effect on history in my case," Dark Walker said gently. "General Washington, remember?"

"Yeah, but you don't think of Rudolph Gaida the same way you do George Washington!"

"No, you don't. But we've all seen enough to know by now that *anybody's* life can have quite a large impact on things . . . given the chance." Hunter appeared lost in thought for a moment. "Greg's right, you know. Even if we clean out Hendricks and his whole gang, it won't change things, not now. But there's another option."

King looked puzzled. "I don't see any options here, Lieutenant. We'd have to figure out what it was that Gaida did after Perm, then do it ourselves. We don't know what he did, other than oppose Kolchak, and that's too vague."

"We have another option," Hunter said. He nodded toward the Soviet time machine. "At least we do as long as we control *that*."

Rachel's eyes widened as she guessed what Hunter was thinking. "You mean . . ."

"Exactly. We can travel back in time one week to Christmas Day, in Perm. We'll find Hendricks's people and stop them from killing Rudolph Gaida."

The plan, once unfolded, seemed simple enough. With Rachel to operate the downlink's controls, they could go back and change history *again,* undoing what Simms and his men had done by killing the Czech general. Gaida would survive . . . and go on to do whatever he'd done in the original version of history. The Reds would triumph and Communism would be established in Russia, but at least the United States would be spared the grim, gray dictatorship the Rangers had glimpsed in their recon to 1980. None of them enjoyed the prospect of losing the opportunity to end the Communist threat to the free world once and for all, but it was the only way to undo the damage already done . . . the only way any of them could see to set things right.

There was only one problem with the plan, and Rachel, with her understanding of how time and time travel worked, was the one who pointed it out.

"I'll stay behind," she said. "I *have* to, to run the equipment. And I won't be able to bring you back after you do what you have to do in Perm, because then you'd be caught *here* when the Transformation Wave hits. Anyway, you lost your beacon . . . there's nothing we can lock on to, and we can't afford to try for either of the ones Hendricks has.''

Hunter's expression transformed itself to one of horror. ''Wait a minute! You're saying that you're going to vanish when things change again?''

''That's exactly what I'm saying.''

''No!''

''Yes. Listen to me.'' Patiently, she explained it to them.

Hendricks and his men had interfered with history by killing Gaida in Perm on Christmas Day. As a result of that assassination, history had been rewritten, ending, ultimately, in the triumph of Nazism throughout the world. Now they were proposing to go back and rewrite history again, blocking Gaida's murder and creating, in essence, a new universe—one in which the news that arrived in Omsk after the victory at Perm reported that Gaida was alive, not dead. Hendricks's actions upon hearing that news would be different than they had when his plan had succeeded. Simms and the other assassins would not return. That whole week and all of its events would vanish—replaced, they hoped, by something closer to the original time line that Hendricks had tampered with in the first place.

''It's like we talked about before we came here, Travis,'' she said. ''Remember? I . . . the Rachel Stein who lived through this past week—who tried to rescue Sarah and couldn't—will cease to exist when this universe does. I'll reconfigure along with everything else. You won't change because you'll be coming from outside. But I will. Do you see?''

Hunter seemed to be struggling with her reasoning. ''But you'll still exist in the new time line, the one where Gaida survives . . .''

''Yes. It'll be the same me . . . right up to Christmas Day when the change is made. After that, for the next week, it'll be a different me, with different memories. I'll be here . . . waiting for you to return from that 'secret mission' they told me you were on.''

''Wait a minute,'' Gomez said. ''What about the rest of us? If there's another Rachel back there . . . are we going to be running into ourselves?''

''No,'' Hunter said. He kept his eyes locked on hers. ''No,

we were out of the way, confined up in 2007, remember? The change won't affect us. But Raye . . ."

"It's okay, Travis," she said softly. Her eyes closed as she remembered Sarah's bruised and swollen face. It was strange to be facing something so like suicide, to know that before long she would cease to be.

Or was it simply that she was being given a chance to relive the past week? She preferred to think of it that way.

"It's okay," she repeated. "By rewriting last week, you'll save Sarah from what happened to her. You'll save me from *them*. You *will* come and save us, won't you?"

Hunter grinned ruefully. "If I can convince you that you need rescuing. You might not believe my story when I show up!"

She smiled up at him. "Explain it to me . . . when you see me again. I'll believe you. I won't remember this conversation, but I'll believe you."

Gomez shook his head. "Somebody better explain it to *me*! Rachel is telling us to rescue her sometime last week, and I don't think I believe that at all!"

"What about you, Raye?" Hunter asked. "I mean . . . *you*. The Rachel who has to open that door behind us sometime after the rest of us walk through the machine?"

She shrugged. "Don't worry about it. With the change only a week behind us, it shouldn't be more than an hour or two before the Transformation Wave arrives. I can hold out that long."

"But—"

She placed her fingers on Hunter's mouth. "No buts. This is the best way, believe me! You didn't see what they did to Sarah. This way she has a chance . . . and so do I! So do all of us!"

Hunter shook his head. "I still don't think I understand."

"Then don't try. It's not important that you do! What *is* important is that you change this past week, and restore the United States we knew!"

"Is this . . . good-bye, then?"

She smiled. "Until I see you last week sometime, when you're back from Perm!"

They embraced, squeezing close in a lingering, passionate kiss.

Then the computer signaled full power and a positive lock. Power spat and crackled above the stage, where auroral patterns glowed.

Someone hammered on the boxcar door.

"Quickly!" Rachel said. "Go through!"

"But—"

"The accuracy on a blind transfer like this won't be good," she continued. "But I'm aiming for a bit before Christmas, to give you time to get oriented. Go, quickly!"

Hunter waved his men through. King, Anderson, Gomez, and Walker stepped through the light and vanished.

Rachel gave Hunter a last kiss. "Please go, Travis. I'll . . . I'll be waiting for you. A week younger . . . maybe a bit sillier . . . but I'll be waiting for you. I love you."

"I love you, Raye."

The pounding sounded again. The boxcar door sliding open as someone forced it with a pry bar.

"Quickly!"

Hunter pulled his .45 from his holster and left it on the console beside her. Then he squeezed her hand and stepped onto the stage.

Rachel watched him vanish, then turned as the door boomed open and Hendricks's men climbed through.

Seventeen

King held the radio to his mouth. "Yankee Leader, this is Yankee One. I've completed the sweep in to the center of town. Still nothing."

"*Okay, One.*" Hunter's voice sounded tired and flat. "*Keep looking.*"

"Understood. Yankee One out."

He pocketed the radio, unslung his FN-FAL, and looked at the buildings around him. Perm was a large city, graceful with the Victorian-period flourishes to its architecture, and the sweeping, onion-capped towers of its Russian Orthodox churches. Many buildings showed damage from shell fire, but the beauty of the city remained intact beneath the hovering black pillars of battle smoke and burning houses.

He had to admit that Rachel was right on the money with her setup on the Russian equipment. They'd emerged the evening before not far outside the city limits of Perm. For hours now the Rangers had been split up, searching the city and its surroundings separately. The plan was to find either Gaida and his staff, or Simms and his men, or both.

The equation was simple: Gaida might be prevented from entering the city . . . or Simms might be stopped from pulling the trigger. Either way, things should be set right. Simple or not, the plan's execution was the difficult part. Perm was a city under siege, torn by artillery and machine-gun fire. Gaida's Czechs had forced their way into the center of town, but pockets of resistance remained as stubborn Red defenders elected to fight it out to the last round . . . or the last man.

And Perm was *big*, far too big to be searched, building by building, by five men. The armies, too, numbered tens of thousands of men and were spread across front lines that stretched for miles across the Russian steppes. Knowing that Simms was here—even knowing that Gaida was here—and *finding* either of them were two entirely different propositions.

It was already getting late in the afternoon, and time was running out. He looked around at the buildings towering on every side, grimacing with frustration. There were so damn many places where a sniper could hide!

"Yankee Leader to all Yankees!" Hunter's radio voice cut in on his thoughts. *"I've found Gaida! He's approaching the plaza at the center of town, but he has so many staff officers with him, I can't get close. Start closing in on me. Simms must be close by!"*

King acknowledged and hurried forward. He was already in the area. The plaza was only a few blocks away. Simms, he knew, favored an M-21 with a telescopic sight. That weapon would give him a range of well over a kilometer, though the ideal range would be something closer to five or six hundred yards.

That helped. And if Simms wanted it to look as though the shot came from the Russian lines, he would be on that side of the plaza . . . somewhere in the direction of that Orthodox Church rearing above the street.

King froze. A glitter of light appeared in one of the slit windows, high up in the side of the church's tower. Had he imagined it? No! There it was again!

Sunlight reflecting from glass . . . from the objective lens of a pair of binoculars or a telescopic sight. He spoke into his radio as he ran. "Yankee Leader, this is One! There's someone in the tallest church tower north of the square! It could be Simms!"

"One, this is Leader! I'm still trying to get close to Gaida, but they're keeping everybody back! Check it out!"

"I'm moving. One out!"

The interior of the church was dimly lit and barren, the luxurious furnishings stripped by the Bolsheviks who had occupied the place hours before. The altar had been overturned, and the wooden pews smashed for firewood.

Two American soldiers stood outside the door to the bell-tower stairs. They reacted slowly, fumbling for their M-16s as King charged down on them. "You!" one exclaimed, and then his head snapped back, blood gushing from his shattered mouth. King triggered a second shot as the other soldier scrambled at the tower door. The bullet exploded at the base of his neck, killing him instantly.

Had they noticed the gunfire in the tower? Stray shots from the fading battle continued to crack and bark throughout the city and they might not have been warned. There was only one way to find out.

King took the stairs two at a time, moving silently but as swiftly as he could manage. The stairs wound around and around in a tight spiral, leading up through the drafty tower from level to level. Bell ropes dangled within the spiral's twists, hanging through the openings in a succession of wooden platforms, level above level above level. How much farther? He should be almost there.

"C'mon, Sarge," a restless voice complained from just overhead. "Nail the son of a bitch and let's clear out!"

"Patience, Slick," Simm's voice replied. "Patience. Just a little . . . ah!"

King sprinted up the last twist in the staircase, emerging through an opening in the wooden floor. One of Hendricks's men twisted, swinging his M-16 to bear on King.

The FAL bucked once and the soldier pitched backward. King thumbed his weapon to full auto and squeezed the trigger again. Autofire thunder rang from the stone walls. One of Simm's men triggered a long burst as he collapsed, the rounds going wild. King heard the great church bell high overhead toll twice as 5.56mm ricochets struck it.

The FAL's magazine went empty as King tracked the weapon across the chamber, trying to hit Simms as he bounded away from the narrow window and rolled across the wooden floor.

Simms was the last of the Bravo troops alive. He came up

to one knee, swinging his M-21 to his shoulder and drawing down on King's chest.

"You shoulda thrown in with us, buddy boy," Simms said. A grin spread across his face as he tightened his finger on the trigger. There was an explosion of sound, and King tensed against expected pain.

But there was no pain. A small, neat hole had appeared in the center of Simms's forehead, as the top and back of his skull vanished in a splatter of red gore that painted the wall of the bell tower behind him.

Dark Walker appeared at the top of the stairs. He must have seen Simms through the opening in the center of the floor where the bell ropes hung, and taken the sergeant out with a single shot from his Galil—a difficult shot.

"Thanks."

"Don't mention it." Walker grinned. "Teamwork."

King looked at the bodies sprawled across the dark wooden platform. American bodies. "Yeah. C'mon. Let's go find the lieutenant."

Hunter pressed his face against the glass of the rail-coach window, straining to see ahead past the locomotive. It was evening on the last day of 1918, one week after the battle in Perm and the death of the Bravo Team troopers sent to kill Gaida. *One entire week . . .*

He'd hated every minute of the delay, but the wait was necessary. A grateful Rudolph Gaida had provided the Rangers with a platoon of Czech soldiers under their friend, Captain Anton Dubcek, and one of the Legion's armored trains. The five Rangers would not be going against Bravo Team and Hendricks's White Death alone.

Again he wished they'd been able to bring their recall beacon through with them from 1980. He would have liked to have been able to call Thompson for reinforcements before the Transformation Wave cut him off from Time Square . . . or return to the Chronos Base and have Thompson re-insert them in Omsk.

Perhaps it was just as well that they were still cut off from 2007. What would have happened, he wondered, if he'd used a beacon to contact Thompson a week before the general released him and his men from house arrest? The Rangers might have been released a week before they actually were.

Hunter drew back from the window, shaking his head. *That* kind of thinking led only to headaches. Even theoreticians like Rachel's father didn't understand the ins and outs of time-changed universes yet; if Dr. Stein couldn't follow the twistings of temporal paradox, Hunter would be damned if *he* was going to meddle with them!

At least the Rangers had stopped Simms. Gaida had not died at Perm. The Rangers' intervention there had created a whole new time track.

Hunter could only pray that it was the right one.

Right or wrong, they had a date with Hendricks and Bravo Team. That bastard had to be stopped before he twisted history so badly out of shape that an army of Rangers couldn't put things straight.

A door at the far end of the compartment opened, and King entered, swaying slightly with the rocking motion of the train. He pulled off his parka and dropped into the seat next to Hunter. "Almost there," the master sergeant said. "The lads know what to do."

"Good."

"I'm still not sure about this, Lieutenant. What about Hendricks?"

"The warehouse first, Greg. Hendricks could be anywhere in the city . . . maybe there. If we can capture the warehouse first, we'll have the beacon and can call for help if we need it." *And pray we're not screwing ourselves up in some damned time warp*.

"But the VBU train . . ."

Hunter suppressed an inner pang. *Rachel* . . .

"We'll take it, but only if we can do it quietly." Hunter scowled. "If we got tied up in a firefight at the depot . . . Hendricks could use the recall beacon to escape."

"Yeah, but we'd have the VBU equipment. If he got away, we could follow him."

"If we could get it running in time, Greg." Hunter closed his eyes. "I don't know. I've been over it and over it. My best guess is to try for both the train and the warehouse . . . and hope like hell we can catch Hendricks's people by surprise."

"Think that's going to work? Hendricks must know things went sour in Perm."

Hunter smiled. "Yeah. But he doesn't know *what* happened

. . . that we just shifted universes on him. If he heard Simms was killed, he can't know it was us who did it. That may be our one advantage, and I intend to milk it for all it's worth."

King was about to reply when the far door opened again and Captain Anton Dubcek entered. The blond giant brushed ice crystals from his beard, grinning. "The engineer says Kulomzino is thirty minutes," he said in German. "My men are ready."

"*Sehr gut, Herr Kapitan,*" Hunter replied. "Be ready to move out smartly."

"*Ja wohl, Herr Major!* At your command!" The grin broadened as he saluted and left. The forms of military discipline were not to be ignored. A problem had presented itself when Hunter, a lieutenant, found himself in charge of a contingent of Czech Legion soldiers under the command of Captain Dubcek. General Gaida had solved the difficulty quite simply by field-commissioning Hunter on the spot as a major in the Czech Legion.

If only promotions were that easy in his own time, he thought ruefully.

Beside him, King stretched back in his seat, looking thoughtful. "Once we wrap Hendricks up, where do we go next?"

"We still have a VBU force of unknown size and composition out there somewhere," Hunter replied. "Of course, at this point, we may be able to leave them alone. We can't carry out the original Backlash mission . . . not now."

"That's for damned sure!"

"The way I see it, we take care of Hendricks and Bravo, get our beacon back, and hightail it uptime to Chronos to report. Things ought to go pretty much the way they did originally after that. And we can leave before the VBU shows up."

"Might be smart to leave someone here to keep an eye on things, just in case."

"Maybe. Or we get Thompson to set up some sort of base before 1918, so that if there *are* any more changes as a result of tonight's action, we have a force safely tucked out of the way of any Transformation Waves that can set things right." He shook his head. "Time enough to work that out later. First we take out Hendricks."

"I reckon so, Lieutenant. Uh . . . Major." King smiled. "But I sure as hell hope the VBU stays clear until then. That would be a bloody mess, having to deal with Hendricks and the VBU too!''

Hunter could only nod agreement.

''There is no doubt, Comrade Major. That is our train.''

''*Da!*'' Andryanov smiled wolfishly. ''See the power leads between those two boxcars and the lighted coach? That car houses the reactor; the other holds the downlink.''

After an epic journey they had finally reached their destination. Crossing the front lines near Ufa, the VBU team had used forged passes to join a White supply train as railroad workers, and so made their way to Omsk. Now Obinin and Andryanov, both clad in civilian workers' clothes, stood out of the wind in the shelter of a toolshed in the station yard at Kulomzino and watched the train parked on its siding near the depot.

Obinin reached for his pocket. ''Should we call Vasilov?'' The third member of the trio had been left in a crude hut outside of the capital with shortwave radio gear. He was their link to Colonel Zamiatin's spetsnaz contingent.

''*Nyet.*'' He shook his head. ''Not yet. Remember, complete radio silence, unless absolutely necessary. It will be several more days before the colonel can reach Omsk.''

''The city is heavily defended. Recapturing the train may be beyond our means.''

Andryanov shrugged easily under his heavy coat. ''We wait and we watch, Vadim Sergeivich, until the colonel brings his unit up.''

''*Da.*'' His sigh was an explosion of white vapor. ''But the waiting is hard.''

''What is the proverb? 'All things come to him who waits'? We know precisely where the Americans are now. When we are ready to strike, they will never know what hit them.''

The Czech train pulled slowly into Kulomzino Station with wheezing, shrieking gaps of steam. Legion soldiers were climbing down off the cars before the locomotive had braked to a complete halt. Like all Czech trains in Russia, the railcars on this one were gaily painted with religious or patriotic themes. The color made a strange contrast with the gray, snowbound squalor of the rail yard.

Hunter stepped off the train and peered through wet darkness as the other train pulled up on its siding near the depot. The VBU train had not been moved during the past week, and there was no sign that it was heavily guarded. He caught Dubcek's elbow as the big man came up. "Remember, Captain," he said, "don't approach the other train until the alarm has been given. We don't want some eager sentry over there to alert Hendricks before we're out of the depot."

"We have it—how do you people say—'in a bag.' "

"Good."

"Our engineer says he must bleed off steam to take on water, *Herr Major*."

"That's a routine operation, isn't it? Shouldn't cause any excitement."

"Yes, sir. We will take on coal as well. We have way out if things go bad."

Don't even think that! Hunter wanted desperately to find Rachel. She would probably be with the downlink, but it would be dangerous to approach the train now.

Pushing the thought aside, he signaled King, who was standing with the other Rangers, together with a company of Czech soldiers. "We'll be back as quick as we can."

"And we will be waiting for you! *Viel Glück, Herr Major!*"

"*Danke*, Anton. We'll need all the luck we can get!"

Five minutes after their arrival, the Rangers and twelve Czech soldiers were quick-marching along tracks beaten into the snow, heading toward the warehouse at Number 12 Market Street. So far no alarm had been given, and their only witnesses were occasional White soldiers braving the cold of the town's streets as they made their way to a bar or some other place of warmth. The cold was pervasive, bone-numbing, and keen. A wounded man, Hunter reflected, would not last long outside before he froze to death.

The small Legion unit rounded a corner onto Market Street, moving double time, more for warmth than for the need for speed. Ahead, Hunter saw the warehouse, warm yellow light spilling from the windows, and a half dozen guards huddled around an oil-drum stove outside the front door.

Why so many guards? Hunter saw the answer almost at once. Major Landry, one of Becker's staff officers, had departed for the past after the Rangers' semi-arrest in 2007. He must have landed *here* . . . and been promptly killed or imprisoned by Hendricks, who would be trying to preserve his isolation in time until he could change history and eliminate Time Square. The Bravo Team leader would have seen to it that the warehouse and the recall beacon were heavily guarded; he would not have dared to switch the beacon off—not and risk warning Thompson and Becker—but he would have made sure that anyone who did come through would receive a warm welcome. General Becker, Hunter recalled, had departed for Omsk a few hours before Thompson released the Rangers. He wondered if Becker had already arrived in 1918 . . . or was due to come through later.

It didn't much matter, except, of course, to Becker's well-being. The Rangers had to secure that beacon, not matter how many of Hendricks's bully-boys surrounded it.

"Halt!" One of the sentries stepped away from the fire, his M-16 at a sloppy port arms. He spoke heavily accented Russian. "You are not permitted here!"

"Who is in charge?" one of the Czechs demanded in German. The Rangers remained quiet. They didn't want to alert Hendricks's men that they were no longer up in 2007 . . . not yet. Their Czech spokesman kept talking, winning precious time as the column closed on the warehouse door. "We have special message for your commander."

"What the hell?" another American growled, hefting his assault rifle. "The general wouldn't send no goddamned locals . . ."

"It's a trick!" Gunfire spat in the night, bursting wildly above their heads.

Shit! Hunter had hoped to take the outside guards quietly, without alerting the troops, which must still be inside. He remembered the old maxim about plans surviving contact with the enemy and shouted, "Take them!"

The lead Bravo Team soldier stumbled backward against the oil drum as bolt-action rifles cracked. A second American swung his M-16 around to fire, but Hunter snapped up his Uzi, triggering a burst into the man, which sent him sprawling in the snow.

The other Hendricks guards died, and King hurled his shoulder against the warehouse door. Inside all was confusion as Bravo soldiers were caught still groping for their weapons.

Dark Walker sent a round from his Galil through the eye of one trooper with an M-16 while Anderson's heavy M-60 thundered close by, smashing a pine crate to splinters and killing a pair of soldiers hiding behind it.

Then the battle broke down into complete chaos. One of Hendricks's men hurled a grenade, the steel baseball clattering across the wooden floor and bouncing from the wall near the door. The blast momentarily deafened the attackers and killed a pair of Czech soldiers outright. Hunter lowered his head and raced forward as gunfire hissed and snapped past him.

A second explosion sent shards of glass tinkling across the room. Hunter threw himself flat as gunfire erupted from a new direction. Several of Hendricks's men were squeezing through a window shattered by the blast. Hunter squeezed off a burst in their direction, then let them go. They would warn Hendricks, but he would confront that worry later. He *had* to secure the beacon before one of Hendricks's men wrecked it with a stray bullet or grenade!

There it was! The familiar blue aurora shimmered in the air above it. Hunter's eyes widened. Something was materializing, taking shape as the aurora contracted into a glowing whirlpool of light.

Hunter leapt to his feet and scrambled forward. General Becker stepped out of the portal, blinking uncertainly as he looked around the warehouse. Hunter tackled him at the waist, driving the general back and down as autofire crackled past them. They landed in a heap on the floor next to the body of one of Hendricks's men.

Becker's eyes were wide. "Good God, Hunter! I just left you back—"

"Save it, General!" Hunter rolled off the man and triggered his Uzi at a running Bravo Team soldier. The man skidded and went down. "We'll sort it out later!"

But the battle was already over. Slowly Hunter stood up as the rest of the Rangers and Legion troopers emerged from cover. Seven Bravo soldiers lay scattered about the warehouse. At least two more had escaped through the blast-shattered window.

"You'd better explain yourself, Lieutenant!" Becker exploded. "I came back here to check up personally on your allegations! How did you get back to 1918 ahead of me?"

"That's not the question just now," Hunter said. "Right now our problem is 2007."

"Eh? What are you talking about?"

Hunter stepped across the floor, stooping to retrieve the recall beacon. It dangled in his hand, the plastic case shattered, bits and pieces of its interior circuitry dangling from the holes where a 5.56mm round had gone clear through the device, wrecking it. Hunter remembered Thompson commenting that Time Square had lost touch with 1918 shortly after Becker went through. This explained the silence quite well. When Hunter had knocked the general aside, one of the rounds aimed at them had smashed the beacon.

"There's still the downlink," Gomez said, coming up. "And Hendricks has one."

"Yeah," Hunter agreed. "Let's get back to the train . . . fast."

A growing dread gnawed at him. Their only link with their own time now was aboard the train. And as soon as Hendricks learned what had happened here . . .

Eighteen

"The Rangers! Here?" Hendricks groped for his trousers. The Russian girl, Tanya, had recovered after her first scream and sat upright now, naked in the bed. The Bravo force commander ignored her. "Where the devil did they come from?"

"Maybe the question is when," Malloy replied. He'd rushed to Hendricks's hotel room with word of the attack at the warehouse. "It happened right after a train arrived from Perm. The Rangers must've been on it. You know what that means?"

"Yeah! They're the ones who killed Simms!" He began pulling on his trousers, then reached for his other clothes, scattered about the floor. "Dirty sons of bitches! I'll kill 'em!"

"I sounded the alert, Swede. Our boys are mustering now outside the hotel."

"Okay! Get as many of our guys and White Death Commandos together as you can in the next five minutes. Then head for the train station."

"The VBU train?"

"Yeah. And put a guard on the civilians. They'll be our insurance."

"Fitzpatrick too?"

"No. I'll keep him with me. But grab the girls. And have

the engineer get up steam—fast! We're gonna do a fast fade!''

''*Pahzhahl'stah!*'' Tanya chirped. ''*Gospodin* Swede! What is happening?''

''Nothing to worry about, Beautiful,'' Hendricks replied in Russian. ''I'll be back with you in no time at all!'' He pulled his coat from a hook on the wall and questioned Malloy with a raised eyebrow. ''All set? Let's roll!''

Tanya was great fun and he hated losing her, but there were plenty more girls to be taken, and he couldn't be slowed down by civilians now! He followed Malloy down the hotel stairs at a breakneck pace.

''An attack, Comrade Obinin!'' Andryanov touched the Skorpion machine pistol in its holster beneath his coat. ''This may be our chance.''

''Is it the Reds?'' Obinin looked tense, nervous.

''I can't tell.'' He raised binoculars to his eyes and scanned the panorama of sheds and buildings and huts filthy with coal soot. ''It appears to be Czechs fighting Americans and Whites, but that makes no sense.''

''Little in this war makes sense, Comrade Major. Shall we radio for instructions?''

Andryanov considered the question for a moment. ''*Nyet*,'' he said at last.

''But, Comrade Major—''

''*Nyet!* In this instance, Comrade, we are expected to exercise our initiative! The colonel is fifteen hundred kilometers from here, and we are on our own! What is our primary mission?''

''To keep our train under observation until the main force arrives!''

''Then that is precisely what we will do!''

''Huh? What?''

''We are dressed as civilian railway workers, *da*? Let us see if they have work for us aboard that train!''

They hurried out into the cold wind, running as the sound of gunfire crackled above the snowy streets of Kulomzino.

Hunter ducked as machine-gun fire yammered from up the street and bullets slammed into the side of the building at his back. *The natives must be getting used to periodic coups by now,* Hunter thought. *Still, it's a hell of a way to celebrate New Year's!*

He turned to Gomez, crouched beside him. "Think you can quiet 'im down, Eddie?"

The Hispanic Ranger grinned for answer and chambered a 40mm grenade. The machine gun continued to blast, firing blindly. Gomez brought the M-203/M-16 combo to his shoulder, his finger curling around the grenade-launcher trigger ahead of the assault rifle's magazine. There was a dull thump, followed a moment later by a blast of snow and smoke and noise a hundred yards away. The machine gun's bark fell abruptly silent.

"Okay," Hunter said. "Move! Move!"

Hendricks's people were thoroughly alerted now. That machine gun was the third time they'd been pinned down since they'd left the warehouse.

The battle had spread to the rail yard by the time they reached it. Dubcek met him near the Czech train with word that Legion troopers had boarded the other train as soon as the gunfire began in the city. There had been some stiff resistance, but both were now held by the Legion. "Is good you come," Dubcek said. "Hendricks's men, they come!"

"Have you found the . . . civilians on board?"

Dubcek nodded. "Still aboard, keeping heads down. As you ordered, *Herr Major.*"

"Good. I'm going to want both trains moved out of here as fast as your men can get them moving."

"For that one, no problem." Dubcek said, pointing at the VBU train. "Engineer and two coal men aboard already, with orders to get up steam. For our train . . . need water, and time to get up new steam."

"How long?"

"Two hours? Maybe more."

Hunter looked across the yard as a fresh volley of firing broke out. That would have to do, he decided. The only way to get Hendricks into the open now was to draw him out with the VBU train, his only hope of escape from Omsk. If Hunter could actually get the train out of the city, it would be easier to defend.

The deep-throated growl of a heavy engine brought him around! Now what?

The armored car burst into the open on the far side of the train station. The contraption looked almost comical, a 1914 model car with wire-spoked wheels and fender-mounted headlights, an open truck's back and a squat, angular turret above and behind the armor-plated cab. Hunter had read of such machines; this one was a Rolls-Royce, originally built in England, one of a number shipped to Russia during World War I. Its .303-caliber Maxim gun winked and chattered as the turret cranked ponderously around. A group of Czech soldiers standing beside the VBU train scattered as the fire cut into them. Three men went down, one shrieking hideously.

Gunfire erupted from the train, but futilely, as rounds sparked and pinged off the armor. The Rolls swung parallel to the VBU train, its machine gun sweeping men from flatcars and sending others fleeing for more substantial cover.

Then the White Death attacked.

The Czechs were superb soldiers, but they were badly outnumbered and caught in the open by the Whites' mad rush. The armored car clanked to a stop, the turret still traversing as its gun cut down the running Legion troops.

Hunter stood, raising his Uzi. A strong hand on his shoulder dragged him down behind a stack of lumber. He turned and found himself looking into King's eyes. "It's no good, Lieutenant. We need Eddie and his thumper."

Hunter nodded reluctantly, swallowing the bile that threatened to choke him. "Get him up here! We've got to take out that Rolls!"

In the rail yard and across the station platform, White soldiers were swarming toward the armored train. A few of Dubcek's men, cut off from the rest of their forces, fought a bitter last stand among the railcars. Gomez ran up, bent almost double to stay below the stray lead that was whistling through the night air. Hunter pointed and Gomez replied with a thumbs-up sign. He brought his grenade launcher to his shoulder and fired.

The blast shattered the wooden cargo compartment in the back and rocked the armored chassis violently, but the machine gun continued shouting death. Gomez cursed and broke the breech on the M-203, slapping another round home. Hunter caught a glimpse of men dashing from the shadows of the rail yard buildings, men carrying the familiar shapes of M-16s and other modern weapons. Behind them, a building erupted in smoke and yellow flame, momentarily silhouetting the running troops. Hendricks and his men were making their escape while the *B'yelee Smert* bought them time.

There was a shrill, piercing blast from the VBU train's whistle, and the *chuff-hiss-chuff* as the heavy locomotive began grinding forward on the tracks. "They're moving!" Anderson yelled from close by. He stood with his M-60 braced on his hip, spitting flame at the White Death Commandos. "They're leaving!"

Eddie fired again. This time the grenade detonated underneath the chassis, just behind the front tires. The detonation lifted the heavy vehicle from its wheels and toppled it over on its side with a thundering crash. Flames licked at a shattered fuel tank.

The explosion lit up the rail yard and sent chunks of burning debris hurtling a hundred yards. A cheer rose as the Legion soldiers, those who were left, surged forward, gunning down the last few commandos of the *B'yelee Smert* who stood in their way.

But the VBU train was gathering speed now. Too late, Hunter thought of closing the siding switch and blocking the train's escape, but the switch was on the far side of the train, and gunfire from the White troops still clambering aboard made any such move impossible.

The armored train was swiftly swallowed by darkness as it swung onto the main line of the Trans-Siberian Railway, thundering east.

Hunter stood, his Uzi useless in his hand. He recognized Dubcek's tall and brawny form. "Captain! We have to follow them."

"*Ja*," the giant growled. "They have killed too many of my own." His eyes were bleak as they met Hunter's. "But it will take time to get water and coal . . . and make steam, *Herr Major*. Too much time . . ."

"Then let's get started." A new thought occurred to Hunter. "There are Czech garrisons all along the Trans-Siberian Railway, aren't there?"

Dubcek nodded. "They hold most of the line as far as Baikal," he said. "Most of the Legion is still in the process of withdrawing to Vladivostok."

"Okay. Get to the telegraph office here in Kulomzino. Hendricks and his people won't get far without stopping for coal and water themselves. Maybe one of your garrisons can hold them.''

Dubcek shook his shaggy head slowly. He pointed across the rail yard to a building blazing furiously against the night. "They have destroyed telegraph station."

Hunter sagged. "Then all we can do is go after them."

"That, my friend, we can do. We *will* do it."

But will it be enough? Hunter wondered. He could barely hear the rumble of the armored train now, far off in the darkness to the east. That train held the Rangers' only hope of returning to their own time.

And Rachel . . .

Andryanov held the Skorpion up for the engineer to see. The body of the coal man had been rolled out of the locomotive cab moments before, and the white-faced engineer pressed back against the steel frame of one window, terrified. Outside, darkness roared past the speeding train, though the first traces of dawn were visible to the east.

"You have nothing to fear if you do precisely what we tell you," Andryanov said. He knew the local would not recognize the Skorpion, a weapon that would not be invented for another fifty years, but the ugly little machine pistol *looked* deadly and backed up his words with vicious promise.

"Pa-pahzhahl' stah!" the frightened man stammered. "I have no politics! I am only a train engineer!"

"Then you will do what you know how to do. But if you give warning . . ." The Skorpion threatened again.

"Nyet! Nyet! I promise!"

"Comrade Major!" Obinin waved his small transceiver. "Vasilov says the colonel has acknowledged! He congratulates us on our quick thinking in boarding the train!"

"His orders?" Andryanov did not take his eyes from the engineer.

"To stay with the train . . . and to alert him as we draw near to his position!"

"Excellent!" Andryanov smiled. He gestured at the engineer with the Skorpion. "Best to keep your eyes on the track ahead, Comrade. We have a long way to go.''

The light of the first day of 1919 grew stronger, setting the eastern sky aglow.

Hunter watched the night give way to day, the featureless darkness replaced by the almost featureless monotony of the snow-covered prairies of southern Siberia. It was a monotony broken only rarely by patches of forest or a solitary cabin squatting under a pillar of wood smoke from its chimney.

He berated himself for the failure at Kulomzino. Fifteen Czechs were dead or seriously wounded because he'd under-estimated Hendricks's response to his attack. Worse, Hendricks had escaped with the armored train; taking with him his own recall beacon as well as the VBU downlink. The Rangers would be stranded in this savage and bloody war if they could not catch up with Hendricks and bring him to heel.

And Hendricks had Rachel, Sarah Grant, Brian Fitzpatrick, and the historian, Lynn Colby. He had an unknown number of his White Death Commandos with him, plus at least twenty-five of his own soldiers, armed with assault rifles and machine guns.

Against the renegade Americans, the Rangers had Dubcek and thirty-two Czech Legion soldiers, all who could still fight after Kulomzino. The Czech train was as fast as Hendricks's but lacked the armored van with its turret-mounted cannon. The Czechs did have one surprise weapon aboard, a boxy, fabric-and-plywood contraption which Dubcek had the audacity to call an airplane.

The struggle for Russia's political future had seen a number of strange technological adaptations, Hunter knew. The world's first use of aircraft carriers could be traced to float planes launched by both sides from barges on Russia's strategically critical rivers. The Anatra DS was a similar experiment, rigged to be broken down for storage atop a railway flatcar, then assembled and sent aloft from any convenient open field. It was a two-seater observation plane with a top speed of less than ninety miles per hour . . . not much faster than the train they were chasing, and Hunter was not certain how they would be able to use it.

The problem was, they couldn't use any of their combat assets until they caught up with Hendricks and the VBU train. Repeated attempts to telegraph warning to Czech outposts along the way had been frustrated time and time again . . . probably by Hendricks's people tearing up the wires ahead. Sooner or later Hendricks would run out of track—at Vladivostok and the Sea of Japan if no sooner—but the fear that the renegade would somehow shake off his pursuers dogged Hunter with grim relentlessness.

If Hendricks did escape, if Rachel or the other civilians aboard that train were killed, if the renegades succeeded in changing history either accidentally or to their own purpose, it would be *his* fault, and that realization was grinding him down.

Hunter looked up as Becker entered the coach. "Hello, General." He tried to keep his voice light.

"Don't get up," the general said, holding up a hand. "Mind if I join you?"

"Not at all, sir."

Becker had been much subdued since the firefight in the warehouse. Hunter's explanation of all that had transpired— of the alternate future with its Fascist America, of the return to Perm, of Hendricks's men lying in ambush for people coming through from Time Square—had shocked the man almost into complete inactivity. He had insisted on boarding the Czech train with the Rangers, but for a long time afterward could only sit by a window, murmuring, "Poor Landry."

Major Landry must have been murdered the moment he stepped through the portal into the warehouse.

The general sat and watched the passing scenery for a moment. Black smoke briefly smudged the sky above the bleak and level horizon. Most of the fighting at this point in the war was in the west, but there were continual Bolshevik raids all along the length of the Trans-Siberian Railway, interspersed by White or Czech counterraids that were no less savage and bloody. It could hardly matter to the peasants, Hunter reflected, whether their towns and homes were burned by Reds or by Whites.

"I . . . just wanted to let you know," Becker said at last. "You're in command here . . . and now."

Hunter said nothing. In his own mind he had never relinquished command, but that was hardly the sort of thing a lieutenant said to a man with two general's stars pinned on his collar. He'd been afraid that Becker might try to take charge of the motley Ranger-Czech force and had been wondering just what he would do if it happened.

"I really screwed this one up," he continued. "It was my fault Hendricks got as far as he did. My recommendations—"

"You couldn't have known, sir."

"I could have run checks . . . like Thompson did. I should have *known,* dammit! Hendricks was a phony, start to finish."

"He's not finished yet, General." Hunter felt uncomfortable. If lieutenants do not fail to relinquish command to generals, neither do generals confide in lieutenants. This was hardly a normal situation, however. Hunter could sense that Becker felt totally lost in this new environment. The reality of *being* in the past, of actually seeing it through one's own eyes, could come as a staggering blow to someone who had only known the past through books or movies.

"Hendricks was important to me, Hunter," Becker went on. "Important *politically*." His mouth twisted in an unpleasant attempt at a grin. "You'd think that with America hanging on the ropes we'd be able to put aside the career scrambles and the political bickering and get on with fighting the common enemy, wouldn't you? But you see, Hendricks's success at Berthoud Pass was *my* success. I had put him there. He was under my command. The warning broadcast from his post before it was overrun let me avoid a nasty Russian trap, and win the victory we needed. His victory showed the Joint Chiefs what a great general I was. What a great tactician. *Bullshit!*"

"Sir, I—"

"That's all I wanted to say. That . . . and I'm sorry. If anyone can get us out of this mess, son, you can. I just wanted to let you know that I'm counting on your good judgment . . . where mine failed."

Hunter watched Becker leave. That Becker felt the same pain, the sense of responsibility that Hunter did, left the Ranger thoughtful.

Hendricks strolled among the twisted bodies, probing with the toe of his boot for signs of life. There were few survivors . . . a couple of Czech soldiers he'd ordered spared to load coal aboard the train, plus a handful of terrified women who'd been staying with the Legion garrison. All the rest were dead, killed in those few seconds of nightmarish fury.

"They were trying to delay us, Danny," Hendricks said. It was colder here, on the fringes of the mountains, and each breath burned in his lungs. "That nonsense about problems up the track . . . that was bullshit to hold us up."

Malloy nodded. "Hunter, you think?"

"Yeah." He looked up at the wires that drooped between lonely evenly spaced poles along the tracks and extending clear to both horizons. "They must've patched into a telegraph line along the way and signaled ahead."

"They must be pretty hot on our tail."

"I want to be fueled up and outa here in an hour, Danny. No more."

"Right, Swede. What about the prisoners?"

"When you're done with 'em . . ." He jerked his forefinger across his throat.

Another of Hendricks's soldiers approached, a heavyset corporal named Ludowicz. "Hey, Gen'rul," he said, sketching a salute. "The guys were wonderin' about all those women we captured. Think we can give 'em the Italian treatment?"

Hendricks looked away toward the shed where the women were being kept. "Italian treatment" was local slang the men had picked up from their Russian hosts who, with limited experience of the rest of the world, believed that anything Italian must be lewd or sexually suggestive. It described the practice, Red and White, of taking all of the pretty girls from a village aboard a military train and raping them.

"No, Luddy. Not this time."

"But, Gen'rul—"

"I said no, dammit! We're gonna spring a surprise on the Rangers at the next tunnel, and I want the men on their toes, not screwing the locals! Wait until their men finish loading the coal, then kill them! All of them!"

"Y-yes, sir."

He glared at Malloy. "I don't want any witnesses, understand?"

"Sure, Swede. No witnesses."

"No!" The new voice shrilled behind him. "No, you can't do that, Swede!"

Hendricks turned and looked down at the slight figure of Lynn Colby. "What the hell are you doing here?"

"Swede! What's . . . what's happened to you? You can't just kill these people!"

"War is hell, Lynn . . . or didn't you ever read that in your history books?"

"This isn't war! It's cold-blooded murder!"

"Sometimes there's not a hell of a lot of difference. Get back on the train, Lynn. You shouldn't have gotten off."

"No! I will not! You've twisted me and manipulated me and gotten everything you've wanted out of me, but I'm not going to be a party to this!"

The ghost of a smile touched Hendricks's lips. "What else can you do?"

Her shoulders slumped. "I . . . don't know. Swede, you've got our only way back home. Please, won't you let us go? Sarah and Rachel and . . . and me? Stay back here if you want, but you don't need us. Let us go back . . . please. . . ."

Hendricks appeared to reach a decision. "No problem."

Colby's eyes narrowed, as though trying to fathom his change of heart. "You . . . mean . . ."

"You can stay right here." He reached inside his parka, tugged his Colt .45 from its holster, and snicked back the slide. The historian screamed and stumbled back a step. "No . . . please . . ."

"You're right, baby. I don't need you now." The pistol barked once, and Lynn Colby twisted, then slumped across the sprawled body of a Czech soldier. Hendricks stood above her, a savage light in his eyes. "From here on out, Lynn, I make my own history!"

A few yards away, two Russians peered from the locomotive cab at the sound of the gunshot. "He is ruthless, that one," Andryanov commented.

"How much longer, Comrade Major?"

"Not long now. Colonel Zamiatin reports that the ambush is ready. All we need do is take control when he gives the word." He studied Hendricks for a time. "It seems a pity, though. That American would be a splendid asset as a VBU field operative."

Nineteen

"He's gone as bad as the Russians," Hunter said. He tore his eyes from the grotesquely twisted bodies and tried to focus on the mountains looming above the tiny depot of Tartaretz instead.

Dubcek cocked an eye at him. "It is not the Russians, *Herr Major*. It is the *fanatics* on both sides, who make things . . . like this."

Hunter nodded. "I know, Anton. But it's hard to understand. I know the guy." *But I can't really say that. I know him . . . but I've never understood him.*

"Some of these bodies are still warm, *Herr Major*," Dubcek said. "They lay here an hour . . . no more. We just missed them."

Hunter turned away and started back toward the Czech train. The colorful paintings on the side of the cars seemed obscene amid so much blood and death.

There was a terrible temptation to blame himself for this fresh round of murders. Only a few hours before, they had stopped at Krasnoyarsk, fifty miles to the west, and telegraphed instructions to Tartaretz to hold Hendricks's train when it came through.

The result was the slaughter of the garrison. From the look of things, few of them had even had a chance to reach for their rifles. One stack of twenty bodies near the coal pile had the look of people who had been lined up in a row and machine-gunned where they stood.

But why in God's name had they killed the women too? Not a solitary living thing was left at the station. The wind shrilled down from the mountain peaks ahead, a ghoulish, lamenting wail.

No. He would not give in to that temptation. There was a subtle distinction here between responsibility and guilt. But he had to reach Hendricks before there were any more murders as senseless as these.

"LT!" Anderson was kneeling in front of the train station. "LT! Over here!"

It was Lynn Colby. "Is she alive?" he asked, hurrying to join him.

He read the answer in the slight shake of Anderson's head. "Yes..."

She was alive and conscious, then, but not for long. The wound was high in her shoulder, but the subzero cold had nearly finished the Chronos historian.

Her eyes fluttered open. "Lieutenant?"

"Yes, Lynn. It's me."

"You've got to stop him, Lieutenant. You've got to."

"I know, Lynn. We'll catch him. And when we do—"

"You don't understand! Heard them...talking..." She was growing weaker as she spoke. She had lost a great deal of blood. Her face was paste-white, her lips so badly frostbitten that she could hardly talk. "Ambush," she said after a short struggle. "Heard them. Ambush...you. Next tunnel..."

And then she was dead.

Hunter stood up slowly. He met Dubcek's eyes. "You have your map case?"

Dubcek nodded. "Aboard the train."

"Good." The fury churned in Hunter's gut, warming him against the Siberian wind. "I want to see where the next tunnel is. And...better round up your pilot, I think we'll want to break out your observation plane for a bit of scouting."

Dubcek wiped at the ice encrusted on his eyebrows. "Risky ...in this cold."

"I don't care. The bastard is turning to face us. This is our chance to nail him."

Eddie Gomez could no longer feel his face. Despite the goggles, despite the wool scarf muffling his mouth and nose and neck, the cold seared through his clothing like the fiery blast of an acetylene torch. The windchill factor . . . he didn't want to think about it. Siberia in January experienced from the observer's seat of a biplane flying at eighty miles an hour held no charms for the California native.

The Anatra went into a bank, its 150-horsepower Salmson engine straining in the cold air. *I sure hope they put plenty of antifreeze in that thing*, Gomez thought as he listened to the rotary engine's stutter. *Come to think of it, I could use some antifreeze myself.*

He shifted his position, trying to work some warmth back into his legs. The observer's cockpit faced the plane's tail. A 7.62mm machine gun was set on a pintel mount, but Gomez had long since decided that if he needed a weapon, he would depend on the M-16 wedged into the cockpit next to his leg. The machine gun was crusted over with ice.

He fumbled for a moment, his hands clumsy with cold and the heavy gloves he wore. He almost lost his radio before he managed to open a channel. "Yankee Leader," he said, forcing the words between numbed lips. "Yankee Leader, this is Eagle!"

"Go ahead, Eagle!" Hunter's voice was almost lost in the roar of the plane's engine. Gomez burrowed lower into the cockpit, trying to escape the cold wind. Gomez could see the double tracings of the Trans-Siberian Railway a hundred feet below him, a dark slash through the eye-burning brilliance of the Siberian snowfields.

"Still nothing, Chief," Gomez said. "The tracks are twisting a lot as they go up higher into the mountains. Rugged ground . . . bare rock, cliffs, and broken ice." Gomez turned in his seat, following the tracks with tearing eyes. He tried to smear the rime of ice from his goggles with the icy finger of his glove, then gave up.

An insistent thumping sounded from up front. Gomez contorted his body enough to see the Czech pilot, who was pounding on the side of the plane to attract attention and pointing.

Ahead, Gomez could see a dark gash in the face of a sheer rock cliff.

He raised the radio again. "Hold it, Chief! I see the tunnel! Wait one . . ."

The pilot banked again, swinging ninety degrees to give Gomez a better view. The Ranger raised a pair of binoculars, straining to make out detail through the murky smear of ice on his goggles. He finally gave up and pushed them up on his face. A few moments' exposure to this wind would give him severe frostbite, he knew, but he was next to blind wearing the heavy goggles, and right now he needed to *see*.

"Yankee, this is Eagle," he said after a moment's study. "Target confirmed. They've backed the train into the tunnel. Looks like they've shifted the cars around so the armored van with the turret is last. *Dios!* They're laying for us with that cannon."

"*Roger, Eagle,*" Hunter replied. "*Get on back here . . . double quick!*"

"On my way, Yankee. Have the ice picks ready and a warm fire going, okay?"

The Anatra completed its turn and raced back toward the Czech train at better than eighty miles an hour.

An hour later Hunter bent over a map table in one of the Czech railcars. Anton Dubcek and General Becker were there, along with the Rangers. Gomez huddled in a corner, wrapped in a heavy blanket, sipping at a steaming cup of thick, black Russian tea.

"He'll catch us as we round this curve," Hunter said, his forefinger probing at a map. It was an old, Czarist military engineering map for this stretch of the Trans-Siberian Railway, already heavily annotated and corrected by scribblings in English, German, and Czech. It was not very accurate but would serve to help the Czech-Ranger force counter Hendricks's ambush.

"Your idea is to come down this cliff?" Dubcek frowned. "I do not question your abilities, but . . ."

Hunter smiled easily. "We've had special training." Inwardly he hoped he and his men were up to it. Rangers were highly trained in rappeling and other mountaineering skills, but they did not have the harnesses, strong and ultra-lightweight lines, and the other high-tech gear they were used to. They would have to make their descent with substitutes available in 1918.

"Even so," the Czech officer said, "you will bear the brunt of combat until my men can reach the tunnel entrance."

"We'll be after the armored van and that cannon," Hunter explained. "Eddie will rig us up some satchel charges as soon as his fingers thaw. We'll take out the cannon and any machine guns they have covering the approaches to the tunnel. That ought to give your men a straight shot into the tunnel."

"Much depends on your people's abilities on the mountain, then, *Herr Major*."

"You'll have your part to play, too, Anton. If your people don't show up, there're going to be four Rangers squatting up there at the end of an armored train with a large number of very angry Whites coming out of that tunnel."

Dubcek smiled. "We will be there, my friend."

Becker spoke for the first time. "It would help if we could get the Czech train closer before the attack," he said. He pointed to where the track curved around a spur of mountain, in full view of Hendricks's cannon for nearly half a mile before swinging left to approach the tunnel entrance.

"True," Hunter said. "But I don't see how . . ."

Becker straightened, holding Hunter's eyes with his own. "It's my fault that Backlash has come to this," he said. "And my responsibility. I want one last chance to talk to Hendricks. Perhaps he'll give himself up."

Hunter's stunned expression brought worry to Dubcek's face. Becker had spoken in English, and the Czech had not understood the exchange. "What? What did he say?"

Hunter repeated Becker's words in German, still not believing them. Dubcek shook his head when Hunter finished. "Hendricks . . . he will not listen."

Becker smiled as Hunter translated. "Perhaps," he replied. "Look, if I can talk some of his people around, that's all to the good." He shrugged. "At worst, I buy you boys time, and we edge the train a bit closer so the Czechs don't have to run so far in the cold."

Dubcek listened, his face softening. *"Taw ye nadherneh!"* he exclaimed finally, extending a hand to the American general. "Magnificent! To know such men . . ."

Hunter turned to look at Gomez. "Eddie? How're the face and hands?"

"Getting there, Chief. Another coupla gallons of this winter-weight oil and I'll be ready to go."

"You don't have to, you know."

"No problem, Chief. I'd rather fall out of an airplane than off a cliff any day. Besides, it might take some time getting the stiffness out of my fingers." He grew serious. "I can do it, Lieutenant."

Hunter nodded. He'd already asked Gomez if he would go back up in the biplane once the attack was set in motion. He wanted an airborne pair of eyes to watch for a countermove by Hendricks on that mountain. Once the Rangers began their descent, they would be vulnerable if Hendricks had thought to leave men in hiding among the rocks above the tunnel entrance. Gomez would be their insurance against such a move . . . and a way to keep track of Bravo Team if they decided to fire up their train and head for the other end of the tunnel. The little Anatra biplane, carrying an observer who spoke both English and German, would be invaluable if Hendricks decided to run for it.

"Okay," he said at last. "We'll go. Anton, have your people find something we can use as a truce flag. It's about time we paid Hendricks a social call."

Hendricks stood in the mouth of the railway tunnel, watching the approaching Czech train. It had first edged around the far bend in the tracks several minutes before. He'd been raising his hand to give the order to fire when Sergeant Malloy pointed out a man standing on a low, railed platform at the front of the locomotive, waving what appeared to be a white flag.

"So . . . they want to talk," he said.

Malloy stirred at his side. "I don't like it, them getting that close."

Hendricks chuckled. "What can they do?" He slapped the cold steel plate of the armored van's turret. "We can blast them anytime we feel like it, and they know it!"

"They could get close enough to rush us. Hunter must have Czechs with him . . . no telling how many. See the paintings on the cars? That's a Legion train."

"With a 75mm cannon looking down their throats, plus

machine guns on both sides of the tunnel mouth, there's not a damn thing they can do about it!''

He looked up at a faint, droning buzz. The biplane was back, circling above the other train. Hendricks had been concerned when it had been sighted earlier, since that meant his ambush had lost its surprise. *Move and countermove,* he thought. *That's okay. We'll let them spin things out with this parley of theirs . . . and then smash them flat!*

The Czech train ground to a halt a hundred yards from the tunnel, chuffing clouds of steam billowing out on either side of the locomotive in the cold air. The man standing at the front dismounted and began walking up the tracks, still waving the white flag.

Hendricks started, then brought his binoculars to his eyes. "Oh, shit!"

"What is it?"

"That's Becker! How the devil did he get here?"

"Maybe he came through with the Rangers . . . from wherever they came from?"

"That must be it."

The only explanation for their setback so far was that Becker and Thompson had released the Rangers in 2007, then sent them back to Perm to kill Simms and save Gaida. Just how they'd figured out where Simms was and what he was doing was still a complete mystery, but there was no denying that they'd somehow interfered with Hendricks's plans. Now it appeared that Becker had been in with the Rangers all along.

Hendricks glowered at Malloy. "You know, Danny, I'd still like to know what went wrong in 2007. You told me the Rangers were under arrest!"

"I swear, Swede! Becker was set to throw the book at them! When I left, he was talking like he was going to have them shot!"

"Well, it looks like they talked their way out of it . . . and talked *him* into comin' with them. Tell the boys to get ready. This'll be short and sweet."

Malloy snapped an order, and the clack and snick of drawn rifle bolts sounded from either side of the railway embankment.

Hendricks reached under his parka and drew his .45.

• • •

Becker was out of breath by the time he approached the waiting men. The last stretch of track before the tunnel mouth was straight but led slightly uphill, and he was not used to the exertion. His breath billowed around his head in white puffs, and his heart pounded.

He let his eyes flicker once toward the top of the cliff. There was no sign of the Rangers, but then, there wouldn't be. Hunter and his men had been dropped off beyond the bend in the tracks a mile away and would be moving swiftly along the crest of the long mountain ridge now. They had promised that they would not attack until after he tried to convince Hendricks to surrender. Becker was sincere in his offer to buy the Rangers more time, but he was sincere, too, in his desire to talk to the renegades.

Hendricks and Bravo Team were *his* responsibility, and Major General Richard Becker did not turn his back on his responsibilities.

"No closer, General," Hendricks called from forty feet away. "What do you want?"

"Just to talk." Becker kept his hands in view, the scrap of bed sheet that served as a flag fluttering fitfully in the wind. "Can I come up?"

"I can hear you fine right where you are." Hendricks gestured with the .45 automatic in his hand. "Get those hands up. Higher!"

Becker complied, placing his gloved hands on his head because his arms were already tired from holding his hands up where they were visible.

"Can we talk now?"

"Fine by me. Talk."

"You can't keep running, you know. You'll run out of track at Vladivostok . . . and then it's a long swim to America. You wouldn't like America in this period, either."

"Can't be much worse than the America we came from."

Becker was sharply aware of the droning of the biplane behind him. Gomez and the Czech pilot would be doing their best to keep the attention of Hendricks's men focused out and away from the cliff behind them. He wondered if his peripheral vision had just caught an instant's flicker of motion high up and had to force himself to keep his eyes rigidly on Hendricks's smiling face.

"Put down your weapons and come out," Becker said. "If you don't, you'll all die . . . either here or when the Reds catch up with you. You can't survive this war . . . or this time!"

"Seems to me we've been doin' pretty well, Becker. We really have to thank you for all you've done!"

"For all I've done . . . ?"

"Sure! We've got us a time machine now. We've got the chance to go anywhere, any*when* we want! And it's all thanks to you!"

The pistol fired, and Becker felt the bullet hammer into his sternum. He sprawled backward on the rail bed, aware of the warm gush of blood from his chest.

Oh, God . . . forgive me . . .

Hunter launched himself over the edge of the cliff seconds after the shot echoed from the rock walls around them. He'd had only a glimpse of Becker dropping the truce flag and staggering backward, of Becker sprawled on the tracks with blood soaking the front of his parka.

With a length of cotton rope snugged tight across his back, he dropped his feet, swinging in toward the cliff face until his boots connected with rock. Playing out the line from his left hand, he kicked off and dropped again, descending in slow-motion bounds toward the railcar below. Ten feet to his left, Dark Walker repeated Hunter's moves in an acrobatic mirror image, his Galil tightly strapped to his side out of the way. Both men had satchel charges slung from their shoulders. Gomez had assembled four of them, canvas bags stuffed with TNT and armed by M-60 pull-ring fuse igniters. Gomez had cut the fuses to different lengths; Walker's for a few seconds, Hunter's for longer.

Fifty feet below them, the van was halfway out of the tunnel, with only its sloping, steel-plated sides and the eggshell-shaped turret exposed. With the rest of the VBU train hidden, Hendricks had found a perfect defensive position, presenting the Czech gunners with a minimum target while affording a full field of fire to the 75mm turret-mounted artillery piece.

Two bounds, and stop. He swung close to the rock, securing the line around one arm as he clapped both hands to his ears. Twin steel spheres hurtled down from the rim of the cliff. Seconds later, twin explosions flashed and roared on either side of the armored car, buffeting the two climbers and plunging the soldiers milling around at the base of the cliff into immediate and total confusion. Two more grenades exploded and the White troops bolted for the safety of the tunnel, leaving their dead and wounded lying in the snow.

Hunter exchanged nods with Walker, then kicked off again, dropping the end of his rope and rapidly sliding down its length.

They landed close by the armored car just as the artillery piece mounted inside the turret fired, a thunderous hammering. The stink of cordite filled the air as an explosion blossomed against snow and rock just above the Czech train one hundred and fifty yards away.

Hunter had his Uzi up and firing, cutting down a White soldier emerging from the tunnel. He checked left and right. Gray-clad bodies lay in still, twisted heaps. The grenades lobbed from above had taken out machine-gun nests on either side of the tunnel.

Dark Walker had already leapt to the side of the armored van, his satchel charge dangling from one hand as he yanked the fuse igniter and swung it into the slot in the turret from which the cannon muzzle protruded.

The fieldpiece fired again, and Walker tumbled back off the car. Down the slope, a portion of the roof of a gaily painted boxcar vanished in flame and whirling splinters. Shouts rose from inside the turret as someone noticed the canvas bag.

The explosion tore ragged, gaping rents in the turret and sent flame boiling up the face of the cliff as Hunter and Walker lay flat and let the tidal wave of noise roll over them. From the side of the mountain, small rocks and chunks of ice danced and skittered across the tracks, debris dislodged by the blast.

Moments later Anderson and King arrived at the base of the cliff, weapons in hand. The attack, precisely planned and timed, seemed to have caught the Russians and Bravo soldiers completely off-guard. With their attention held by the Czech train and Becker, the four-man assault down the face of the cliff had been totally unlooked for.

Hunter paused long enough to glance back down the tracks toward the other train. Czech soldiers were visible now, bursting out of the clouds of steam that enveloped the locomotive and racing up the hill toward the tunnel. The fight would be at close quarters now, and that suited Hunter fine. Though there was no way to be certain, it seemed likely that the Czechs outnumbered Hendricks and his White Death Commandos, assuming the Whites even wanted to continue the fight once they saw that it had turned against them.

In fact, the only advantage Hendricks had now was the fact that he still controlled both the downlink and the civilian technicians, and Hunter was determined to correct that small problem right now. He snapped a full magazine into his Uzi's handgrip. "Let's move it, men!" he cried. Each of the Rangers had his own target. Weapons ready, they plunged forward into the tunnel.

High above the mountain ridge, Gomez leaned over the edge of the observer's cockpit and pulled the goggles back from his eyes. He had seen the death of the valiant Becker, had seen Hunter's and Walker's descent as Anderson and King cleared the way for them with grenades. He signaled the pilot by thumping on the biplane's hull, then pointed. According to plan, they would move now to the far side of the mountain, watching for Hendricks or his people to try to escape that way. Gomez reached down and grasped his M-16, checking to see that both the assault rifle and M-203 had rounds chambered.

The Anatra cleared the top of the ridge, engine sputtering and gasping in the thin air. Rocks and ice flashed past, twenty yards below . . .

Gomez heard the pilot's yell above the engine noise and turned. What he saw made him turn far colder than the frigid wind that clutched at the bare skin of his face.

It was a train, a third train, moving with slow deliberation up the hill toward the tunnel, but on the side opposite from where the battle was taking place. Soldiers were already dropping off railcars all along its length, clutching at their weapons and running toward the tunnel.

The biplane roared low over the small army that was deploying along the tracks. Gomez, with his binoculars, could pick out every detail.

The soldiers wore heavy winter camouflage uniforms unlike any he had yet seen in 1918, and they carried AK assault rifles in gloved hands.

The VBU had arrived, and in full force aboard yet another captured armored train!

Twenty

Rachel heard the cannon fire and grenade blasts at the rear of the train and felt the car sway slightly with the shock. The soldier guarding them turned, his M-16 shifting in his hands as though probing for danger.

It's an attack, she thought. *But who?*

There were plenty of possibilities, she decided. Reds, Whites, Czechs, bandits, the VBU . . . For at least the thousandth time she wondered if Hunter and the Rangers were still alive. Hendricks had told her they were off on a secret mission, but she no longer had any reason to believe the man. Bravo Team's leader had displayed his true colors days before, when he had ruled the warehouse off-limits to all personnel except for his guards and ordered Rachel and Sarah both to be held under what amounted to house arrest in the coach. Since that time a guard had always been present, and Rachel and Sarah both wondered when Hendricks would drop the pretense and declare them both to be his captives. They'd not been mistreated—not yet—but the two of them had watched in silent horror from the coach as Hendricks shot Lynn Colby at the Tartaretz depot. The senseless slaughter of the Czech prisoners and their women moments later had simply piled horror upon horror.

Hunter, Rachel decided, had been right about Hendricks all along. The man was a monster, vicious and unprincipled. The question that haunted her now was whether Travis was really off on a secret mission somewhere . . . or whether Hendricks had murdered him and the other Rangers out of hand.

What does he want us for? she wondered. *Simply as hostages? Or does he want us to work the VBU downlink? Fitzpatrick ought to be able to do that . . . and the little bastard has been working for Hendricks all along.*

The guard was a husky, pug-faced man the others called Lenny. Rachel hated and feared him, a soldier who enjoyed spending the time he was called on to guard Rachel and Sarah leering at them, talking about what he would do to them when they had the chance. He was obviously under orders not to touch the two civilians now, but it was equally clear that he was looking forward to fewer restrictions in that regard in the future.

Lenny was scared now, though, his piggish eyes starting from his head as he rushed to the nearest window and bent over to peer out. "What the shit's goin' on?" he muttered. It was dark inside the tunnel, with only the faintest light filtering in from the entrance, and there was nothing to be seen. The cannon fired a second time. Rachel met Sarah's eyes and nodded slightly . . . meaningfully. If they had even half a chance . . .

The explosion, partly focused by the tunnel itself, rocked the coach violently from side to side and threw the guard against the window.

Rachel sprang from her seat, tackling Lenny around the waist just as he bounced off the window, driving him forward and into the glass a second time. She heard the dull crack of Lenny's skull against the glass and prayed she'd knocked him senseless, then she knew stark despair as the soldier's eyes narrowed and he twisted under her, his hands reaching for her throat.

Lenny's M-16 clattered onto the floor as Rachel kicked at his crotch. The blow was deflected harmlessly by the big man's knee, and he bore down on her, throwing her to the floor as his fingers closed under her jaw, pressing her head back . . . back . . .

Sarah stooped to retrieve the M-16, bringing it up behind her head in one smooth motion, then swinging it in a whistling arc that brought the rifle's butt hard against the side of Lenny's skull. Rachel watched as the man's eyes rolled up in their sockets, then he sagged and fell off her, fingers still twitching spasmodically.

"Thanks, Sarah," she gasped, standing shakily. "You swing a mean rifle."

"C'mon, Rachel!" Sarah said urgently. "Let's get out of here!"

"Uh-uh," Rachel said. "Not until we know what's going on out there."

"But—"

"No buts, girl!" Rachel took the M-16, checked the magazine, and stripped in the first round. She'd learned a lot in the months she'd known Travis and the other Rangers. "Look, someone's attacking, but we don't know who. At least now we can jump if we have to, but let's wait it out and see what happens." She nodded toward Lenny's prostrate form. "He's got a pistol. Can you see it?"

"I . . . I think so."

"Good. Take it. You watch that door." She nodded toward the front of the coach. "I'll watch this one. As soon as—"

The rear door smashed open and a man burst through. Rachel dropped to one knee, snapping the M-16 around, her finger tightening on the trigger.

"Raye! Don't!"

Rachel's eyes snapped open—she was not aware of having closed them—and stared up into Hunter's face. "Travis!"

He caught her as the M-16 slipped to the floor. Outside, the battle redoubled its fury.

"Tell him fast!" Gomez yelled into his radio. "Don't worry about what it means! Just tell him: VBU approaching the east mouth of the tunnel!"

"*I will tell him, Eagle,*" Dubcek replied. "*But he is inside and does not answer!*"

"Get a messenger to him, then! He's got to know!"

"*It will be done, Eagle! Dubcek out!*"

Gomez took another look at the advancing Russians. There were at least thirty of them, he decided, and more still on the train, which was puffing slowly up the grade toward the tunnel. This, he decided, was the VBU force they'd detected entering Siberia weeks before. In another few minutes they would be entering the tunnel's eastern entrance.

How to stop them . . . ?

He pounded on the biplane's fuselage and pointed. The pilot nodded understanding and banked the Anatra into a low, fast pass. The Anatra was not primarily a combat plane, but it carried a single forward-facing machine gun ahead of the pilot, as well as the swivel-mounted MG for the observer.

The little plane shrilled as it leveled out twenty feet above the snow. Gomez heard the pilot open fire, a stuttering yammer that pounded above the roar of the engine. Gomez ignored his own machine gun. His M-16 gave him as much firepower and a wider field of fire . . . and the M-203 gave him the capacity for lobbing bombs at the enemy, which ought to come as a complete surprise.

Gomez caught the surprised expression of Russian troops looking up as the biplane howled overhead, and aimed his weapon.

He'd forgotten all about the cold.

Dark Walker dropped to the ground and rolled until the great steel disks of the flatcar's wheels sheltered him. His goal had been the boxcar containing the Soviet downlink, but he'd been stopped and pinned down before he could even get close. He could tell from the sound of the fire that the car's defenders were American renegades with M-16s, though he could see nothing in the near total darkness of the tunnel except for the persistent, stuttering flashes as weapons fired.

He rolled onto his side and pulled out his radio. "Yankee Leader, this is Yankee Three! I'm pinned down west of the downlink car . . . no way through!"

"*Sit tight, Three,*" Hunter's voice came back a moment later. "*Keep them busy. I'll see what we can do here!*"

Hendricks had run for the downlink car when the first grenade had bounced down the face of the cliff and exploded. He'd left a dozen White Death Commandos to hold the mouth of the tunnel and brought his own men here. Now he, Malloy, and Fitzpatrick stood inside the boxcar with its tangled complexity of wires and busbars and power leads. "Well?" Hendricks snapped at the Chronos technician. "Turn the damn thing on!"

"I'm working on it, Swede!" Fitzpatrick whined. "It takes time, and we don't have a solid lock on anything for transmission!"

"I don't care where we go . . . or when!" Hendricks replied. "Just get us out of here!"

"Careful, Swede," Malloy said softly. "One wrong move and we come through a hundred miles out at sea, maybe. Let the guy do his job."

"Well, step on it, Fitz! Those are Czech soldiers chargin' this tunnel, and they're not exactly happy with us for what happened back at Kulomzino!"

What would Fitzpatrick say if he knew I shot Becker? Or that Hunter is leading the attack? He shook his head. Better to escape now, with Fitzpatrick and as many of the boys as possible, and start fresh somewhere—somewhen—else. He slapped the holstered .45 on his hip. A man could make something of himself, loose in the past with modern weapons.

"Okay." Fitzpatrick looked up from the console as a deep-throated hum swelled from the machinery. "We have power gating from the reactor. We've got five . . . maybe ten minutes to wait, and then we can go through."

"Where?" Malloy asked.

"I don't know." Fitzpatrick shrugged. "I'm not good on the coordinate system."

"That Stein bitch knows coordinates," Hendricks growled. "We could bring her in, make her set them for us."

"No time, Swede," Malloy said. "Listen." Outside, gunfire roared and banged just outside the downlink's boxcar as Hendricks's men battled in the darkness with unseen foes. "They've got us . . . do you understand? I say we just go."

"Yeah." Hendricks stared at the maze of wiring, suddenly feeling lost and vulnerable. It wasn't supposed to work out this way. "Yeah. We'll go!"

His mind raced as he figured the angles.

King's FAL barked a short burst and the Bravo trooper standing by the boxcar keeled over, blood pumping from his chest. The boxcar, located near the mouth of the tunnel quite close to the armored van, looked like the car the Russians were using as a barracks car when the Rangers first captured it. Since then the Rangers had used it to store supplies and equipment . . . until they'd been sent back to 2007 and Hendricks had seized the train.

The hope was that Hendricks was still using the car to store equipment. Perhaps Hendricks's recall beacon was there now?

The door to the boxcar gaped open. King hitched himself up and swung inside. It was empty of people, but the wooden floor was strewn wall to wall with filthy mattresses. The White Death Commandos had converted it into a passenger car again.

A quick search failed to turn up the recall beacon or anything else of use. King was just dismounting when a Czech runner arrived, breathless, carrying Gomez's warning, relayed through Dubcek.

The Anatra biplane sideslipped as it banked, the engine screaming protest. Below, VBU troops scattered as their aerial tormentor stooped for another strafing run. "Ha, turkeys!" Gomez yelled into the wind as he triggered his grenade launcher. "You can run but you can't hide!" The explosion cut down two VBU troops near the tunnel entrance and clawed broken rock from the cliff.

A fusillade of gunfire reached toward the little aircraft, plucking at its fabric wings. Gomez couldn't hear the shots, but he saw the wink of a dozen AKMs as the plane raced overhead, and there were certain to be light machine guns down there as well. The plane shuddered. He heard an unpleasant shredding sound, saw gaping holes appear all along the length of the plane's lower wing. The engine took on a new note—ragged, gasping, as smoke boiled from under the cowling.

Hunter pulled out his radio. His passionate embrace with Rachel had been interrupted almost immediately by the device's insistent call.

"This is Yankee Leader! Go ahead!"

"Yankee Leader, this is Yankee One," King replied. *"Relaying from Eagle!"*

Hunter scowled as King passed on Gomez's report. It was just plain bad luck that they'd run into the VBU main force just when they'd caught up with Hendricks . . . and the Soviet time travelers were going to complicate this battle horribly.

"I've searched the car we thought held equipment," King concluded. *"It's not here!"*

"Understood, Yankee Two! Help Walker with the downlink car! He reports he's pinned down by Hendricks's people there!"

"Roger! On my way! One out!"

Where was the recall beacon hidden? He had no doubt that Hendricks would hold on to the device. Now that it was possible to tie in to a beacon through a VBU downlink, the small unit was more important than ever. And in this wild firefight, the Soviet time machine could easily be damaged. Then the *only* way out would be the beacon.

Hunter looked around the coach. "Raye, where did Hendricks stay? What did he use for an HQ these last few days?"

Rachel gestured with her arm. "Right here. Mostly he kept us locked up in our quarters, except when he wanted to guard us close, like just now. This was his office."

"Then his beacon is here somewhere! He wouldn't have taken it outside . . . not and risk having it shot like the last one. He's hidden it somewhere, and I'm betting it's *here*."

Rachel and Sarah looked around doubtfully, and Hunter knew what they were thinking. The coach was still richly furnished. There were so many places where a device the size of a large book could be hidden.

"Quickly!" Hunter said. "Start looking!"

Anderson was farther up the train, flattened against the roof of a boxcar with less than a foot of space between his head and the tunnel ceiling. The locomotive, his goal, sat amid billowing, impenetrable clouds of steam just ahead. Briefly he wondered if the engineer he'd clubbed into unconsciousness during his first assault on the train was still there . . . and what he would say when Anderson showed up again.

The Texan had taken to the tops of the train cars when he realized that the tunnel was becoming filled with unfriendly strangers. Faintly through the steam, he could see the light of the eastern end of the tunnel several hundred yards in the distance. A wet-sounding slap-slap-slap echoed above the hiss of the engine as someone approached from that direction.

Russians!

Light from the locomotive cab cast just enough illumination for Anderson to make out their snow camo garb. There was no mistaking the AKM assault rifles they carried.

The VBU had arrived!

In the next moment Anderson held his breath as a pair of train workers stepped from the engine, their hands up.

Now what . . . ?

"Ch'yornee Ahgohn!" Andryanov cried, his hands held high as he stepped out of the locomotive. The Black Fire code was their contact password; now it saved the VBU major from being gunned down as the spetsnaz rushed into the tunnel from the eastern entrance.

"Who are you?" a spetsnaz sergeant demanded.

"Never mind! Quickly! Follow me! We must reach the downlink!"

Andryanov and Obinin had waited out the opening of the battle hidden by the darkness of the tunnel, crouched in the locomotive cab until the first handful of Zamiatin's troops had pounded up the tunnel from the east. The darkness was a comforting shelter now, close around the VBU agents as they raced toward the west and stabbing flashes of gunfire where Czechs battled Whites at the rear of the train.

If they could take and hold the downlink, Andryanov had the coordinates and operational codes to connect with the Soviet base in the past. If he could open the gate to 2007, they could bring reinforcements through inside the tunnel . . . right where they would catch the Americans and Czechs by surprise.

Machine-gun fire thundered in the narrow confines of the tunnel, the heavy weapon's muzzle flash stabbing from the roof of a nearby boxcar. One spetsnaz trooper went down . . . then another. Andryanov whipped up his Skorpion and triggered a burst. Obinin joined him, along with the surviving spetsnaz troopers. Bullets splintered the top edge of the boxcar, sparked, and shrieked as ricochets skipped from the tunnel ceiling.

Something made of metal, long and heavy, skittered off the boxcar and crashed to the ground a few feet away. The gunfire from the boxcar ceased.

Andryanov approached the object and saw it was a battered American M-60 machine gun. There was blood on the butt just behind the receiver.

"Now!" he called to the others. "Let us go!"

Twenty-one

The Anatra DS didn't fall so much as the ground swept up to meet it. The Czech pilot leaned far back, battling the stick, struggling to bring the nose up as the biplane's wheels skimmed the icy upper crust of a snowfield.

Then the Anatra struck with a hammer blow to Gomez's spine. The plane bounced once, pancaked, then slammed with a head-wrenching crunch into a snowbank as the engine tore free of the fuselage, struts snapped, and the wood-and-fabric wings folded like the wings of a great stricken bird.

Gomez waited until a growing awareness of the aches and pains throughout his body combined with a sensation of smothering cold convinced him he was alive before he emerged from a pile of snow. The biplane had crash-landed several hundred yards north of the east tunnel entrance. He could see the new VBU train, a red-and-green painted locomotive trailing a long string of armored coaches. It was motionless now as more VBU troops dismounted. Those who had escaped Gomez's strafing and bombing runs were picking themselves up out of the snow and moving toward the tunnel. It looked as though they were assuming the occupants of the biplane were dead.

They were almost right. The Czech pilot was slumped in his

cockpit, his neck snapped clean. Gomez pulled his M-16 from the observer's seat and started wading through the snow back up the hill toward the tunnel.

Andryanov spotted the boxcar with the downlink sitting just beyond the reactor car. He saw lights on inside the coach as he led his men past it but ignored the shadows he glimpsed moving inside. Time enough to mop up later.

They caught Hendricks's men from behind, opening up with full-auto fire that moved through the American renegades and cut them down even as they continued to exchange fire with unseen attackers farther up the tunnel. The downlink car's door was slightly open, and light was spilling from inside. He couldn't hoist himself inside while holding his Skorpion. He holstered the weapon, then snapped an order to the spetsnaz sergeant and had Obinin and himself boosted up into the car.

"Hold it right there, Russian!" Andryanov found himself facing the tall, blond, bearded American named Hendricks, and a Colt .45 leveled at his face. The VBU man froze, his hands open and empty.

"I am unarmed," Andryanov said in accentless English. "Do not shoot."

"Don't you worry, Russkie," the American said. Behind him, two other men stood by the downlink controls. Andryanov could hear the hum of raw energy, could tell that the machine was powering up to open a gate. "I'm glad you came, actually," the American continued. "I was hoping to get to talk to you people."

"Oh?" Andryanov's response was guarded. He would not be able to reach his Skorpion easily, not with the weapon holstered under his coat. He glanced sideways at Obinin, who was watching the American through narrowed eyes. "Why would that be?"

"Because I figure we could cut a deal, you and me! We got your train back for you, and your time machine! Right now *I* control your downlink. I should tell you I also have one of the U.S. recall beacons and a couple of prisoners you might be interested in . . . all tucked away safe and sound."

"And what would you expect in return?"

"Well, for a start, you can take care of our noisy neighbors out there. Then we can tell you one hell of a lot about the U.S. time-travel program.''

"Indeed?" Andryanov smiled. "Perhaps we can do business!" He dropped his hand.

"Watch it!" Hendricks warned, his knuckle whitening on the trigger. "No tricks!"

"No tricks," Andryanov agreed. "May I reach for my radio? I will have my troops guard this car. I will use English if you do not know Russian, so you know what I say."

"I understand Russian just fine, mister. Go ahead."

Andryanov glanced at Obinin and nodded. He unfastened his coat and slipped his hand inside, reaching for the butt of his Skorpion.

Obinin knew that Andryanov's radio was in his coat pocket, not on his hip. The VBU agent lunged forward as Andryanov made his move. The American fired, the report painfully loud inside the narrow room. Obinin shuddered and went down, but not before Andryanov yanked the Skorpion free and swung it up, spitting flame and empty casings.

The blond American whirled back against the console as bullets tore into his shoulder. A second American soldier clutched at his stomach, dropping to his knees as blood gushed from his nose and mouth. The third American crumpled to the floor, unhurt but covering his eyes, whimpering fear as spetsnaz troops clambered into the car.

"Mount guard outside!" Andryanov ordered. He singled out one private and indicated the two surviving Americans. "You! Watch those two. We need them!"

He turned and strode to the control console, checking the gauges, adjusting coordinate settings. The machine was nearly at full power, and it would take only a few minutes more to open a direct link to the Soviet time base in the past where spetsnaz reinforcements would be waiting.

The battle would end when those troops poured through from the future.

"I appreciate the offer," he said over his shoulder a moment later as he entered a final string of coordinates. The wounded American stared up at him with pain-glazed eyes. "But you see, we already have you . . . and all the information you possess that could possibly be of interest to us. I'm sure you will be more than willing to discuss matters with our interrogators, once we get you to our home base.

"It should be only a few minutes more."

"Got it!" Rachel exulted. "I got it!"

Hunter looked back over his shoulder from where he'd been guarding the coach door while the two women tore up the interior of the car. The plush cushions of the window seats and furniture had been scattered across the floor, and an ornate liquor cabinet on one wall smashed open. The chair Hendricks usually sat in during briefings in the coach had been overturned, revealing a long, deep slit in the bottom through which some of the stuffing of the seat cushion had been removed.

The beacon had been shoved inside and the hole repaired with electrical tape. Rachel had noticed the crude nature of the repair, ripped off the tape, and reached inside to claim the prize.

"Does it look okay?"

Rachel studied it carefully. "Seems to be. Switch it on . . . it should work."

"Okay, girls," Hunter said. He went to a window and peered outside. "It's busy out there. I think we're going to have to play it cagey if we're going to get out of here."

Anderson rolled over onto his back, blinking blood out of his eyes. His head rang like a church steeple, and white fire hammered at his left temple.

He had just opened fire on a group of spetsnaz, he remembered, and killed at least two of them, when return fire had driven him back from the edge of the boxcar. He blinked at the rock ceiling of the tunnel a foot above his face and decided that a round must have struck above and ricocheted into his head. He was still bleeding freely from a nasty scalp wound, but he seemed otherwise unharmed.

His M-60 was missing.

No matter. His goal was still the locomotive, and right now he was mad enough to take on any VBU troops he might meet with his bare hands. Moving cautiously—blood and shock dimmed his vision and made his hands slippery—he made his way to the ladder running down the end of the boxcar and climbed down to the floor of the tunnel. The coal car was next, and then the locomotive. Steam from the waiting engine boiled around him, no longer hot enough to scald but drenching him with hot droplets of water. He reached the cab ladder and climbed aboard.

The engineer blinked at him from the floor near the firebox, fear mirrored in wide, rheumy eyes.

Anderson recognized him. "Hello again, friend," he said in Russian.

"Nyet!" the man cried. "Don't hit me!"

Anderson decided that his looks must have frightened the man as much as anything else . . . soaked, blackened by soot and smoke, and wearing a mask of blood. He grinned fiendishly and reached for his radio.

"Yankee Leader, this is Yankee Two!"

"Go ahead, Two!" Hunter's voice was muffled, as though he were trying to be quiet.

"I've got the engine," he said proudly. "And the engineer!" He decided not to add that he was, for the moment at least, also completely unarmed.

"Up, you." Andryanov made a savage gesture with his Skorpion. Reluctantly the American prisoners rose from the floor of the car. Other American prisoners huddled nearby, under close guard by several spetsnaz troopers.

Blue light glowed and wavered on the transport stage . . . an open gateway into the past. More Soviet commandos were stepping into the car from the Russian base in the past—reinforcements, battle-ready and heavily armed.

"Through there," Andryanov said, indicating the pulsing light. "Quickly!"

The blond American licked his lips uncertainly, then seemed to arrive at some decision. "Okay, mister. But I still think we can cut a deal!" He walked into the light and vanished. He was followed in turn by each of the other prisoners, including the small, frightened American technician.

Andryanov grinned at the sergeant in command of the spetsnaz unit. "I'll be back," he said, "as soon as I deliver these prisoners. Keep the time gate open."

"Da, Comrade Major! We will wait for you!"

This haul should restore his standing with the VBU high

command! Andryanov laughed as he followed his prisoners into the glow.

Hunter had pulled Rachel and Sarah underneath a flatcar when he'd seen the first spetsnaz troopers begin jumping from the downlink car ahead. Russian railroad tracks are spaced a full five feet apart, and there was plenty of room for the three of them to lie huddled together on their stomachs as the Soviet reinforcements began streaming out into the tunnel. The ties pressed uncomfortably at their chests and hips and knees, but in the smoky darkness they were invisible to the soldiers swarming around the train cars ahead.

"Like a circus," Sarah said softly. "Clowns coming out of a Volkswagen . . ."

"I've never seen circus clowns with AK assault rifles," Hunter said. He reached for his radio. "Yankee One, this is Yankee Leader! Come in, Greg!"

"Yankee One here. Go ahead!"

"What's your sit, Greg?"

"Still pinned down, Lieutenant! The bad guys were replaced by more bad guys . . . and I think they've got help coming through the downlink."

"That's affirmative," Hunter replied. "I'm watching them from here. They must have the portal open. Can you get them with grenades?"

There was an uncomfortable pause. *"If you're that close to them . . ."*

"Right, One. I see what you mean." The tunnel was like a vast but narrow shooting gallery, and Hunter and the two women were downrange of anything King and Walker might throw their way.

"Travis!" Rachel exclaimed. "Roy said he was in the locomotive!"

"Yeah . . ."

"Right!" Sarah agreed suddenly, her eyes seemed almost luminous in the darkness under the flatcar. "They had their downlink locked on space-time coordinates!"

Hunter shook his head. "I still don't . . ."

"What happens if their mobile downlink becomes really mobile?"

Hunter thought, then looked up as the realization struck him.

"They move in space . . . and the coordinates change!"

"Exactly!" Rachel exclaimed. "Not by much . . . but even a few yards ought to be enough to make their focus drift . . . make the lock get fuzzy. It's worth a try, anyway!"

"That it is, Raye!" He brought the radio to his lips again. "Hang tight, One! Yankee Leader out!" He switched channels. "Yankee Two! Roy! Are you there?"

"Right here, LT," the Texan answered. *"Shoot!"* There was a drawl in his voice that suggested Anderson must be worried.

Quickly Hunter explained the idea to Anderson.

"So see if you can get the train moving, Roy!" he concluded. "Don't worry about stopping. Just get her rolling and jump for it!"

"Will do, LT! You just get clear before she goes!"

"That's a roger. Yankee Leader out!"

In the locomotive cab, Anderson replaced his radio and turned sharply. "How do you get this overgrown toy moving?" he demanded of the engineer.

"Don't hurt me."

"Goddammit, I'm not going to hurt you!" Anderson wavered on his feet, holding himself upright with one hand against the wall as he wiped blood from his eyes with the other. He didn't realize that he'd lapsed back into English. "Just get the sucker rolling!"

Words, and the meanings behind them, can sometimes cross linguistic barriers. The engineer stared at Anderson for a moment, then turned to the controls, closed a pair of bright red valves, released the hand brake, and eased up the throttle. Perhaps as much from habit as anything else, he yanked at a cord above his head, filling the dark tunnel with the shrill, ear-piercing shriek of the engine's steam whistle.

There was a deep-throated chuff as the drivers turned over . . . followed by another, and another. The train lurched, then began rolling slowly and ponderously forward. A chain reaction of cars thumping cars made its way toward the rear of the train, where men fought to the death in darkness and smoke.

The creak-bang of the train starting to move was deafening to Hunter and the two women in their hiding place under the flatcar. One massive wheel groaned past Hunter less than a foot where he lay, followed moments later by another.

The train began to pick up speed.

"Stay here!" He shouted at the women. He passed the recall beacon across to Rachel. "If anything happens to me, get back to Time Square. Maybe they can put together a team to come in and pull the others out!"

"Wait!" Rachel yelled. "Where are you going?"

But Hunter had already timed the slow and stately passing of the next set of train-car wheels and rolled over the rail and onto the roadbed outside. The clack-clack of the cars sounded beside him as he rose to his feet.

His satchel charge still hung over his neck and shoulder. He removed it, gripping the M-60 igniter ring. Gomez had cut his fuse long, he remembered. Ahead, spetsnaz scattered as the train pulled out. Hunter spotted the downlink boxcar by the light spilling from the open door in its side. The car was drawing closer . . . moving faster . . .

Gunfire barked from between the train's wheels and a Russian soldier running out of the darkness staggered and went down. Rachel and her M-16 . . .

The downlink car rumbled past Hunter. He twisted the arming ring on the satchel charge, grasped it by its handle, and slung it through the opening. The bag sailed through the opening and landed with a dull thud inside.

The train rumbled on.

Gomez killed another Soviet soldier breaking from cover, then started forward toward the tunnel. He stopped as he heard the wail of the locomotive's whistle and dropped to his knees, watching, his rifle at the ready.

The train exploded from the tunnel mouth in steam and noise an instant later. The green-and-red engine thundered into daylight, pushing a single flatcar, then followed by car after car. Two shapes hurtled from the locomotive cab as it passed. Gomez had a blurred impression of Anderson and another man, a civilian, landing in a snowbank nearby.

Down the hill, the VBU train sat on the tracks, a helpless, immobile target.

Locomotive struck locomotive head-on with a volcanic roar of bursting boilers and tons of colliding metal. Gomez glimpsed one massive driver wheel sailing like an immense Frisbee through the air as a mushroom cloud of steam and rolling smoke erupted into the sky. Car followed car, each piling into the next. As the locomotives appeared to merge in exploding steam, flame gouted from one of the boxcars, blasting out its sides in smoke and whirling chunks of wood and debris.

The blast wave struck Gomez and knocked him down. As he tried to stand again, ammunition in the westbound train exploded, hurling burning pieces of railcars high into the sky, trailing smoke and flaming debris.

The explosions went on and on and on . . . .

Anderson struggled up to his hands and knees a few yards away. "Good God!" he said. Snow and blood so completely covered his face that Gomez knew him only by his voice. "Good God in heaven, what was that?"

"That," Gomez assured him, "was one hell of a bang."

Explosions continued to echo from the surrounding mountain peaks.

The surviving Russian spetsnaz began surrendering. Gomez didn't blame them. It was cold here, and a long, long walk to the nearest town.

Epilogue

The fighting had long since ended on both sides of the mountain. Inside the tunnel, now grown silent, blue light flared and danced above the recall beacon. Hunter stood at Anton Dubcek's side as Time Square MPs herded a line of Soviet spetsnaz two by two through the portal and into the future.

"I do not understand, friend Travis," Dubcek said slowly, shaking his head with wonder. "A tunnel . . . through time?"

"Don't try to understand it, Anton." Hunter laughed. "We'll be leaving you now. You'll be able to carry on your fight without us."

Dubcek's eyes narrowed, bright with speculation. "If you are from the future, as you say, you must know our future. The Legion's . . ."

Hunter shook his head. "Only in general, Anton. No specifics. I'm afraid you never made it into the history books."

"That does not sound like a particularly comfortable place to be."

"The Czech Legion will get out," Hunter continued. "Most of it, anyway. You've got some hard fighting ahead of you, though."

It would be—*was,* Hunter corrected himself—such a waste.

217

Shifting politics and alliances had ended foreign intervention in the Russian Civil War less than two years after it began. The last American troops, for instance, would leave Russia for home late in 1919 . . . to become a forgotten chapter of a miserable, forgotten war. Russian would continue to kill Russian until 1922, and then would come the purges and mass killings executed by Stalin and others. The Soviet Union's internal political agonies would continue for decades yet.

And politics had nearly spelled the ruin of the United States in a second intervention in the Russian War. Operation Backlash was a complete and abject failure because one man had blindly chased political ambition, while another succumbed to the quest for raw and naked power.

Those quests had nearly killed all of them.

Dubcek passed his hand over his eyes. "I don't think I can watch this, Herr Major Travis. It makes me dizzy, seeing men vanish like that. I will say *Zbawhem* . . . good-bye." He took Hunter's hand.

"Zbawhem, friend Anton. *Auf Wiedersehen!"*

A young Chronos MP saluted Hunter as the Czech walked back down the tunnel toward his waiting train. "All the prisoners are through, Sir! General Thompson says you men can come through anytime."

"Very well," Hunter replied formally. "Tell him we'll be right through."

Rachel stood at his side. They watched as Sarah helped Anderson, his head heavily bandaged, walk into the portal's light.

"I let you down, Travis," she said softly. "I . . . I let what I wanted blind me to what Hendricks was."

"I'd say you redeemed yourself, love," Hunter said with a small grin. "Several times, in fact."

"What do you mean?"

"I'll tell you later. It's a long story." He was still unsure of how he was going to tell Rachel—*this* Rachel—of the valiant sacrifice an alternate version of herself had made.

"Ready to go, Chief?" Gomez called from near the beacon. "I'm cold! Let's go home!"

"On our way, Eddie!"

Gomez, King, and Walker vanished, and the two were alone on the windswept Siberian hillside. Rachel shivered.

"What do you think happened to him?" she asked. "To Hendricks? Was he on the train?"

Hunter's eyes sought the still burning wreckage down the valley. "Maybe. Or maybe the Russians took him. His body wasn't in the tunnel . . . that's all we know."

And with that kind of ambition, Hunter thought. *God! What could he make of himself if he'd gotten loose in time?*

"Come on, Rachel," he said at last. "Let's go home. I have a feeling I'm going to hate winter for as long as I live."

Together they walked through the portal.